About This Book

The author was a quiet academic, publishing learned articles on Kafka and suchlike, until his first novel, *A White Merc With Fins*, came out worldwide in 1996. In 1998–2000 he helped turn his second best-seller, *Rancid Aluminium*, into 'the worst film ever made in the UK' (*Guardian*). He is now divorced and lives quietly in Cardiff, with his son. His third novel, *Dead Long Enough*, is in film development. He is learning Welsh.

by the same author

A WHITE MERC WITH FINS
RANCID ALUMINIUM
DEAD LONG ENOUGH

White Powder, Green Light

James Hawes

Jonathan Cape
London

Published by Jonathan Cape 2002

2 4 6 8 10 9 7 5 3 1

First published in Great Britain in 2002 by
Jonathan Cape
Random House, 20 Vauxhall Bridge Road, London SW1V 2SA

Random House Australia (Pty) Limited
20 Alfred Street, Milsons Point, Sydney,
New South Wales 2061, Australia

Random House New Zealand Limited
18 Poland Road, Glenfield,
Auckland 10, New Zealand

Random House South Africa (Pty) Limited
Endulini, 5A Jubilee Road, Parktown 2193, South Africa

The Random House Group Limited Reg. No. 954009
www.randomhouse.co.uk

A CIP catalogue record for this book is available from the British Library

ISBN 0-224-06322-7

Papers used by The Random House Group are natural,
recyclable products made from wood grown in sustainable forests;
the manufacturing processes conform to the environmental
regulations of the country of origin

Typeset by Palimpsest Book Production Limited,
Polmont, Stirlingshire

Printed and bound in Great Britain by
Mackays of Chatham PLC, Chatham, Kent

To Owain

PART ONE

Scenario

Solitude is a torment not threatened in hell itselfe

John Donne

Shopping @ £60

Paul Salmon, the thirty-six-year-old Producer of the recent lo-budget/no-budget teenslasher drugs'n'guns cult schlocker, *Suzi Got Whacked,* and Co-Producer of the upcoming fab new Britpack Russian mafiya heist caper, *Base Metal,* trotted happily across Soho Square in the last, dull glow of the late-February sunshine. Behind his titanium glasses, his pale blue eyes seemed dreamily lost, leaving his autopilot to pick out the smoothest and straightest path for his soft, black shoes between nervy crackheads, exhausted backpackers, *Big Issue* salesmen and the newly arriving evening shift of amateur rent boys. Darkness was already in the wings, but Salmon's long, pale face was jasmine-fresh from a Full Exfoliation & Revitalisation Session @ Skin Heaven in Wardour Street (£60) and above his two-tone black/blue slim-fit suit it gleamed in the sunset, a strange, unnatural pink.

Salmon was happy: he had been shopping all day for free.

He was carrying several expensive pastel-shaded carrier bags, and each of them had one of those small, witty logos on it. They contained: airsprung sports shoes (£120); a titanium squash racquet (£180); a nice selection of antioxidant vitamins (almost exactly £60, bizarrely enough); and an Egyptian cotton tracksuit (£89.99). But all these splendid things had cost Salmon *nothing at all*: every time the bags bumped up against his soft knees, they reminded him of happiness.

His new life had just begun, and now all he needed

was a big new Project to pitch at Alan Barony on Monday afternoon, a scenario he could persuade Barony to take an Option out on right away, a modest commitment up front, a little hit of liquid cash, and he was home and dry, safe and sound, done and dusted . . .

—Save the planet, sir?

—You what?

Salmon returned to earth and found himself confronted by an intense-looking young man. No, not quite young any more, even by today's standards of eternal teenagery. The not-quite-young-any-more man wore a dark green anorak, bore a shaven head and carried a plastic ID card around his neck. Before Salmon's nose he brandished a Greenpeace brochure as if it were some legendary artefact that could at any moment annihilate the vile, materialistic West End. From beneath the multiple piercings on his eyebrows, he gazed at Salmon with the slightly unnerving zeal of a lost male who has recently found Meaning and a Home in this bedsit-ridden, loveless world of old socks and bleak, greasy sheets.

Salmon was surprised that this ridiculous little git had dared to accost him: normally, his well-trained, LA-style, W1 body language was enough to tell lost tourists, whingeing beggars and Buddhist hippies to fuck off and bother someone less important & busy. But something about this laughable little pain in the arse reminded him vaguely of a Movie Angle he had thought of earlier. Business. So he stopped, set down his bags, crossed his plump arms and smiled indulgently.

—OK, OK, you're lucky: today, I'm happy.

—Good for you, sir, smiled the other, revealing his filed and studded teeth. (He was known to his friends, or at least to the people he drank cider with

4

and took drugs with and hung about with at festivals, as Skanky.)

Good indeed. And true. Salmon *was* happy. And no wonder. He was on his way to do the sort of things that millions of human beings daydream of doing: he was off to the Groucho (where his subscription was from now on free) to meet The Gang of famous British actors, artists and journalists for a couple of hours and drink for free; he might well meet a piece of posh media totty called Sheina (hence the exfoliation) unless she had really been sent off to cover the Welsh Oscars in Cardiff, poor cow. If he did meet her, he might well take her for a free dinner in a signature restaurant.

He might well even get inside her little knickers tonight.

And tonight, if he got there, he would be able to get his cock hard, for once.

Salmon was not taking cocaine any more.

He was thus filled with the warm glow of a new life which was to be, no, correction, was *already being*, divided equally between glittering, wealth-bringing work, fitness-oriented consuming/pampering and the dedicated pursuit of a suitable, useful, desirable squeeze. And in not taking cocaine.

—But is *the world* happy, sir? Or is it crying out in pain?

Aha, of course! The *Angle*. Environment, that was it. Yes, yes: a digital, shoulder-shot, *Blair Witch*-style, mocumentary, shoot-em-up, yoofsploitation number based on ecowarriors ('*Today They Call Us Terrorists. The Future Will Call Us: THE SAVIOURS*'): Salmon had thought it up last weekend while lining up the charlie on those handy marble loo-roll shelves in the Gents at the Cobbett Club: a project he could pitch to Alan Barony, something Barony could personally

Green Light without having to go upstairs to LA. Shit, he really *had* to get one of those Psions to write down all this stuff as he went, it was no good getting the Big Idea if you were going to forget it like that! Tax-deductible, obviously. He would go shopping for one tomorrow. Web-connectable. Which reminded him, he must look up that website someone had told him about, *yoofresistance.co.uk* or something like that, sounded like the kind of place to find out what was hot, *coming* hot, with sixteen- to twenty-four-year-old males. *They* are the only Market Sector that matter at the Box Office, after all: if you can second-guess what the male sixteen- to twenty-four-year-old cohort is going to want to watch twelve months down the line, you are soon going to be taking *that* call from Hal Scharnhorst . . .

—OK, friend, you just bought your three minutes. Pitch it.

—Sorry, sir?

—Hit me with it, Salmon smiled condescendingly.

Salmon had been not taking cocaine all week. Well, not since Sunday night, and that had only been a couple of lines to be sociable. Of course, Salmon knew that the easy part had finished now. Now, the weekend was coming, and it is only the weekend nights that count, isn't it? Anyone can not do *anything* in daylight, there is always shopping to do and things to look at and missions to invent, by daylight. And as for weekday nights, well, they pass quickly by, they can be sidestepped lightly: Tuesday, a red-wine dinner with the kind of old friends who would think *a bit of the old Salvador Dali* means a book of art-shop prints; Wednesday, a quick and handily dutiful trip to the parents; Thursday, a night of mortal (but coke-free) tedium at the theatre watching a bunch of grant-funded idiots shouting a lot, rolling about with no clothes on and playing the saxophone badly. Whatever. There are all sorts of things to get you through the week – especially if you didn't sleep at all on Sunday night because of the powder.

The weekends are another matter. Very.

But Salmon had got through Thursday OK, and Thursday counts as the weekend, at least in W1 it does, doesn't it? Indeed. And now he was obviously going to make it through Friday night too and if you can crack Friday, well, Saturday is going to be a piece of piss, isn't it?

Obviously.

Salmon exulted internally. He had done it. Knocked Coco the Clown on the head. So in a *very real sense*, he was making money just by standing here in the cooling Soho sunshine, listening to some sad little fuck spouting bollocks about humpback whales, ozone layers and Siberian tigers. Just by virtue of being alive and not taking cocaine, he was *quite literally* making £60 every couple of days.

Things were good. They were undoubtedly getting better.

And the best thing, the most amusing thing that Salmon had discovered was that as soon as you stopped taking cocaine, the world suddenly appeared to be filled with pleasant, healthy, desirable things that cost exactly the same as a gram. Or multiples or fractions thereof. So he would probably only ever wear those stupid new shiny £59.99 jeans he bought yesterday once, so what? How many times do you sniff a given gram of chang? The moment was all that mattered, the feelgood hit, however you got it, whether it was the sleek, cool touch of your new jeans on your arse when you wore them out for the first (and maybe only) time, or the cold, creamy bite of the coke up your nose.

The hit, the moment, the impact.

What other reason is there to do anything?

What lasts, anyway?

Salmon had very nearly bought a ridiculous jumper today, simply because he quite liked it for a second or two, and it was £240: now he had chucked the gack, he could have a jumper like that *absolutely free*, once a fortnight, if he felt like it.

Why not? So what?

Once every week or so, in fact. Not *every* week, of course, things had never got *that* bad. Anyway, he had always spread it about royally, he probably only ever actually *took* about half what he bought, really, *less* than half, probably. Most of what he spent on whiff was just sociable, oiling the wheels, you know, it was no different to buying rounds, when you thought about it, more of an investment than an expense. Indeed. Because what is the difference, really, at the end of the day, between providing a gram of ye olde morale-raising flour in Soho House to keep The Gang smiling while the deal settles down, and getting in a big round of Sea Breezes? Apart from the coke being cheaper, especially in Hoho bloody House, ha ha! And, well, the thing is, people simply *remember* the person who chopped them out a nice fat line in the bog far longer than they remember some bloke who just shoved them yet another Sea Breeze along the bar . . .

—Yes, got to oil the wheels, after all, mused Salmon.

—Sorry, sir?

Salmon returned again to the real world and Soho Square, to find that he had just spoken out loud and

8

had no idea at all what he had been listening to for the last three minutes.

—I'm getting bored, friend. Better close now: clock's ticking.

—Well, yes, sir, of course, *oil*, yes, for the foreseeable future we will need *some* use of non-renewable resources, such as oil, but surely the challenge for us now is to . . .

—Yes, yes, yes, snapped Salmon, suddenly irritable. – OK, friend, let's cut to the chase, shall we? Now, would *you* cheer if we killed Japanese whalers?

—Ha ha, sorry, sir?

—Would *you* cheer Japanese whalers being machine-gunned? Would you? Would your friends? Well?

The not-quite-young man's intense gaze had, up till now, been slightly glassy as he droned out his pre-learned sales pitch. Now, however, he appeared to wake fully up. He looked nervously at Salmon's shining suit, and his resplendent shopping.

—Well, sir, obviously, Greenpeace policy is *officially* non-violent.

— . . . Non-violent? When did *non-violent* ever work? You kidding?

—Well, yes, sir, I mean . . . The cider-blasted, ecstasy-enhanced eyes now seemed to light up from within with a flickering mixture of suspicion and hope. They zipped swiftly around Soho Square. —I mean, yeah: *non-violence*!

—We are on the same wavelength, friend. When did non-violence ever sell seats, eh?

—Seats, sir?

—You think grown-up people pay their seven quid to see *non-violence*? To see people being *nice*? Jesus Christ on a mountain bike! Did Sophocles do *nice* stuff? Is *Hamlet* nice? What do you think gets people away

9

from the cable TV on a rainy Tuesday in November? What makes them go out the door and get wet and cold and hang around on a tube platform full of psychos, and then get wet again and queue up in the rain and pay their seven hard-earned, tax-paid quid to sit in a big dark room, and then give some nutter who can't speak English another twenty-five quid to take them home in an old Toyota with no seat belts that smells of last century's vomit? *Nice* stuff? They do all that so they can see *nice* stuff? You kidding? You *stupid*? People go out and pay to see other people doing *bad* stuff, idiot, they pay to sit there chewing popcorn and swilling Coke, I mean *Coca-Cola*, while they watch good-looking, forty-foot-tall people doing one of two things. You know what those two things are, friend?

—N-No, sir. (The eyes now shyly meeting Salmon's had long since lost any sign of comprehension; but they glowed darkly with instinctive deference to his pure conviction and his palpable status.)

—Extramarital shagging or permanent physical damage. Or both. Both is best. The only difference between the good guys and the bad guys is the good guys get a *reason* to do the shagging and the violence. It's called the Concept, idiot. It's called Motivation. So: is saving the world a good enough motivation to go around doing bad stuff, and I mean *really* bad, I mean *bums-on-seats* bad? Well? Sell me the fucking Concept, schmuck!

—Me, sir? But . . . *saving the world*, yeah, sir, sir, what, what *bad* stuff?

—Stop! Don't tell me, I see it myself, why in God's name do I bother hiring morons? Here it is, come with me. OK: a Japanese whaling ship. Hey, you. You coming with me or what? You listening?

Skanky's intense stare had broken off for a second to flick nervously around Soho Square again. Now he

10

shuffled hesitantly closer, his head bowed, his eyes imploring.

—I'm listening, sir. A Japanese whaler? Yeah, yeah, I'm listening. This is, like, yeah: you *been* there sir?

—Shut up and come with me. Here we go. OK: we power-zoom in across grey seas, and find a Japanese whaler. Blood everywhere, serious shit, whale meat bigtime, slant-eyed guys slicing huge fucking mammals, blubberfest. It's hard-core sicko, but we'll get a PG certificate no problem, because it's real, it happens, right? Well?

—Right, said Skanky, —too fucking right, sir. Bastards.

Skanky's eyes had by now locked on to Salmon's in that alarming Young Male Worship mode so frequently seen at grunge rock gigs or in photographs of the Hitler Youth on parade. Or in chimps near the pack boss. But Salmon did not see this: his own eyes were turned fervently inwards, on his Scenario.

—Yeah, bastards. Big bastards. OK, OK, wait for it. Yeah. Right. They're after another whale. A *mother* whale, shit, of course, she's guarding a *baby* whale, ha ha, that's good. And here comes the whaling ship for another run, brrrrrrm, slant-eyed gits load harpoons, other slant-eyed gits smile, horribly.

—Fuck them.

—Yes! Exactly! See? It's working. You're *with* me. The Bad Guys. Then *whoosh*! a Greenpeace boat zips across their bows, it's full of pretty blonde girls and wimps with beards, shouting and waving and crying, trying to stop them. The Good Guys, right?

—The Good Guys, sir.

—Yes. But the slant-eyed whalers just fucking *laugh*. Ha ha ha, ohhh, sca-ry, *non-violent* protesters, save us! Wimps!

11

—Yeah, right, sir.

—The Greenpeace girls are weeping, yeah? Blonde teens with big tits in surfy wetsuits, crying their eyes out. Fab. Perfect. We're with them. We are sooo with them. The whaling ship closes, the harpoon is locked and loaded, mummy whale gets her body in between the ship and baby whale, she *knows* what's going on here, oh yes!

—Y-You *been* there, sir? (Once, Skanky had stood quite close to the guru Hans von Porris himself at a Greenpeace rally: then, as now, he had felt himself glowing, as if blasted by some benign irradiation, in the presence of a true Silverback.) —You got the footage?

—Hey, not yet, ha ha, but don't worry, we can do mummy whale in CGI, you know, computer-generated images, yeah? Big Disney eyes, the works. OK, so where were we? Oh yeah, the cute Greenpeace girls are weeping helplessly, and mummy whale is in the harpoon sights; no escape; she is halfway to margarineville.

—Cunts!

—Exactly, exactly, see? It can't fail. *And*. And what? Well?

—Sir?

—Heh heh. Now: in come the low trumpets. You know: *Independence Day* trumpets, *The Patriot* trumpets, the-torch-song-is-coming trumpets, yeah? No? You don't know about the trumpets? OK, don't worry about the trumpets, the trumpets are piss, any stupid fucking ten-grand-a-score composer knows what I mean about the trumpets. And? And from behind an island, or an iceberg, an iceberg, yeah, we can CGI an iceberg in ten, this other boat appears. The trumpets harden. What is this boat? Who are these new guys?

—Who? breathed Skanky.

—The Saviours.

—The Saviours! Oh fuck, man.

—You like it? Does it do it for you?

—The *Saviours* . . . Oh, man . . .

— . . . Yes! The weeping Greenpeace girls look at each other with that whatyoucallit, yeah, *wild surmise*. Good. Good. The trumpets grow. The whaling ship doesn't even flinch, they aim the big harpoon, so what, they think it's just another bunch of fucking hippies on their gap years, what do they care? They laugh, ho ho ho. But as they aim the harpoon, something's going on aboard the new boat: a tarpaulin is pulled aside, we glimpse dark metal, we see the eyes of the new-boat guys and girls: these are no ordinary loved-up peaceniks! A strong arm, a hard eye, a *semper fidelis* tattoo, yeah, yeah, you see it, friend?

—Shit, man . . .

— . . . More trumpets. Horns and trombones. Mummy whale is right in the cross-hairs, Mr Slant-Eyes licks his lips, his finger whitens on the harpoon trigger, and . . . BUDABUDABUDABUDABUDA!!! blood-bags everywhere, the guy at the harpoon just blows apart, the other slant-eyed whaling bastards reach for their guns, but the strange new boat, oh boy, now we see it fully at last, and it's mounting a fuck-off, all-American Browning 0.5, it just *wastes* them, splatters the whole show, peeowpeeowpeeow . . . KaBOOM, the whaling ship goes up.

—Yes! Yes, sir!

—Yes! Exactly. Major petrochemical explosion time, and . . . and? And what happens? I tell you what. The sixteen- to twenty-four-year-old boys and girls cheer, my man. Cheer. They fucking *cheer* these whaling bastards being chewed apart by lead and fried up for breakfast. *Would* they? Would they cheer? They would, wouldn't they? Or wouldn't they? You *know* they would. Well?

Salmon paused, arms flung wide, eyes huge.

—Yes, sir, yes! cried Skanky, and seemed about to fling himself prostrate at Salmon's feet, his face locked in a primate smile of devotion and subservience. But then Salmon seemed slightly to deflate. He shook his head at his own stupidity.

—I know, I know what you're going to say. *But will it play in Singapore*? Problem with the slant-eyes eh? OK, OK. So they're *Norwegian* whalers. Ha ha! Yes. Nazis, you know, tall, blond, blue-eyed Nazi bastards. The flag on the boat says *Norwegian*, but the pictures say: *Nazis*. Much better. If you ever get to choose the bad guys, friend, choose Nazis every time, believe me, no bad guys play like Nazis. You copy?

—Norwegian Whaling Nazi Bastards, muttered Skanky, his eyes lowered in hypnotised respect, nodding his head to Salmon's half-heard words as he had nodded it so often, for timeless hours on end, to the infinitely repetitive four-square loop of solstice trance music in damp Cornish fields.

—Yep. Nazis play everywhere. Even Germany. Ask the guy that wrote *Captain Corelli*, and if you don't believe him, ask his accountant. We may have a problem in Norway, but who ever heard of a show going down because *it didn't play in Norway*, ha ha!

—Right, ha ha! Fuck *Norway*, man.

—Unless you're applying to the Nordic Film Fund, obviously. Shit! Hit me, man. I did it again! I forgot about the *love*. I always do. Got to remind myself: *sex and violence sells, but love cleans up*. So true, so true.

—Yeah. Love, man. (Salmon did not see the eyes burn more deeply still.)

—OK, so we get a close-up on the love interest in the Greenpeace wimp boat right at the start, yeah, we establish Her at the top of the film. Let's see, let's see. OK, yeah, she's a blonde who's kind of harder-core than the other wimps, but still worried, she's *conflicted*, she doesn't want violence, but she wants to save the world. Hmm. Is blonde too last millennium? Do the sixteen- to twenty-four-year-old kids go more for redheads, these days? Maybe a redhead with kinda dreadlocks, yeah?

—Red Dread Girl, murmured Skanky, his eyes wide with dark yearning, as if Salmon had ushered him gently up to a peephole in the very gates of heaven. Then he seemed to awake, and bowed his head, crestfallen at his own inability to serve the new guru:
– I'm sorry, sir, I don't really, you know, *women*, sir, I don't, I haven't really, not for along time, I . . .

—Forget it, said Salmon, and turned to pick up his shopping and leave.

—But, sir, you can't go, you, I mean, The Saviours, man, where can I meet these guys, I got to . . .

— . . . Watch this space. And spread the word.

—Don't leave me, sir. I want to do this thing.

—Got to run, friend, clock never stops ticking.

Salmon disengaged himself from Skanky's helplessly respectful grip. But as he bent heavily to grab his bags, his face passed close to the Greenpeace brochure, and his eye (which was used to checking out the bottom line first in any deal) automatically, unconsciously located the tear-off form where it actually said *exactly* how much they were going to hit you for, after all the flannel and soft-soap and pandas.

He stopped dead. He dropped his bags and stood up straight again. His hand came down upon Skanky's shoulder like a royal sword. Skanky froze hopefully.

Salmon reached out and grabbed the Greenpeace sign-up form. He stared. After all, he could write off a membership of Greenpeace against tax, as legitimate research on *The Saviours*. And surely it was the hand of Fate itself that had written: *Standard Annual Donation: £60*.

Brown Bread and Leeks

Dr Jane Feverfew, the new lecturer in Spanish Literature, was sitting in her new office at the University of
Pontypool ('Quality Through Excellence in an Industrial Heritage Environment') trying to make her new
Option proposal ('The Vision of the Text') seem *fun*
(and easy) to a group of some half-dozen second-year
students, so that they would sign up for it when the
new semester began next week.

As she chatted away in the required youthful +
carefree manner, Jane was actually fighting back the
horrible certainty that she had been wrong to ever come
to Wales.

She had arrived a month ago, from London. Being
a single woman of thirty-five in a new place is not a
good thing, especially at the weekend; being a single
parent of thirty-five in a new place is not a good thing
either, especially at the weekend. Jane was divorced,
with a five-year-old boy called Bryn, and she alternated
Bryn-care weekends, so she was sometimes a single
parent and sometimes a single woman, which is just
plain psychotic, at thirty-five, in a new place, especially
at the weekend.

—Sounds like the *coolest* Option, said one of the
girls.

—Yeah, sounds *fun*, said one of the boys.

—Should be, said Jane, her autopilot selecting the
correct degree of bored, chilled, pleasure. She wanted
these students, and she was going to get them.

Jane was a popular lecturer wherever she worked

because she had carefully trained herself to pick up the slightest hint in the students' chit-chat, dress and TV habits. She had known when it had been *cool* to say *Oh my God, they killed Kenny* in her lectures, and when that had suddenly become *so not cool*. She said things like *Puh-lease, this is such utter fucking crap* and *How much of a heap of stinky pants* is *that?* at least once a lecture. This was just the sort of stuff students anywhere liked to hear. First-year male students everywhere especially liked that kind of thing, especially if it was said by a thirty-five-year-old female lecturer who always wore knickerline-tight black jeans with big turn-ups (a different brand every day, but always tight and black, always big turn-ups) and boots (different boots every day, but always boots) and whose red lipstick and dyed-blonde hair never changed their shade. Jane also knew that it was important to seem as if she did not really give a damn whether they signed up or not.

In fact, she cared a great deal. If enough of them chose her Option, she would be allowed to run it. If not, she would be landed with the Business Language Class. Jane did not want to teach the Business Language Class. And it was vital that Jane's work-life was not *too* vile right now, because Jane's life-life was not really going very well.

Last night, she had been on her first Date in Wales. It had not been a success.

As she chatted coolly away to the young people across from her, Jane suppressed a graphic shudder of memory. He had not been too bad-looking, true; he had not even been *too* boring, at first, for an Economics lecturer. And after all, Jane had been out with enough men to know that if you want a man, you are just going to have to discount *boring* in advance. (Autism is almost always male; Jane darkly suspected that it

18

is really just another name for extreme maleness.) But since she had not expected much, the evening had not been horrendously depressing, really, at first. He had been English, so naturally they had been able to laugh about Wales together. Except then the waitress brought the basket full of ghastly so-called fresh-baked French bread and her Date, this plain, balding, boring man of forty for whom she had actually bloody dressed up and put on make-up and lied about how happy she was (*Argh! The Shame!*), stopped the girl and quietly asked for *a little bit of brown bread*. And as he asked for his *little bit of brown bread*, he smiled at Jane, a hideous, shy, smugly pleading smile of complicity, and he said:
—Well, *better*, you know.

Even remembering it now, Jane shivered. She might be getting too old for a man with *The Rough Guide* in his backpack, but she was not ready for a man with *The Roughage Guide* in his car coat . . .

. . . Jane shook herself back to the present and said the sort of thing she knew the students liked hearing:
—Yeah, film and TV is the only way to look at literature these days. I mean, would Shakespeare write *stage plays* today? Like, *really*, yeah?
—We're, like, up for it, yeah, guys?
—Def.
—Cool, said Jane, bringing the meeting to an end. Then she waved them coolly away, coolfully turning down an invitation to join them for vodka and Red Bull down the Students' Union bar on the pretty damn chilled-out grounds that she had to take, like, a couple of calls.
—*Like*, said Jane to herself: —Christ almighty.

Jane stood in her office for a few moments, resisting a wave of hopeless regret at having left London, and then went out across the corridor to the departmental noticeboards, in order to place her Option Proposal formally on the Year 2 section. There were, as always, no free drawing pins, so she started pinching some from her colleagues' Option sheets.

—You *what*? screamed a very Welsh male voice nearby, and Jane jumped guiltily. Spinning around, however, she realised that the yell had not been aimed at her at all: —You *read* your bastard contract?, it continued, nearby but unseen, bawling out from Professor Evan Evans's office. Jane began hastily to tiptoe back across the corridor, to the sanctuary of her own office.

—Well, yes actually, said a second voice, a desperate voice, an English voice trying pathetically to defend itself without *making a scene*. —Yes, I have. Actually. And my contract clearly states that my duties are . . .

— . . .*States*? States, does it? Does it state that you have a *right* to teach the useless bloody crap that only *you* care about? Well? And you stay right there, Janeygirl. I want a word with you too.

Jane stayed. A tall, thin, bearded man had retreated out into the corridor: one of Jane's new colleagues, a Senior Lecturer whose name she did not yet even know. Professor Evan Evans now appeared in the doorway of his spacious office, short of stature, large of belly and broken of nose, as befitted a former Wales Schoolboys rugby hooker. His thick, curling hair, years since turned a silvery white but still worn long and with imposing sideboards, in homage to the Grand Slam heroes of his bachelor days, lent him a curious resemblance, after one of his longer lunches, to a red-faced koala. Now, as he stood and confronted the wretched Senior Lecturer, Evans seemed to delight in his own fury.

—Well? So you've read your contract, have you? *Read*, can you? Duw duw, there's qualified. Thank

God for a good old-fashioned Cambridge education, eh? Worth every penny of the poor bastard miners' taxes that paid you to go and ponce about with posh poofs on punts for years, eh? And don't tell me you don't secretly wish you were back there, eating roasted sodding swans and buggering about in a stupid bloody gown. I know your sort. Slumming it here, you are, that's all, and dreaming of posh fucking quadrangles. *Read*, can you? Well, I can read too and I remember what I read because I was brought up to read and remember the bastard Bible on pain of my father's belt on a Sunday morning and I'll tell you what your contract says, shall I? It says you shall fulfil *'such duties as the Head of Department may require'*. Not the bastard *University*, see? And not the bastard *Union*, right? The bastard *Head*! Me. I could have you washing my bastard car if I wanted. But do I? No. All I ask is that you get off your high English horse, roll up your posh little sleeves, and pull your weight with the bastard Business Language Course, which just happens to be the only thing which keeps (a) this bastard department afloat and hence (b) posh Cambridge sods like you in jobs where a grateful state pays you, for some Godunknown reason, to pursue so-called Research that isn't worth a tart's fart to anyone else on earth. Do I make myself clear? Well?

—Yes, said the Senior Lecturer, sounding as if he were about to choke on his own impotence. He walked stiffly away, like someone who is trying very hard not to run, quite unable to return the utter conviction and joyful outrage that blazed in Evans' gaze; as he passed Jane, the two of them carefully avoided doing anything which might indicate each other's presence on the same planet.

Professor Evans shook out his shoulders, his arms and his chins, then turned his head slowly and menacingly towards Jane. He smiled, showing satisfaction and teeth.

—Nice boots, Janeygirl, growled he.

—Ah, said Jane, guardedly.

—Well? Got your poncey Option sorted?

Jane was still holding the paper which she had been about to pin to the noticeboard. Evans grabbed it and skim-read. When he had finished, he grunted and plonked it back into Jane's hand.

—All right if you have the IQ of a fourteen-year-old, I suppose. Which makes it a dead cert with the Second Years. Fair play to you, Janey. Should get plenty to sign up for that. Keep you safe from teaching the Business Language Class, eh?

—I just want to, you know, *teach my own speciality*. After all, it's the best use of my work time, for the department, and, well . . .

— . . . And you don't want to teach the bastard Business Language Class.

—Well, yes, Business Spanish isn't really my speciality and I thought . . .

— . . . I know you lot, none of you bastards wants to teach the Business Language Class. Or the First Year Beginners Options. Especially you poncey bloody English girls. Think you're too good for the coalface, don't you, just want to piss about doing your clever postmodern crap, eh? Posh English bastards.

—Posh English? Me? I'm half Scots and I went to comprehensive school, for God's sake, said Jane. —You saw my CV.

Jane was very keen to get this point firmed up. The Scots bit was a bit dodgy, since she was really only a quarter Scots and had lived there merely for some half-dozen, half-forgotten years of her childhood, but posh she was certainly not.

Jane's trouble, her never-ending trouble, was that she had been locked at birth into the body and face of a brainless, upper-class, horsy-tweedy girl. All her life, she had been doing battle with (a) her own hips and (b) people who assumed that she was posh. The hips were tough going because she loved food and drink; the posh was always a problem because her parents, teachers who had believed in Harold Wilson and Progress and suchlike, had moved up and down, from England to Scotland and back again and round about, all through her childhood, leaving Jane with one of those nowhere-and-nothing accents that sound *posh* to people who have real, proper accents from somewhere. There is no point looking and sounding like that unless you have the money to go with it, and Jane did not. Being an allegedly posh cow is not a very sexy thing to be as a seventeen-year-old at a bog-standard northern comprehensive, and it doesn't much help when you are applying for crap, menial jobs after college either. True, she had been able to sneak in for amazingly cheap lunches in the Medical Staff Dining Room at University College Hospital, when she was a penniless postgrad, without anyone ever doubting that she was a Hearty Young Doctor, but that was the only good her looks and voice had ever done her. Now, she was *not* going to let Evans get away with typecasting her as posh right from the start.

—Posh I am not, said she, with unusual firmness.

—All right, Janey, all right, point taken. Now, what else was it? Oh yes: shagging.

—Sorry?

—Shagging.

—Um . . .

23

—Departmental Policy regarding the shagging of students.

—Oh. Well . . .

— . . . They'll come into your office when everything's quiet and start asking for *just a few pointers to the kind of finals questions we might get on your Option, Dr Feverfew*, or rather *Dr Jane*, I bet you make them call you *Dr Jane*, eh? (Evans laid his head on one side and did a very fine impression of a young male student looking up at her with imploring, fuck-me eyes.) —Showing their flat little six-packs off, eh? Prancing about in their baggy trousers and sandals, is it?

—Ah, said Jane.

Actually, it *had* occurred to her. In London, she had taught a couple of male finalists who could do quite good impressions of real human beings. At twenty-one, they were just entering that brief window between Spotty and Seedy, that short decade when you can have sex with a man without knowing that he is going to run straight back to his mates so he can boast about it, or run straight back to his wife and kids so he can lie about it. She could hardly remember what a cock was *like*, for Christ's sake. And they *did* have flat stomachs and downy, breastless chests, and . . .

—I don't give a monkey's toss *after* the finals are in, said Evans. —Once it's too late for them to get clues, you can shag as many of them as you like, then they can piss off to Thailand to *find themselves*, God help us.

—Right, said Jane.

—I know, you're going to say: well, who says you can't just shag them and then *not* give them clues for the finals? They could hardly complain. Well, I'll tell you a funny thing, Janeygirl: it just *doesn't happen like that*, does it?

—I suppose not, said Jane. Professor Evans suddenly looked at her in a new and more guarded manner.

—Here, Janey, *you* never did *that* to student, did you? Shag them and then *not* give them any clues? You didn't? Did you?

—I've never shagged a student, actually, said Jane, trying not to feel absurdly ashamed.

—What, *never*? asked Evans, genuinely amazed.

—I'm not even legally *divorced* yet.

—Oh, I see. Oh. Sorry, girly. See, I assumed you got divorced *because* you shagged students. That's the usual way. Oh, well, there we are. Well done on the Option. And don't trip over your turn-ups on the stairs.

Jane returned to the noticeboard, where she pinned up her Option Proposal and scanned it wearily as the melancholy sunset blazed fitfully into the empty corridor through the Pontypool rain.

Friday afternoon.

Jane could tidy her desk, grab her bag, set off for her home in Cardiff, and be *free*.

Totally, utterly *free*.

All weekend.

Hoo-bloody-rah.

Jane had already discovered that Wales has the same number of intelligent, sane, attractive, interesting, straight and free single men over thirty who actually like kids (as opposed to pretending to like kids to get inside girls' pants) as anywhere else in Britain: that is, none at all. Even London has none, but at least in London you could sit alone and stare out at the sodium-lit darkness and tell yourself comfortingly that The Right Person must be out there *somewhere* in all those teeming, yearning millions. You never *know*,

Jane had been able to murmur softly, as the rain fell from the orange London half-night. But here, you *knew* all right . . .

—*There* you are, said a voice behind her, as if on cue. Another Welsh male voice; Dafydd Thomas's voice; her husband's well-known, once-loved voice. Jane swung to see him coming up the corridor. She had not seen him for two days, and now she looked at him with a strange, clear sense of distance, as if she were observing him approach her through a wall of highly polished glass.

He was carrying a small booklet with a Welsh title, and a single large leek.

For a short but unnerving moment, Jane wondered if he was about to go down on one knee, thrust the leek romantically into her hands and start quoting Welsh bardic poetry at her in an attempt to get them back together.

For a shorter but even more alarming moment, she caught herself wondering what she would do if he did.

I mean, why not? If you have given up on love?

Who would you call on 11 September?

The other parent of your only child, of course.

Yeah, but who would *he* call?

His mother, of course.

Jane and Dafydd were presently waiting for their decree nisi to come through. They were *doing things amicably*. This was quite easy because in London they were naturally too poor to buy anywhere to live, even with both of them working, and spent all their wages on rent and childcare. So when they realised that they had neither laughed out loud together nor made love for more than six months, so they had better split up to avoid wasting their lives, there was no house and no money to be amicable about anyway.

They agreed to do whatever they could in order to avoid ruining Bryn's little life.

They agreed to come to Wales.

They agreed this because Dafydd's family was large, chatty, close-knit and rich in children, while Jane's family was small, tight-arsed, far-flung and not. They thought that by coming to Wales they would be able to give little Bryn something like a proper life with other real humans and children in it, not just crèches and videos. And be able to both afford little houses with little gardens for him to play in. And actually, Jane liked Dafydd's family, she always had. More actually, she had always liked Dafydd's family more than she had liked Dafydd himself. Especially, she liked one of Dafydd's great-uncles called Gwyn, who was always fascinated by how much Jane had *moved about* in her life.

—Duw duw, there's a lot of bother. Me, I was born here in Ponty, Janeylove, *and I have never moved*.

(Jane imagined him, as a baby, not moving as his thirties terrace was built about him; as a toddler, motionless in shorts as his mam and nan ferried plain but substantial, ration-cooked meals to him; as a boy, immobile as his prefab school was constructed about his person by Italian POWs; as a young man, self-consciously statuesque in his best wedding clothes, smoking a Woodbine as a chapel sprang up behind him and a shy girl in white came down to his side to be photographed; solid as a rock as he sank gradually, vertically, unmoving, into a newly nationalised mine; and then arose again, an elderly man now, perfectly, perfectly still as the mine was filled in beneath his ascending feet, his helmet removed from his head and replaced with a cap, the mine closed down and turned into a Heritage Experience complete with bilingual signs, and the slag heaps landscaped all around him. Before him, a table was placed by women, resplendent meat and vegetables awash with dark, sweet gravy were set before him. He *had never moved . . .*)

. . . Perhaps little Bryn would never have to move, now? Perhaps he would have that strange, lost, mythical thing called a *home*? Perhaps, if she really *did* shove Dafydd off a handy cliff, they would sort of adopt *her* as well as Bryn? She might never have to move again. She could sit here, quite still, and let the world spin on about her. She might, one dim and distant day, even wake up to find that she had lost her stupid bloody posh accent and gained what we all long for: someone else's Big Family.

No Big Families, no Big Stories.

Ti-tum.

. . . And so, as she looked at Dafydd now, as he advanced, leek and book in hand, Jane allowed herself to think the two Forbidden Things that everyone who has ever been stuck amicably between decree nisi and decree absolute will have thought. Should she (a) drain his brake fluid one night, right now, while they were still legally married, so she could cash in his life insurance and have a full-time nanny for her child instead of a part-time bloody father? Or (b) get back together with him so that Normality and Comfort could return to her life?

I mean, why not?

What had she broken up with him *for*? Freedom? Freedom for what? So that she could spend another three thousand nights alone in her little house in Cardiff with Bryn? So that she could get drunk with gay men once a week if she was lucky? So that she could maybe, just maybe, have the odd night with a man who was not *too* old and boring and who would be decent enough

28

afterwards at least to lie half convincingly about why he was running away so quickly? What the hell was she after? For *that*, she had given up all Normality and Comfort? She and Dafydd got on OK, they were amicable enough, so if he asked, if he really, *seriously* asked, maybe, after all, she was not sure that she would not . . .

. . . Dafydd, however, did not go down on his knees and plead with his leek for the return of Normality. Instead, he looked Jane up and down.

—God, Janey, you *still* wearing those black trousers? (*OK, OK, brake fluid it is.*)

He now did indeed present Jane with the leek, though in an entirely unromantic way, but before she could ask what exactly it might be for, he also shoved the booklet into her hand. Jane immediately recognised it, because she had already found copies of it three times in her pigeon-hole since arriving here.

It was a booklet from the University Staff Development Board, inviting her to take Welsh classes. The classes were, it was ringingly announced, *free*; it was hinted that unclear but attractive future benefits might be expected from learning Welsh; it was also subtly noted that anyone who did not want to spend a mere few hours a week learning Welsh, when it was *absolutely free*, had *only themselves to blame*. It did not say exactly what these insanely anti-Welsh-language people would have themselves to blame for, but the menace, like the bribe, was unmistakable, if vague.

—Yeah, I know about that, but I'm too busy with work right now, said Jane, and she waved her leek firmly in the air, like an African dictator with a ceremonial fly-swish.

—Well, you'll have to learn Welsh sometime now Bryn's at Welsh-language school, or you won't be able

29

to talk to your own son, will you? So you may as well do it while it's free.

—Look, Daf, I was thinking. (The leek now slumped, pleadingly, at Jane's side.) —If we really want him to be bilingual, we could bring him up speaking Spanish instead, couldn't we?

—*Spanish?* Good God, why?

—Why? Well, because I teach it. And then he could talk to about four hundred million more people in the world. Instead of just another half-million people in Wales who he can already talk to anyway.

—There's Patagonia too. They speak Welsh in Patagonia. And they *don't speak English*. Ha!

—No, but they do speak Spanish.

—Eh?

—So if I teach him Spanish he can even speak to the Patagonians, if he ever wants to.

—Yes, well, that's not the point, Janey: we don't *live* in Spain.

—No, but we're all global now, and *international*, and anyway it's ridiculous, I can't even pronounce the name of my son's school.

—What, Ysgol Mynydd Ynys-y-bwl?

—I can say it when *you* say it, but every time I *read* it my brain explodes.

—So learn Welsh. You learned Spanish.

—But there's a *point* to learning Spanish.

—You are *so* bloody English, Janey.

—I am not!

—If it was *Icelandic*, you wouldn't think it was pointless.

—If I was in Iceland I wouldn't send my son to an Icelandic-only speaking school if three-quarters of everyone in Iceland had stopped speaking Icelandic a hundred years ago and they spoke English now

30

instead and even the ones that did speak Icelandic spoke perfect English as well.

—They probably already bloody *do*, said Dafydd, bitterly. —Do you *want* the whole world to speak nothing but English?

—Daf, I *teach Spanish*, remember? I love languages, I just . . . Oh, for God's sake, said Jane, suddenly tired. She could feel that familiar Anglo-Saxon rush of hopelessness in the face of pure, unembarrassed, guilt-free, Celtic Authenticity. She already knew she was going to lose. Again.

—Janey: we came here so our son could grow up at home in Wales, with a family around him, yes?

—Yes, yes, said Jane.

—And we both hope he'll stay here and feel *at home*, yes?

—Yes, of course. But, Daf, most of your family don't even speak Welsh. You've only been learning for three months yourself.

—Don't start that again, Janey. I didn't bloody realise how things have changed here, did I? No one cared about Welsh round here when I was growing up. Socialism and rugby, we cared about. The Pontypool Front Row and J.P.R. Williams, we sang about. In English. But not any more. Welsh, you got to speak now: the rest of us are trash. What's the point of us giving Bryn a home here if he has to bugger off to London to get work because he doesn't speak bastard Welsh? I hope he wants to stay here when he's older, and if he does want to, I'm not having him kept out of all the decent jobs by a bunch of bloody Gogs.

—Gogs?

—Northerners.

—Oh yes, I remember. The *Gogs*. The ones that talk through their noses.

31

—Yeah, them. Bastards. Right. I'll bring him round to your place for teatime on Sunday. And Monday is St David's Day, so *do* remember to dress him up in costume for the afternoon procession, won't you? It's expected, at the new school.

—Costume? What costume?

—An old cap, braces, boots and a waistcoat. And a leek, of course. I got you the leek.

—Yes, I noticed. What do I do with it?

—You pin it to his braces.

—Daf, where the hell do I get child-sized braces?

—There's a whole window display in the Cardiff House of Fraser. Everything you need. Or a Welsh rugby shirt would do instead. They do imitation Seventies Grand Slam Years shirts in boys' sizes, very nice, get him the number 10 jersey if there are any left.

—But this is ridiculous. I'd never dress him up for St George's Day.

—Of course not, this is St David's Day. Well, it's up to you. If you really want our son to be the *only one in the school* not dressed up for it, if you think it's OK for him to feel *left out*, and for all the other kids to think he's *funny* and *English* and *posh* . . .

— . . . All right all right, where did you say I get the stuff?

After Dafydd had left, Jane locked up her office for the weekend, stuffed the leek into her handbag (the leaves stuck out a clear foot) and stood for a while in the corridor, staring out of the window at the rain and at the wet, Welsh, green hills beyond. On the ancient lino, her sexy boots squeaked quietly, pointlessly, barrenly.

Friday night.

A free weekend.

Great.

She did not want a free weekend. Being a single mother with no family or pals about her was hard, but Bryn was lovely; her only fear was that Bryn would soon start to prefer his weekends with Daddy (and Daddy's brothers and sisters and aunties and uncles and nephews and nieces) to his weekends with Mummy (and Mummy and Mummy). On her free weekends, though, when Bryn was with Dafydd (or rather, with Dafydd's family), Jane was as lonely as any shy, friendless, first-year student. Quite probably, she would not say a word to another human being between now and Monday morning unless she went and bought stuff she did not need, argued uselessly with Dafydd, or went to a bar on her own and let some fat slimy git talk to her because he wanted to look at her tits.

—Oh, balls and arse and death, sighed Jane.

Standing quietly in the corridor, she looked idly at one of her new colleagues' doors. She had not met this colleague yet. She had not met many colleagues yet: you don't, at universities. The door had on it a big photograph cut out from the *Abergavenny Chronicle*: it showed two bearded lecturers, daringly holding up pints of beer in dimpled glasses. Beneath this picture, the unknown colleague had written, big and proud, with a red felt-tip pen: '*Would you buy a used degree from this dodgy duo?!*'

Jane felt strangely ill.

Her trousers felt strangely tight.

She was going to have to learn Welsh.

Christ, why had she left London?

OK, OK, the students *had* to sign up for her Option Course. She was not teaching the bloody Business Language Class on top of everything else. They *must* believe she was cool. Jane glanced around the corridor shiftily. There was no one about: they had all gone off to their unfree weekends, the lucky sods. Right, then.

At her previous university, Jane had so cunningly persuaded her students she was cool (rather than a quiet, studious person who had spent her twenties in studies and libraries, not in clubs and on beaches) that the stupid little sods had changed the name on her office door. Perhaps it would help if she did it here? It might. They would assume it had been done by other students. Quickly, Jane reached up with a pen and worked away. Then she pocketed the letters she had prised away and, blushing with shame and guilt, head down in case anyone had seen her, walked swiftly away, leaving on her office door a nameplate that now read: *DJ FEVER*.

Soft Money

By five o'clock, Salmon was sitting upstairs in the telly room at the Groucho, with Kev, Max, Dorian and The Gang, downing his free vodkas and smoking his free cigarettes and fingering his skimpy, press-out Greenpeace temporary membership card with a certain glow of sentimental pride, gloating over the fact that he was saving whales and rainforests and whatever bollocks else *for nothing*.

So here he was, not taking cocaine. Fine. Curious, but fine. No sign of Sheina or her mates. Oh well. So what? Salmon had already planned his fall-back evening: a video he really *ought* to see, the best takeaway in Chinatown, the finest wine and porn in Old Compton Street. The minicab was, as always, self-evident: fuck *public transport*. It would all hardly add up to more than the gram he was not going to take tonight.

All free.

Sorted, then.

—*Or rather, not*, chuckled Salmon, as he sucked deeply on his vodka and tonic, lit up another fag luxuriantly, laughed broadly along with the others round the table, without having the faintest notion of what he was laughing at, and laid his substantial weight further back in his chair with the smug air of a man who, unlike practically every other bastard in the place (to judge by the frequency and convivial manner of their trips bogwards) is not taking cocaine. So that was all right. He would have a good, clean, weekend; he would spend the whole of tomorrow and Sunday working out his Big New Pitch; come Monday, he would blow Alan Barony away with it.

Salmon allowed his vodkas to hit warmly home and luxuriated in a mellow, gold-lit vision of himself calmly sitting in his flat, smilingly working out the easy details of his Pitch over good coffee and fresh croissants; he saw himself on Monday morning, purified and cleansed with antioxidants, in white-pressed running gear, doing his two kilometres in ten minutes on the machine, emerging from the sauna, shaved glassily clean and glowing with aerobic health, taking a light but tasty (and dry!) lunch, rocket & Parmesan or some such suitable bollocks, and finally breezing into Barony's office, radiating irresistible success.

Things were going to be fine.

His life was bright and clear: it followed a pure, inevitable line (no, a *track*, Salmon corrected himself hastily). His long march had started on that lucky day back in the eighties when he had first been sent by sheer chance, as a young accountancy temp, into a movie office in Wardour Street, where he had quickly noted that anyone who can simultaneously crawl to The Money, flatter The Talent and cook The Books has got what it takes to Produce. His career since then had been a logical progression towards triumph. *There is a place to get to, but no path; what we call the path is merely hesitation; as you take the step, you are already there.* Who said that again? Must have been one of the Chink flicks, that's the good thing about Chink scripts, you can get away with any kind of philosophical bollocks, mmmmm, maybe *Chinese* ecowarriors?

Whatever. He had all the time in the world to work stuff out, now he had stopped taking cocaine. It had been so easy, really. Which just went to show he was no way actually *hooked* on the stuff, obviously . . .

—Christ, said Sheina, breezing in beside him. —Hiya, Max. Paul, darling: *what* a day, I could murder a line, she said, just like that, shaking out her hair and lighting up a red Marlboro before she had even sat down. —Alan is *such* a bore. He almost made me go to some ghastly awards thing in *Wales*, for God's sake. Apparently, they're having their own sort of *extra*ordinary Oscars in Cardiff tonight.

Sheina air-kissed Salmon: her kiss was already full of perfumed cigarette smoke. The smoke passed by Salmon's nostrils; his hand rested for a second on the mild swell of her hip; his eye flicked for an instant over what was on show of her small, pale breasts. Then she sat down, chattering, and Salmon listened and smiled, determined not to be a *bore*.

Bore, he knew, was Sheina's highest term of disapproval, the number-one sin in her and her friends' eyes. Being *bored* was the absolute worst thing that could happen to someone. Boredom was the opposite of fun: lots of *fun* was what Sheina and her pals said they were going to have with their next project, whatever it was.

Salmon knew with half his brain that when they said *fun*, they meant *money*; when they said a man was a *bore*, they meant *poisonous little sexually abusive power-crazed creep, but hey, a girl's got to eat*, and when they said *a line* they meant *half a g for starters*. But somehow, every time he actually *met* Sheina, all this insight just went out of the window.

—Yes, they're on tonight in Cardiff, said Salmon, pulling in his gut and sitting taller. —The Cymru-Wales Oscars.

—But I thought the population of Wales was about the same as the population of, well, *Greater Birmingham* or somewhere.

—It is, said Salmon, —but don't knock it.

—Well, how hot would the *Top Young Film-Maker in Greater Birmingham* be?

—Sheina, you never heard of Euro-Funds? The Lesser-Used and Traditional Languages Equalisation Fund? The Marginal Lands and Celtic Heartlands Cultural Project II? The Anglo-Saxon-Franco-Hispanic-Teutonic Imperialism Compensation Initiative?

—Oh yes, I think Alan once said something about looking into that sort of thing.

—Did he? Well, yes, he would. Soft money, if you can get it.

—Golly. Is there much of it about?

—Look, Sheina, it's only 0.013 per cent of the EU Budget, so nobody notices it and no one complains, right? The EU budget is just another EU lake, a money lake, a lake so big you could sink the whole of the Third World debt in it and only the tip would show. *That* side of the dam, who cares if a poxy 0.013 per cent is trickling out each year? No one. Keeps a bunch of sad idiots and wasters happy in the pub when they might be running about the hills in berets, blowing things up and spray-painting government buildings and generally making a nuisance of themselves. Every Bogside bogtrotter and every Basque arsehole who can invent a Cultural Initiative and prove they have no connections to the IRA or ETA gets money chucked at them. Keep the sods quiet; cheaper than cops; value for money.

—Oh. So it's not worth worrying about, then?

—No, no, no! That's the view from *that* side of the dam. But! But if you're standing *this* side of the dam, different story. Get your bucket out, lady. You know how much 0.013 per cent of £500,000,000,000 is? Enough to keep several hundred cute little media businesses in Edinburgh and Dublin and Quimper and Cardiff and Bilbao and fuck knows where else afloat and paying London wages and leasing a nice new Merc every three years, is how much.

—Yes, I see. Coo. So, how do we *get* it? That would be fun.

—We can't. We're the oppressors. You have to be Welsh or Basque or Irish or Catalan or something. Eskimos count as well, I think.

—Eskimos?

—Because of Denmark.

—Oh. Oh well. Not much fun to be had there then.

—I dunno. You only need a Co-Production agreement. Hmmm. Must have a chat with Alan about it on Monday.

—Oh, did you get a one-to-one? asked Sheina, visibly impressed.

—Course, said Salmon, visibly swelling.

—Well *done*, darling. You do know he wants to make Art this time, do you?

—Art? Alan? You sure?

—Ye-es. Well, at least something with *class*. I suppose that means big dresses for the girls and knee-britches for the boys, doesn't it?

—Got to be. Hmmm. *Historical*, then. When's he thinking of?

—He wants it Green-Lighted yesterday and in Pre-Production before Cannes. And for less than £2.5 million.

—Before Cannes? That's impossible. He'd need a script yesterday. And you can't *do* historical that cheap. History costs.

—Well, that's what he *wants*. He's got some big meeting on Hal Scharnhorst's yacht at Cannes, it's *quite* the highlight of Alan's year, and he really, really, *really* wants Hal Scharnhorst to know he's doing something of his own with *class*. But not British. Alan's fed up with that.

—Shit.

—And make sure you say the lead girl always dresses in white stockings.

—White?

—Yes. You know, those thick cotton ones.

—Why?

—Trust me, Paul. I know Alan.

—Wow. Thanks, Sheina. Top data, top bird.

—I thought you might like to know. Oh, look, there's my friend Miranda, I'll bring her over, she works for MaxiPix now, you know. Can I put a Sea Breeze or three on your tab, darling? Mine's just *too* bloody terrifying at the moment. They might *remind* me about it and I don't think I could *stand* that sort of *menacing behaviour* tonight. My hero. Oh, and did you say you were posh tonight, darling? No? Oh, that's a bore.

Salmon had gone to a state school in Maidstone and had never even heard of a thing called a Private Income until he went to Brighton University: he had always been turned on like hell by girls like Sheina and her gang. Girls he had never been remotely able to fuck: until now. She opened up vistas of some pristine world where, once inside, you would be safe for ever. And so the moment Sheina started to speak, started to unleash her natural-blonde English-rose hair, light up a Marlboro, talk merrily about coke, Salmon began to wonder (to shake his head mentally in wonder) how on earth he could ever have been such a bore (a ghastly, lower-middle-class, cheese-paring *bore*) as to worry about whether or not he (*he*, the Producer of *Base Metal*, *he* who was going to seal his next deal in a one-to-one meeting with Alan Barony on Monday; *he*, the friend of Dorian and Kev and Baz and Joni and The Gang) was going to take a couple of little lines tonight (or just finger-dabs, maybe, yeah, dabs don't really count, everyone knows that).

How pathetic.

How idiotic.

How *boring*.

OK, so he was actually broke at the moment (not Sheina-world-broke, but real-person-broke), so what? So it would have to go on his tab with Fatty, so what? This was the world he lived in: *fun*.

How extraordinary of me, thought Salmon.

Extraordinary was Sheina's other big word. Salmon knew what *Ordinary* was to her: Ordinary was inheriting a nice flat in north London, was walking by some sort of social osmosis into a job with Alan Barony Film Distribution Ltd, was skiing in Val d'Isere where someone or other could always put you up. *Extra*ordinary was anything else: living in Walthamstow, signing on, having to consider money.

Working.

Worrying.

Thinking.

Salmon did not want to have to work, or worry, or think any more. OK, he was only thirty-six, but shit, it was time to get set up, found a Production Company, hire twenty-two-year-olds on the make to do the work and cream his Management Fees off the top. He had done his time. He was fed up hustling. He wanted to be taken up now, here and now, amid the clouds of Sheina's golden hair, to live in the padlocked, paddocked realms where the sheets are always crisp and clean, the cream-coloured Aga is always warm, the deals are shoved happily back and forth among friends and nothing can ever be worse than *boring* ever, ever again.

So when Fatty texted Salmon just then (*our spanish surrealist mate is in town + looking very handsome*) and Sheina just said *Oh good!* like a schoolgirl with sweets, Salmon found himself replying to the message before he was aware of having made any conscious decision. As he texted, he watched Sheina's mouth as she chattered happily away to Miranda. She seemed very far away, and he thought (as his front teeth were already numbing up slightly in anticipation, it was the last real thought he had that night) *It's OK. It's OK. Just a bit of a laugh, just a couple of lines, dabs rather, then home. Maybe with Sheina. Take it easy, get it up. Got the whole weekend to work out the Pitch. It's OK. A costume drama, Gary Winchester's just flogged one to MaxiPix. History is the new Sci-Fi, Barony will eat out of my hand, there's acres of stuff out there, I just need to think for a bit. Not British? Some Chinese shit. Or the ecowarriors thing. Yoofresistance, or whatever it was called? A Historical thing about Chinese ecowarriors? And don't forget love, idiot!! Christ, I fancy her. That tight fucker! How the fuck does he expect anyone to do historical for that kind of money? Shit. Whatever, still got the whole weekend, it's OK . . .*

Aggressive Compliance

Jane pulled over to the kerb, realised she still had the leek on her lap, hastily stuffed it underneath the passenger seat, leaned over from the driver's seat and opened the far door of her car (the central locking had given up months ago, but Jane had never got used to living without it: every time she had to reach out like this to let someone in, she still felt that she had somehow become trapped in some incredibly annoying seventies TV series).

The person who slid in beside her was Dicky Emrys of the Office Supplies Department. He was a friend of some of her gay friends in London, and so she had looked him up when she arrived here. They had got on well, and since they both lived in Cardiff (like almost all the other staff) they had agreed to try sharing lifts.

—Friday! Hoorah! said Dicky. —Nice big cuddly rugby-playing Valleys boys ahoy!

Jane laughed politely and drove out of the University of Pontypool into the jam of traffic that was queuing at one of the many sets of lights on the main arterial road into Cardiff from the Valleys. After several times of doing this commute, Jane was still unpleasantly surprised to find herself caught in a passable imitation of real, genuine, rush-hour traffic. Some four months ago, looking at the map of South Wales in her and Dafydd's rented flat in Streatham, she had fondly imagined herself sailing out of Cardiff to work each morning and back home again from Pontypool each evening against whatever negligible, provincial flow of cars there might be.

—I told you, Janey, said Dicky Emrys, —our commuting is the opposite of yours. In southern England, you go off to work in London every day and come out home at night because no one normal can *afford* to live in real proper London; in South Wales, we go off out to work in the mornings and come back to Cardiff at night because no one normal can *bear* to live in real proper South Wales.

—What do *you* know about normal people, Dicky? said Jane.

—I was speaking about income, lovely, not sexuality, said Dicky. —No one is normal when it comes to sex. Predictable, maybe, but not *normal*. Duw, no. By the way, Janey, did you know you've got a very large *leek* stuck under this seat? What *are* you intending to do with it? Didn't you once tell me that the Spanish for *leek* is also the Spanish slang for *cock*?

Before Jane could explain her leek, there was a *whumpa-whumpa-whumpa* and a scabby white BMW drew up beside them at the lights with clearly hostile intent. In its rear side window was a sticker saying 'IF ITS 2 LOWD UR 2 OLD'. Jane immediately whipped out a pair of shades from the glovebox and plonked them on to her nose.

—Never mind the leek, quick, try to look straight.

—Straight? *Me?* How? And why?

—Enemy at nine o'clock, said Jane.

—What enemy?

—Look tough.

—But I haven't taken my steroids today.

—Just glare at them.

—What, like this?

44

—No, no, no, that's an 'M' glare. We need an 'S' glare.

—Oh. This?

—That'll do.

—But what have they done?

—They're the Enemy. They don't have to *do* anything.

—Janey, what on earth are you doing with your jaw?

—Pretending to chew gum.

—I always *knew* straight people were mad.

Jane smoothed her hand through her short, bottle-blonde hair and blatantly adjusted the rake on her powered seat: as she was eased electronically backwards, she moved her head in time to the thudding music from the BMW and allowed her gaze to slide in and out of contact with the eyes of the driver.

—It's working, she whispered. —Keep glaring.

—But I don't *fancy* white-trash boys. Too many spots.

—Shut up and glare.

—*Whose* enemy are they again?

—You never read the papers, Dicky? *Question:* what two words will you find in every report on Nazi Skinheads, Urban Rioters, Soccer Hooligans, Car Thieves, Ethnic Cleansers, Drive-By Gunmen, Suicide Bombers? *Answer:* Young and Male, discuss. Whose enemy? Ours. Everyone's.

—But I *like* young men.

—No, you *fancy* young men. Different thing. Watch, this is the perfect place, my favourite, see: we go down to single lane about fifty yards ahead.

—What are you going to do?

—Ruin their day.

—Why?

45

—Why? Because I have to say yes sir no sir three bags full sir to Yoof every day and sometimes I just get sick of it.

—Well I never.

Jane yawned theatrically and stretched both her arms above her head, thus making it clear beyond any doubt that neither of her hands was on the wheel or the gearshift, and that she had distinctly meaningful breasts.

—Don't get *them* in Tesco's, said Dicky, with rather horrified admiration.

The Enemy responded by lighting up a cigarette and sticking his right hand out of the window and up on to the roof of his car while he smoked hard with his left hand. He revved his engine.

—I don't believe this, said Dicky. —You're *manipulating* him.

—Male + Young = Stupid, discuss, said Jane. —Well, he can hardly sit there, with his right hand on the wheel and his left on the gearstick, watching me, can he? Of course not. That is *so not possible*, as he no doubt says.

—You're *so* Stone Age, Janey, I had no idea. I thought you were just the regulation-issue fag-hag academic.

—The Stone Age only just ended, Dicky, and it didn't end because we ran out of stones: it ended when someone invented metal spears.

—I'm amazed, lovely. I had no idea you were so *wicked*.

—Only fighting back in the name of the over-thirties.

—Just because you were never a cheerleader.

—Who said I was never a cheerleader?

—If you'd been a cheerleader, you would never have

spent your twenties sitting on your bum doing a PhD, would you, lovely? Too busy shagging and surfing, you would have been. All you bluestockings are the same: you really just long to rule the world through sheer power, beauty and sex.

—Well, it's not fair, is it? cried Jane. —My generation were forced to talk about colonialism and Derrida and shag skinny idiots with little white beer bellies. Today's girls are allowed to have uplift bras, red lipstick *and* brains. And they can demand six-packs and personal grooming. And the worst thing is I'll probably end up shagging one of *the Enemy* just because he's young and muscly and innocent and pretty.

—Well, yes, if you put it like that.

—Anyway, you just watch, little do they know that this car may be ancient and it may have a child seat in the back, but it's automatic and it's got an intercooler.

—What on earth's an intercooler?

—Well, I don't know exactly, but it says on the back that I've got one, and something makes a very loud sort of *hurrying* noise when I do what we're going to do now, so I suppose that must be it.

—Oh dear, said Dicky. —I *knew* I should have written my will last night.

The lights went amber. Jane smiled at the Enemy, flexed her breasts and, with both hands still clearly off her wheel and gearstick, floored it. The Enemy dived for his gear change and clutch, but he was too hasty by far; he stalled.

—Yes, oh yes, oh thank you, God. I mean, Goddess, laughed Jane.

—Bitter, bitter. Dicky shook his head in mock sorrow.

—This is the best bit: prepare for Aggressive Compliance.

—For *what*?

As soon as they reached the single-lane part of the road, with the Enemy's BMW closing rapidly behind them, Jane slowed hard, with a confidence born of her ageing but reliable ABS, to an exact 29 mph, in the exact middle of the carriageway. The BMW hurtled up behind them and almost locked its wheels to avoid a shunt. The teenage driver screamed insane, disbelieving, silent-film abuse, leaned on his horn and flashed his lights; vainly, he hunted from side to side for an impossible gap to overtake amid the oncoming lorries. Jane pressed a button and her sunroof heaved itself creakily open; she raised one hand into the rain, waved merrily, and then made the roof slide clunkily closed; she sat back in her big seat with a smile of deep satisfaction.

—And now all we need is an LCD screen on the back window so you could type in 'UR CAR IS SHIT AND UR MATES R THIK'. Then he'd just *have* to kill himself trying to get past us, wouldn't he? I must patent it. Well, *that* should help the spot price of Brent Crude a bit.

—She shoots, she scores, she wins, said Dicky admiringly. —How *are* the testosterone implants? When did you invent that act?

—I didn't. It was invented by a barrister called Percival.

—A *barrister called Percival*? How fifties. He sounds *wonderful*. Marry him immediately.

—He already is. Well, I assume he is.

—I want to meet him. See if he's good enough for you.

—You can't. I only know him on the Net.

—What, web-sex, eh?

—No, no, no, for God's sake, it's just a silly open site, resistyoof.co.uk, I heard about it on Radio 4 a few weeks ago. We just swap stories about how to annoy Young People. It's completely innocent and normal.

—Of course it is.

—What do you mean?

—E-chat has flirting *built in* to it, Janey. I've been talking to a boy from Goa and in three messages he's got *utterly* disgusting. Wants me to go over on holiday. He *swears* he isn't a rent boy. But would *you* believe a rent boy from Goa?

—I've never met a rent boy from anywhere, so I wouldn't know. Hmmm. So what is it about e-mail? Is it perhaps something to do with the very de-sexualisation of a technological nexus of impersonal yet individual communication in the post-industrial world, do you think?

—No, lovely, it's because in cyberspace no one can hear you lying.

—Oh. Anyway, I'm not *flirting* with Percival. Or anyone else.

—Of course not.

—Shut up, Dickie.

—Janey, I'm worried about you, you're getting cabin fever, you *gorra* come out drinking tonight, lovely.

—I'll see.

—Unless you're too busy playing with your *leek*.

—Please.

Jane had drunk often enough with gay men in London (naturally) to know that while it would be fun, Dickie and his friends would eventually hit Escape Velocity and quite suddenly come over all impatient to go away to places that were even more woman-free than Victorian gentlemen's clubs. It was faintly disturbing. Not disturbing about *them*, disturbing about *her*: at that time of night she always wondered, half drunkenly, why *she* had deliberately chosen to spend *her* evening drinking and talking with men who could never be more than friends. The kind of friends that left you alone too early, wondering what exactly the hell you were doing with your life.

—Hel-lo? said Dicky.

—Sorry, said Jane. —Just thinking.

—Good God, lovely, don't want to do too much of that. Oh, and talking of flirting, did you want one of those stools you sort of *kneel* on to type? We just got a big delivery of them. Do you know, it's very strange: they come with a health warning on every box: *This equipment is intended for use by One Person Only and no responsibility is accepted for any Injuries which may occur through Multiple Use.* Why do you think they needed to put that notice on their silly little chairs? Multiple use? Presumably they got sued by people who took one look at them, felt the irresistible desire to shag the office slapper doggy-fashion, and ended up with dislocated pelvises. I suppose it might work. What do you think?

—Ugh, said Jane happily, trying to avoid a pleasant daydream of herself, in her office, with the blinds down, abusing her kneeling stool with an impossibly good-looking and adoring male student. Or two, perhaps.

The road now returned to two lanes: the BMW blasted past them, its driver and his friends gesturing wildly, making wank signs with the murderous impotence of young men who know they have been publicly humiliated.

—Poor boys, said Dicky. —Poor little mad, straight, fucked-up boys.

—Yes, get me one of those typing chairs, said Jane.

And home they went to Cardiff as the evening fell.

Artichokes

—Dai, I been thinking think it's time Rich *went for it* a bit. Time we sent him out beyond Offa's Dyke, to fly the flag.

—Broader canvas for our Rich, is it, Aled?

—I think so, Dai.

—Here he is.

—Well done, Richyboy!

Dai Jones-Hughes and Aled Morris-Evans, respectively the Heads of Drama at S4C (the Welsh Channel 4) and BBC Wales (Welsh Language Section) and coincidentally brothers-in-law, were sitting at the groaning table paid for by BBC Wales (Welsh Language Section) at the eleventh annual Cymru-Wales Oscwr ceremony at the Millennium Stadium in Cardiff. Outside, rain lashed the city as usual, but here, beneath the mighty, tight-closed roof, all was warmth and arc light.

Jones-Hughes and Morris-Evans hitched up their silk-taped trousers under their bellies and tucked in their white shirts as they stood to applaud. The BBC Wales (Welsh Language Section) table was smack bang on the centre spot of the floodlit turf, so their lead was rapidly noted and followed across the ground. For the first time that evening, Jones-Hughes and Morris-Evans glanced across at their colleagues on the BBC Wales (English Language Section) and HTV Wales tables with friendly agreement, for the Oscwr in question was going to Richard Watkin Jenkins, and everyone liked Rich Jenkins.

Jenkins, spotlit from many angles and throwing a dozen shadows, strode to the podium with that curious gait only found in the Valleys: a big-shouldered, short-legged roll, like a chippy and aggressive teddy bear. Upon the stage, backed by the towering video display, bracketed in limelight, he raised his Gucci shades up over his lustrous black fringe, smoothed a fine hand over his large, horsehair sideboards, hitched his clubland trousers up around his balls, and prepared to accept the Cymru-Wales Oscwr for Best Short Film (Welsh Language). In the previous four years he had taken the Cymru-Wales Oscwrs for Best New Comedy Drama (English Language), Best Documentary (Welsh Language) and Best Adaptation From Welsh (English Language). Rich was big. All around him, the stirring tones of the Welsh national anthem blared out for the twenty-seventh time that night.

The delegate from the Serbian Republic State Television Network (she was here under the European Union Potential New Candidate Small Nations Media Programme) took notes rapidly, highly impressed at this well-oiled display of blameless cultural fervour. She leaned over, her auburn mane flowing down from her shoulders, towards the Head of Public Relations at BBC Wales (English Language Section). He had mistakenly interpreted her bizarre, Slavic eye contact and was also unaware that to anyone north-east of the Adriatic Sea, drinking wine simply does not count as drinking. He now leaned gently, happily forward as he poured for them both, so that he could dwell unseen on her considerable tits. As he did so, he nodded wisely and replied to her questions with that easy volubility that can so quickly overcome a middle-aged man who has had two or three large glasses of 14 per cent Oz red too many and fondly imagines that he is on for a shag

53

with an exotic woman who will certainly never meet his wife.

—This is the greatest young film-maker in your country?

—Yes. Look at him: a charismatic boy, our Rich.

—*Charismatic*. Means what?

—It means men want to drink with him and women want to sleep with him, lovely.

—I see. Like our militia warlords.

—Well, his man loved him, see, and his dad drank with J.P.R., and . . .

— . . . *Jaypeeah*?

—Oh, one of *our* old warlords, lovely, ha ha! Drink up then.

—He defeated the enemies of your nation?

—Aye, love, J.P.R. By Christ, you should have seen him, tearing the English apart, year after wonderful year. He skinned their wingers every time.

—Skinned their wingers? she asked, doubtfully. (Even to a strong girl from the Balkans, actually *flaying* enemy airmen seemed a little excessive.)

—Aye. Tied them up in knots, turned them inside out and skinned the sods alive.

—Alive?

—Buggered them sideways. Great days, great days.

—I see. He is dead now, this Jaypeeah?

—No, he's a doctor.

—Ah, she nodded. —Like our Dr Karadjic.

—No, no, no, he does hips and knees in Bridgend. He was never the same after those bastard All Blacks sliced his cheek off, see?

—Ah, yes, all the bastard blacks. We have Albanians.

—What? Does even Albania play, now? They'd probably beat us, too, these days.

—Leave the Albanians to us, my friend.

—Eh?

—Shh! said someone nearby, for Bryn Terfel's and Bonnie Tyler's pre-recorded duetting voices were fading out, and now the lights dimmed somewhat as Rich Jenkins commenced his acceptance speech. Many cameras, held on the shoulders of fit, scurrying girls or swinging around dizzily on lightweight cranes, closed in to catch his every word and gesture, as well as to record the self-conscious smiles and appreciative nods of his audience: for the proceedings of the Cymru-Wales Oscwr night were being broadcast live, on S4C and BBC2 Wales, to an audience of several thousand.

Rich Jenkins spoke. He spoke first in Welsh.

—Why does all people tonight speak first in *this* language, if many people not understand it? demanded the Serbian delegate, surveying the people around her, a good half of whom had quickly assumed an air of pious absent-mindedness, like non-believers during the boring bits of a church wedding.

—Oh, replied the Head of Public Relations indulgently, —everyone who can speak Welsh speaks in Welsh first here, love. In fact, a lot of people who *can't* speak Welsh speak in Welsh first here. Well, we all want promotion and grants and jobs, don't we? Same in Serbia, I bet.

—Perhaps. You are angry?

—Me? No, love. Worse things to do to get promotions and grants and jobs than speaking a little bit of Welsh into a microphone just to show willing on the big night, aren't there? Even Prince bloody Charles does it, doesn't he? But don't worry, Rich'll say it in the real language of his people next.

—The real language of his people?

—The South Walian dialect of American, love. Then

55

the 75 per cent of us and the 100 per cent of everyone else except Patabloodygonians who wouldn't know Welsh from Albanian will have some idea what the hell he's saying.

—I see. You are becoming angry. *You* do not understand this other language?

—Me? Listen, lovely, my family have lived in Cardiff, loading coal, shifting steel and dredging docks, ever since more than a hundred bloody people lived in Cardiff, and none of them ever spoke a word of fucking Welsh.

—Rich just said something about artichokes, said the Head of Public Relations' assistant, loudly, proudly and treacherously. She had just returned from her month's study leave (all BBC Wales staff are entitled by right, and encouraged by self-interest, to take a paid month off work so long as they say they are taking it off to learn Welsh): she had heard her boss grow dangerously talkative, and she wanted everyone within hearing to know that she, unlike him, was *on the right side of the fence, even if she was English.*

—What? snapped he.

—*March-ysgall* is Welsh for artichokes.

—Why the fuck did they teach you about artichokes?

—I took the New Welsh Cuisine option on my course in Aberystwyth. Very interesting. Artichokes grow beautifully on Caerphilly Mountain, apparently. Well, *hywl fawr*, I think I'll just go and have a word with Gethin Davies . . .

She left, tactically. Her boss stared at his wine.

—Christ. Miners, we used to have. Now it's fucking artichokes.

—You have declared artichokes your new National Vegetable?

—No, that's still fucking leeks.

—I see. So why does your Greatest Young Film-Maker speak of artichokes? Perhaps it is your leader's favourite dish?

—Look, lovely: Rich Jenkins writes about mad old farmers in Welsh, so *they* like him, but he also writes about disused mines and rugby in English, so *we* like him. He's the only one we *both* like. So he can talk about artichokes all night long for all anyone cares. If he publicly stuffed artichokes up his arse he'd get a grant to film it. In Welsh *and* English versions.

—I see. You mean he is the favourite of your leaders?

—Well, yes, you could say that. They love him.

—This is most interesting. Who is *we* and who is *they*?

—North-West is *they*, the *Gogs*; South-East is *us*. *They* don't think *we're* really Welsh because we don't speak Welsh and *we* don't see why we should give a toss about *them* because there's hardly any of them and they're all whingeing inbred sods, and anyway the Gogs don't play rugby so what good are they to anyone?

—These *Gogs* are your ruling clan?

—Yeah, but only because we're still run from bloody England, lovely. The English throw grants at the Gogs just to keep them quiet, that's why. Blow up a pylon and get a job, that was their fucking motto. And it's not even the Gogs who are the worst. They're just *foreign*, it's a four-hour drive to Gogland, give them Anglesey and Gwynedd and good fucking luck to them, say I. They can shag each other's cousins all they want and leave the rest of us in peace. The ones I really hate are the bastards from godforsaken valleys thirty miles from here, who really are *like* us, except they can walk into any job so long as they got two legs just because

57

they speak Welsh. And they reckon people like me are half bloody English just because we don't speak bloody Welsh. Well? English, am I? Were the Pontypool bloody front row English? Well?

—I think they were not, guessed the Serbian delegate.

—Bloody right they weren't. Ate the fucking English alive, they did.

—They were great warriors?

—They were. And if there's one thing I hate worse than South Welsh Welsh-speakers, it's the Welsh-learning Cardiff middle classes. English-paid traitors to their own fucking working class. Half of them *are* fucking English. As bad as those bourgeois bastard Basques and cunting capitalist Catalonians.

—And Turkish-loving, town-living tradesmen, said she, raising her glass subtly.

—Eh? Whatever. I'm telling you, love, you just wait till we're *really* fucking independent. The Gogs and their mates and their grants and their jobs will be the first to go.

—You hate many people.

—Only the English and all Welsh speakers. This country will only be truly free when we all gather around the grave of the last fucking native Welsh speaker to sing 'Cym Rhondda' in Welsh. Like the Irish do it. They got the right idea: everyone *says* they love Gaelic, and no one bothers to pretend they can be arsed to *speak* it . . .

— . . . Quiet, you bloody idiot! hissed a passing, secret, hastily departing friend.

The Head of Public Relations came to, removed his mouth from his glass and looked around blearily. He had not noticed that Aled Morris-Evans had come over to shake the hand of Hugh Pritchard, Head of

Drama, BBC Wales (English Language Section) for the first time that night, to celebrate National Unity (for once) on the occasion of Rich Jenkins's triumph and to discuss the future of their greatest young film-maker. He caught Morris-Evans's hate-filled, slate-eyed glare and saw Pritchard look down in helpless shame. He knew that although Pritchard agreed with everything he had said, and had even said it himself in late, quiet bars, there was no way, these days, you could say it *out loud* in a place like this. Pritchard was his friend; but his days were numbered. And by tomorrow, everyone in BBC Cymru-Wales would know it.

—Oh fuck my granny pink, said he.

The Serbian delegate had been watching closely. A native of Sarajevo, she had been trained from youth to read the ancient fault lines beneath smiling faces, to feel the dark places where the ebb of vanished empires has left unfathomable swamps of vengeance and hatred. She nodded softly.

—Yes, now I think I begin to understand your small country.

—I dunno, Ga, said Rich Jenkins's father, who owned a thriving butcher's shop in Abercwmboi, surveying the assembled Oscwr dignitaries around his nearby table with an indulgent smile and leaning over towards his old friend, the seventies rugby legend Gareth Edwards. —I tell you what: I seen more faggots tonight than a whole week in the shop.

—I'll sort that cynt Murphy, said Aled Morris-Evans, as he lowered his trousers back down on to his bum, returning his bum to his seat and his hand to his glass. —Teach him to keep his cynting mouth shut.

—I always thought he was lower than a corgi's

arsehole anyway. But I tell you what, Aled, I really *do* like Rich Jenkins. You know what I like best about him?

—What's that, Dai?

—The way he says 'we', see? Always 'we' with our Rich, never 'me, me, me'. He really thinks about his country.

—Time for a wider canvas for Rich then. Feature film, is it?

—Why not? We've still got £500,000 of grant support to spend before 1 April. If we don't use it, the cynting English will only roll it over and cut us back next year.

—Better find something for Rich, then.

—Good boy, Rich.

—Can't fault him.

A contented silence fell upon the table, a relaxed yawn of general beatitude, marked only by the gentle tinkle of Australian cava, yellow as melon juice, settling down in fat glasses.

—Right. What's the next award, Aled?

—Best Editor, Welsh Language TV Sports Documentary.

—Who's that this year, your Dewi or my Iestyn?

—Your Iestyn, I think it was going to be.

—There we are then.

White Cotton Stockings

Alan Barony did not give a damn about the Cymru-Wales Oscwrs, but he desperately wanted one of the real, American ones.

Barony was the head and titular owner of MaxiPix's UK arm, a job he had got (as he well knew) only because he was so convincingly English. Eton and the Guards had supplied the timeless look and manner, while his father's taste for young actresses had gifted him a producerial career. That career had in one way or another involved every noteworthy name in British film. And so when Hal Scharnhorst of MaxiPix had, some five years before, felt the need for a truly Brit front-man in order to run the UK movie industry, Barony had been the natural choice. Since then, he had successfully delivered some £42,000,000 of UK Lottery money (which the government had decided would be wasted if spent merely on hospitals or schools) to MaxiPix, resulting in some half-dozen low-budget comedies about warm-hearted and gritty Northern Folk. Hal Scharnhorst was pleased.

But Alan Barony did not want to please Hal Scharnhorst. He wanted to *be* Hal Scharnhorst. He wanted to be American. He had wanted to be American all his life. He was sick of being a Brit, however true. He did not want to be posh and repressed and have to cross his legs elegantly just above the knee. He wanted to sit wide-legged and loose-tied in his editing-rooms in Berwick Street and tell Directors what to cut. He wanted to sprawl in his offices in Soho Square and tell Writers what to write. Most of all, he wanted to lie in jacuzzis in hotel suites and page actresses, *real* actresses, actresses who could do quality stuff, Chekhov and whatever, to come and listen to him talking about movies and then *suck his cock.*

The very phrase made Barony break out in a light sweat.

True, Hal Scharnhorst allowed Barony to personally Green Light one film under £2.5 million per tax year, thus making him the biggest film-maker in the UK. But what does *in the UK* mean? You might as well say you're the biggest film-maker *in Wisconsin.* What kind of actress is going to suck a man's cock if she knows that he has to stand in the queue outside MaxiPix with the rest of the world if he wants to Green Light anything over 2.5m? Only the kind that *calls* herself an actress when what she really does is suck cock for a living. The kind of actress who looks like the real goods but if you said, as Americanly as you could, *Look, honey, I can see you in this part, I truly can, so let me ask something: you ever do Chekhov?* she would think you were asking for a quick *hand-job* (my God, the bloody Yanks even had better *words* for it . . .).

Barony could get that kind of so-called actress any-way. Indeed, he had one calling right now at his flat, at his enormous flat in one of those blocks near the Albert Hall, one of those sandstone monsters that were built back when even flats had to have servants' quarters.

The actress appeared: she was young, she was pretty, and most of all she was dressed right. Madame Joanne always got the girls right for Alan Barony (she had twenty years practice, after all). Blonde. She had to be blonde. Cheesecloth shirt tied under the navel, short denim skirt, platform shoes, and (most impor-tantly) those long-leg socks, almost like stockings, those heavy-knit white cotton things. Sixties, the stuff young Alan Barony had first Chekhov-ed about way back then. The kind of girl his mummy had always warned him about: —They're just common little things who are after your money, darling.

—Hi, said the actress, smiling transatlantically. —I'm Maxi.

—Bad name, snapped Barony, californianally. It reminded him of Hal Scharnhorst, and thus of how Hal Scharnhorst did not have to pay. He *paid*, of course: he hired them, or, if they were somewhat more senior, gave them a Co-Producership on their next movie. He paid, sure: but paying like that is not the same as *paying* paying, is it?

—I'm Jojo? she said.

—OK, OK. Hi, Jojo. What you doing here? You know mummy, I mean *mom*, is home?

—Where is she?

Jojo, who was actually called Kate and was from Walthamstow, was not surprised to hear that Alan Barony's mummy (or mom) was in the flat, nor to hear him almost rupture his tonsils in the bizarre attempt to make himself sound mid-Atlantic. She had been warned. The clothes had to be right, she had to pretend his mother was in the flat, she had to play American. What the hell: he was the biggest film-maker in England, wasn't he? And Kate was an actress. She had recently appeared in a short talking role in a short film that was short-listed for a short BFI season of short films, even. So she hitched up her short skirt to show her thick white cotton stockings, shut the glass doors in her mind, and did American.

She was pretty good.

Normal People

Jane came back to her little terraced house in Cardiff at 10 p.m., having left Dicky and his friends to their cruising before it got *too* obvious that they were itching to leave her and go out into the locker rooms of the night. So now Dr Jane Feverfew, successful academic, loving mother and sex object of many young male fantasies, was half drunk, completely unencumbered and had nothing to do and nowhere to go and no one to do it with on a Friday night. In Cardiff, Wales.

—Hoo-rah for Dr Jane, said Jane.

Jane ate three forkfuls of her 'OnezFun' ready meal, felt sick, watched the news, then sat about for some time on her sofa, trying to work out what exactly she was feeling. It reminded her of something, but she did not know what. Eventually, she worked it out. It was that feeling that comes when you know, simply *know for certain*, that you have left something unfinished, somewhere, but you cannot remember what it was. It turns out to be a half-slice of toast you left uneaten, or a half-drunk cup of coffee you put down without thinking, or a half-smoked cigarette you plonked carelessly in an ashtray. But until you stumble across whatever it is, some deep, ancient sense tells you that you have left *something* undone, and it will not let go.

That was how Jane felt. Except she felt that way about her life: she had put her life down and left it somewhere stupid.

Next, she wandered around her house and wondered what she should do to make it seem as if a decent, normal human being lived here. She wondered this because that was what her little sister had said when she looked round the place.

—Jane, this place says, like, *single girl in need of saving*, soooo badly.

—Oh. I thought it just didn't look like an IKEA ad. Sort of happily chaotic.

—No, it says *girl who's given up*.

—Right. Um, what should I do to it then?

—Well, just, what decent, normal, good people do. Keep the laundry basket empty, for example.

—But I haven't *got* a laundry basket yet.

—Exactly. So *get* one. And make sure it's always empty.

—Right.

—Jane, for God's sake, all you have to do is look at the place and try to imagine you're seeing it through the eyes of a *man coming in here*.

Jane had resisted trying to be like a Normal Human Being until the day she realised, in the nick of time, that she had just sprinkled her and Bryn's dinner (organic chicken nuggets and organic oven chips; OK, it was still minced up chicken necks, but *organic* chicken necks) with foot powder instead of herb salt. It had been very hard explaining to Bryn why his dinner now had to be thrown away and started all over again.

—I want my chips. Why do things go wrong here, Mummy? In Daddy's house, Auntie Blodwen cooks things. My dinner never has to go in the rubbish bin in Daddy's house. Auntie Blodwen makes chips in a pan. I think they taste nicer. Auntie Blodwen can talk in Welsh. Why can't we all live in the same house again, Mummy? If we did, Auntie Blodwen could cook nice sclods for us all.

—Sclods?

—Chips. Welsh chips. In a pan, you cook them.

So then Jane had started trying, at least with food. She had not got round to washing baskets and suchlike yet, however.

Tonight would be the night.

Jane stood in her kitchen and tried to imagine what Normal Human Beings did.

Nice, decent, normal human beings, Jane supposed, did not go out alone on a Friday night at 10 p.m., half drunk. They did not call people who they did not really like, and pretend to like them just so they could have someone to go out with. Especially if they did not know anyone like that anyway. Ho-hum. So what did they do, on a Friday night, alone, these nice, normal, decent, Good People?

Maybe they were simply not lonely: maybe being nice and normal and being lonely simply did not mix? Maybe loneliness is actually a sin?

Aha! Obviously, Good People listened to Radio 4.

Jane found Radio 4, after having some trouble avoiding BBC Radio Wales. After a few minutes, Radio 4 made her feel quite at home; after another few minutes it made her feel terrifyingly, dizzyingly old; so she put on some Joni Mitchell instead, which made her laugh and feel very superior and relatively young.

She washed up.

She cleaned her bath.

She tidied up Bryn's room and changed his sheets.

All normal things.

—I am interacting positively with my domestic environment, said Jane, with a satisfaction that very nearly convinced herself.

After she had tidied up Bryn's room, she stood for a while and stared at the mobile which hung from

66

the ceiling, above Bryn's little, dinosaur-themed bed. It was a luminous mobile of the solar system which she and Bryn had bought at the Science Museum, on their last day in London, before following the removal van up to Wales the next day. That night, they had stayed with friends of Jane's who lived in north London, in Muswell End.

Jane had never expected to find herself thinking of Muswell End as some heaven of Metropolitan delights. But she did now. Jane's friends knew of at least one single man of under forty who genuinely liked kids and was actually quite good-looking really if you didn't mind teeth too much and properly divorced and not *especially* boring and really didn't like football.

—North London; Muswell End, whispered Jane to herself, spinning her nine small planets, as if she were some Eastern monk privately intoning the Secret Names of God while calmly observing the inscrutable mightiness of eternity.

She thought of the Barrister Called Percival, and what he might look like, and how it was a waste to even think that, because he was probably married and just e-flirting and even if he wasn't he wouldn't fancy her and even if he did fancy her he would probably order brown bloody bread at dinner, and smile hideously. And in any case, so what, because he was sure to be in the bloody south-east anyway, like everyone else.

She watched the bright cardboard planets on Bryn's mobile revolve slowly around one another. She thought of how swiftly the years since Bryn's birth had passed; she considered the brevity of life, the inevitability of death, and the unimaginable vastnesses of geological time.

—A year without a baby is a wasted year, she found herself thinking, horrifically.

She fled into her little sitting room and turned on the TV so she could watch upmarket American crap on Channel 4. But she had forgotten (yet again) that you need a special aerial to get *real* Channel 4 in Wales. Jane had not found time to have one fitted yet; she sat, stunned, outraged and disbelieving, in front of S4C.

On S4C, a girl was interviewing a handsome man with dark hair, sideboards and shades, who was holding a large bronze plate with a ghastly modernist rendition of a Greek tragic mask stamped upon it. The girl appeared to be holding herself back, with great effort, from falling on the floor at his feet in a frenzy of worshipful giggles. A grudgingly brief English subtitle read: *Cymru-Wales Oscwr Awards in the Millennium Stadium*.

Jane had never heard of the Cymru-Wales Oscars.

Probably, Dafydd was listening and learning.

Maybe little Bryn would have already half understood what the handsome man and the fawning girl were saying.

A wave of foreignness spread over Jane. Her pathetic, failed attempts to give a pale imitation of a proper life to her child meant that she was trapped for ever in a strange, small land where if you wanted a decent job you had to learn a language which most people had never spoken, where everyone got married at twenty-eight, where you could not get Channel 4 even if you wanted to and where she was permanently surrounded by attractive young men desperate to shag her who she was not supposed to shag.

And she had got drunk with gay men *again*.

Her jeans really *were* too tight.

Jane had only the last refuge of the lonely: cyberspace.

She walked stiffly but quickly into her little study, popped open her waist-button with relief, sat down

68

upon her work-chair and logged on speedily into a happier, if less real, world. A voice which seemed to issue from some whacked-out, robotic Californian hooker announced that Jane Had Mail. And it was not *all* junk, either.

She was not entirely alone, then.

Phew.

Jane dived thankfully into a virtually better world.

Fatty's Gack

Paul Salmon came swanning in from the little circular bar in Soho House, found Pete easily in the lounge and sat down next to him, as if beside an old, if not bosom, pal.

—Hiya, Paul, smiled Pete. —Where you been, my man? How's *Base Metal* coming on?

—Why's Paul talking to that extraordinary greasy man who's *not wearing black*? asked Sheina's school friend from Muswell End Girls' High School, Miranda, who had just come back from her successful Argentinian divorce and had, remarkably, never been to Soho House before.

—Oh, that's Pete. But *we* call him Fatty.

—Ugh.

—Yes, I know. But it saves all that ghastly hanging about waiting for psychos to turn up in some horrid pub. So handy, really. That's why we let him in, of course.

—Oh, I *see*. Oh, *well*, then.

—And he's quite good value for a gossip, he knows everything about everybody. I suppose he has to, so he knows who can pay their bills. I mean, he knew Marcus Dale was coming back to London to do some Shakespeare again, for purely artistic reasons of course, before Marcus even knew it himself.

—Yes, the waves never really got up for Marcus in la-la land, did they? *Definitely* time he got back into boots and knee breeches. Is Paul getting some for us too, do you think?

—Mmm.

—Oh good.

—Anyway, congrats on the divorce.

—Yes, it was all quite fun really. What about you, darling?

—I'm still bloody single and working for Alan.

—Is he still fixated on American girls in white stockings?

—Darling, how did *you* know?

—How do you *think* I know, darling. And how do *you* know?

—Well, yes.

For a brief moment, both girls thought back to their days of struggle. Then Miranda gave a little shiver.

—Let's try not to remember again, darling.

—Let's. Oh God, I'm so jealous of your divorce. My life is getting all so . . . *boring*. I mean, what's the *point* of it all, Miranda?

—Now now, darling. Thresholds.

—But it's so unfair. I know all the right things. I was *born* knowing them: I can tell a Queen Anne rectory from a Georgian one without even thinking about it; I can list you the decent Parisian arrondissements in my sleep; and my hand falls on to the right knife in the three-rosette eatery by sheer *genetic instinct*. But none of it will ever be any use to me at all unless I find some bloody man to cough up, will it?

—Well, really, Sheina, of *course* not. You're an *English-woman*. That's what we're *for*, darling.

—You're so right, of course.

—Oh, look, there's that ghastly weathergirl. *What* a ridiculous dress. Do you know her? She seems to be coming this way.

—Darling, hello! How are the weather fronts doing? Still *fringing in* mercilessly? Byeee!

—God, what a slut.

—Isn't she?

—Anyway, I think your Paul Salmon is quite a hunk. And he's certainly got the hots for you, darling.

—I suppose so, said Sheina.

—I know he's not quite, well, *polished* yet. But I gather he's doing awfully well.

—Ye-es.

Going great, said Salmon. —We're looking for a three-picture throughput umbrella deal with Working Title, and Good Machine are pushing us stateside even-as-we-speak.

—Great, said Pete. —Hope the reviewers like it.

—Reviewers? Who cares about reviews? We'll break even by Cannes. UK box office means jack shit, Pete. US box means a little more. We came in under two point five mil. Thanks to me. Under two point five mil, you can't lose, with the tax breaks and all, provided you got shoot-outs and shags and a petrochemical explosion at the end. You got *any idea* how many Pacific Rim satellite and cable stations there are out there, Pete? You know how many zillion hours they have to fill? Every week? Wallpaper. They cut it however they want, redub, whatever. Who cares? You ever see the Saudi Arabian cut of *The Piano*, Pete?

—No, actually.

—Twenty minutes long. A short moral tale: *Shirty Handicapped Cow won't fuck Generous Hubby; Shirty Handicapped Cow plays Wicked Western Music while Dodgy Bloke looks at her pants; Shirty Handicapped Cow gets her fingers chopped off by Righteous Hubby.* Job done, fade to black, everyone's happy. The guys with the big beards and the wacky headgear and the AK-47s loved it. And they only had to redub into Hebrew, and the guys with the big beards and the wacky headgear and the Uzis loved it too. Who cares? Wallpaper. You know how the Far East buys stuff in, Pete? They send some slant-eyed idiot who can't even speak English over to Cannes, they specially *choose* some idiot who can't speak English, to see if it'll play in Phnom fucking Penh, he sits there with a tray of sushi and a little book and he watches ten movies a day, he counts the shoot-outs and shags, checks his watch, and ticks the special box if it ends in a big petrochemical explosion. Easy. Shit, Pete, who do you think *buys* Jean-Claude Van Damme movies?

—You got that kind of stuff in *Base Metal*?

—Pete, we got six shoot-outs, five shags, a rape and *two* petrochemical explosions, and we came in for under two point five mil. Because we shot it all in fucking Poland. We got half the Polish fucking SAS for a week, for a hundred grand, ammo included. We got kosher tanks and armoured trains and big black limos. And Lari, you know, that holiday-programme girl the *Loaded* boys all like, she gets her tits out, puts her knees behind her ears like a good girl and gets a decent seeing to. Box office? We can't lose. Thanks to me. Reviews? Fuck. And I got this new idea, Pete, you heard it first and you heard it only, a historical idea: History, it's the new sci-fi, Pete. And the Soft Money, the Lottery, the Beeb, Europe, all those idiots, they love historical. They think *historical* means *quality*. Bollocks does it. Fuck quality. Does quality play in the Far East? Does it fuck. You know what *historical* means, Pete? It means heads and guts flying in your face and tits hanging out of big dresses and rape and torture and weird sharp-edged implements and serious leather bondage gear *but* you still get a PG certificate because it's historical, and *historical* doesn't count so bad, see?

—Mmm. How do you get petrochemical explosions in a historical movie?

—Well, we'll make up on the shagging and the gore. For the shoot-outs, the hero gets a multibarrel musket, of course, you ever see a historical movie where the hero *didn't* get a multibarrel musket? Or two multibarrel muskets, fuck, no one counts the shots so long as the blood bags keep exploding. And so who cares if medieval cannons suddenly fire high-explosive shells? I'm not the fucking Discovery Channel, Pete, I'm talking *historical*, not factual.

—And you're on a Fee?

—Does the Pope wear robes? Fuck *percentage points*. We just hand them out to make idiots feel good.

—Great. So, what's the storyline?

—Pete, I don't have to *write* the crap. Not my job. I just pitch the Concept to Alan Barony Monday afternoon, one-to-one. I pitch, we talk budgets and fees, we shake hands, Alan buys an Option, I find some geek with specs and piles who's been living on air for the last six months, he bites my hand off for a couple of grand and three percentage points to write the fucking *storyline*. And hey, Pete: don't talk to me about *lines*.

—Ha ha. Oh, what, you fancy one, Paul?

—Hey, why not, Pete? Actually, Sheina's with me and she's gagging for one. Don't suppose you can help me out with two? Might as well have some on me, you know: oil the wheels. Got to be done.

—Sure, Paul, fuck, no probs. Very tasty too, tonight, though I say it myself. Oh, is Sheina here? Someone said she was being sent in chains to the Welsh Oscars tonight.

—Oh, *you* heard of them too?

—Course. I know the budgets aren't much by *your* standards, Paul, but I gather this Euro funding has done wonders for the film business up that way.

—Yeah, I heard so. You heard of Bollywood? They call Cardiff *Goggywood*, apparently, don't know why.

—Mmm. I been thinking of taking on a partner to cover Cardiff myself, actually. Two was it, Paul? Here you go, my man.

—Great. Thanks, Pete.

(Salmon could feel his stomach loosen ever so slightly at the mere touch of the nice little envelopes. Pete always takes care when he makes up his little envelopes of cocaine, after all, the fat sod is still charging £60 a g when everyone knows the street price is in free-fall, but then again, he's here, he's in-house, it's always half decent, and he makes it feel good, so who gives a fuck? Pete uses pages out of *Dazed & Confused* or *Pure* usually. Good quality paper, just the right thickness, almost like they chose it on purpose, ho ho, and nice photos: the customers get to see shots of their friends' faces and knickers and latest shit design creations as they open up the envelopes and stroke out the coke and chop up their lines, so they can bitch about them in the loo, which is always fun.)

—I'm doing a weekend in New York soon, Paul, and cash is a bit tight, so . . .

—Pete, sure, no sweat. Very soon. Hey, any time.

—Cool. See you, Paul. Good luck with the historical thing.

And fuck you too, you fat greaseball. Still, I only actually took half that last g, not even that much, Sheina had at least half of it, the cow, and she gave her mate a line as well, a big one, I bet, so this isn't really my second gram of the night, and the other one's just in case, I can always shift it late. Yeah, that Miranda works for Hal Scharnhorst anyway, so it's an investment when you think about it, and anyway, what the hell, I'm celebrating, I know what my next project

75

is now, you got to be able to celebrate, haven't you? Yes. Just need to find a good cheap script from an Underlying Work that's already out of copyright. Something Celtic? Never mind. All weekend to do that. I wonder if Sheina will invite me back tonight. Better take it easy on the powder, in case she does. Knee breeches and big dresses. White stockings. Use that lav right downstairs past the kitchens, I think. Too much of a queue upstairs. Funny how half the place still doesn't seem to know about that bottom lav, handy, Baz says he got a blow job off Sheina's mate in there once, she needed a line so bad. Lying sod. Shit, if only I'd thought of filming Jane bloody Austen before everyone else! Will Sheina invite me back? I'll just hold back on the chang for half an hour, pretend Pete had to go get reinforcements, keep her waiting a bit, it's all OK, it's fine, it's fine . . .

Resistyoof.co.uk

Resistyoof.co.uk is unique on the Web because it is nothing to do with money or sex. No one sells anything to anyone and the site has no ghastly, sleazy, private chat rooms or suchlike. It is just a public forum where decent, normal people with no hidden agendas swap tales and advice about how to annoy Yoof. No one seems to know how the site started exactly, but it was mentioned on Radio 4 recently and has been noted in *Outlook* magazine.

Since Jane did not live in N1 or W11, but in Cardiff, she did not know anyone who read *Outlook* magazine: but it was fun to think that she and her unknown friends were out there somewhere.

Midnight now: Jane sat before her LCD screen and gazed at the public chat room of resistyoof.co.uk. She raised her sherry glass contemplatively to her lips, and, discovering that it had inexplicably emptied itself, refilled it generously and sipped deeply before checking her message again before she sent it off (it contained her description of today's Aggressive Compliance Mission).

She just wanted to make sure she had hit the correct e-mail tone, the impression which befitted a denizen of the e-world called DJ Feva (all the chatters at resistyoof.co.uk ironically give themselves the kind of stupid names that Young People invent when e-mailing each other). Yes, she had done it fine: her message sounded spontaneous, relaxed and generally upbeat. After all, no one in e-space ever admits (a) that they are in the chat room because they are so sad and lonely

77

that they have no one human to talk to, or (b) that they have actually *worked* at their reply. It was fine. It sounded right. And she felt sure that KewCPercival (the barrister who had invented Aggressive Compliance) would detect her wittily light-hearted references to his own previous message.

She fired it away.

Unknown friends.

Jane suppressed a tiny, distant whisper of forbidden fruit.

The fact was that KewCPercival had done something rather unusual, if not strictly unheard-of, tonight. His last message (long as usual and, as usual, gently entertaining) had ended by suggesting, very hesitantly, that *'we'* might perhaps try making this virtual network into a real one, by meeting up, sometime, somewhere, *'in the West End maybe?'*

In this, he was pushing the envelope of resistyoof.co.uk, but since his message, like all of them, was for general consumption, it could hardly be misinterpreted as an invitation, a horrid, sleazy, yoof-y invitation to anything un-normal, could it?

Certainly not.

And yet.

And yet Jane was convinced, somehow, that his message was really for *her* alone.

And she was pretty damn certain that *he* knew *she* was writing to *him*. If only the bloody site had private chatrooms so they could . . .

—Oh for God's sake, said Jane out loud, snapping herself out of this pathetic, romantic bubble. What on earth was the point in her meeting a man who thought it was normal to go to the West End?

Of course. The West End. Of London. Where else? *Very* handy for Wales.

And handy so *the Wife* wouldn't see us, no doubt.

Cross, she went back and read Percival's previous message again. She laughed. She smiled anew at his story of how he had forced a McDonald's waitress to serve him with a Happy Meal for his child *before* she dealt with the acne-ed and cap-sleeve-T-shirted twenty-year-old who had *bloody well* shoved straight in front of him.

Jane, her face glowing in the unearthly sheen from her TFT screen, could almost taste Percival's success: surely Happy Meals had never been so accurately named!

Shame about him being married with a kid. Shame about him living in London. Shame she was stuck in Wales now.

For ever.

Well, until Bryn was eighteen.

OK, OK, for ever.

Ho-hum.

Jane logged off, happier. She was still on her own in her little house, but at least she had made some form of human connection. And somehow that had made things clearer.

—Good People do *not* go down the pub on their own, she said firmly.

—Good People do *not* hang themselves, she said, even more firmly. —They think of their child, and their families, and how horrible that would be for them.

So what do Good People do? What do Normal Human Beings do, alone on Friday nights?

—They work, said Jane, very firmly, quite loudly and draining her sherry. —They work because they believe things will somehow get better, one day; they still believe that one day, an impossible, unexpected event will jump-start their heart again.

Then Jane realised she had said all this out loud, and she felt a bit stupid and not very Good and Normal. So she shifted her seat before the computer, quietly, softly, absurdly, as if she might wake up someone else in her little house in Cardiff, and she shut up moaning and she *just got down to work.*

But before she settled in for her weekend of productive loneliness, she had to suppress one last little cheating ray of the thing we can stand least, the thing that makes our lives unbearable, the thing that we long for and which destroys us: *hope.*

Money

Kate from Walthamstow (aka Jojo-from-the-trailer-park) was at work astride Alan Barony. On the pillow beside his head was a large pile of twenty-dollar notes (Alan Barony always paid in dollars), and in her small hand was his pale cock.

They were enacting their little scenario for the third time that night, and Kate was frankly getting pretty bored with it, but then again, she had already made more tonight than in three months of acting and signing on, and the meter was still running. And, actually, it seemed that he really *liked* her (she had been told to expect to do the whole thing only once, or twice for tops!). So she just squeezed and twisted harder, and tried not to giggle. (She had gone beyond gagging with her clients some months ago, but to get over this gagging she had been forced to pretend it was not really *her*, as in *she herself*, that was doing this stuff, and, well, whenever you look at your life like that, as if you are on Mars and observing yourself with a big telescope, the danger is always going to be the giggling.)

—What do you want? whisper-yelled Barony, his mouth pleading, his eyes locked insanely, incredulously, on to Jojo's thick white cotton stockings, or rather, to the very place, the seat of mystery and awe, where those thick white cotton stockings stopped, and her slim, tanned thighs started. Fascinated, terrified, hypnotised, he watched, as if unable to believe that it was really his own hand that was now sliding beneath the soft white cotton and along the smooth, young flesh inside.

—What do you want? he begged.

—You, said Jojo grimly.

—What do you *really* want?

—Don't shout, *Mom will hear you.*

—Oh God, oh God, you have to tell me.

—What do I have to tell you, Alan?

—What do you really want from me? Please?

—Your big fat cock in my tight little pussy.

—No, I know you, you're all the same, Mom warned me about you all, you lying bitches, with your thick white cotton stockings, you don't want cock, I know what you want, no cock is enough to fill *you*, is it, what do you *really* want, oh God, hurry up, now now now, tell me what you . . .

Kate, with splendid dramatic timing, wrenched hard and growled.

—You know what I want. I want *your money honey*!

—Ahhhhhhhhhhh!

Dark Matter

Sheina sat on Paul Salmon's sofa in Kentish Town, waiting for her cab home to Muswell End. Salmon sat next to her. Before them, on the coffee table, lay three little unfolded envelopes made out of pictures from *Dazed & Confused*: all licked quite clean.

Occasionally, they blinked or suddenly sort of shook their heads a bit. They champed their jaws quite a lot. Each was alone in a frozen cave. The taxi sounded its horn outside.

—Sheina, said Salmon.

Sheina was feeling very cold and tired and dried out. She did not really want to go anywhere. She wanted to lie down and stew gently. Her blank gaze fell upon Salmon's glasses as she champed. They were lying on the table beside the dead wrappers. They were expensive glasses, D&G, almost frameless.

He had quite good taste, really. Actually, he was quite fun. And doing well. And he was in with The Gang. You could take him anywhere. Well, nearly. Why not? It would be quite nice to go to bed and wake up somewhere else than her grotty little flat in Muswell bloody End.

He would fuck her gratefully: it might even feel something like love.

A girl needed a rest sometimes.

She might die of boredom on the minicab ride home.

But then, for some reason, she noticed that the little whatsitcalled, you know, those things that balance the specs on the person's nose, those little transparent bits of plastic attached to the frame on little titanium wires, well, she suddenly realised that there should have been a little, a tiny gap, half a milimetre maybe, between those little plastic things and the lenses.

But there was not.

The space was instead filled with some kind of black stuff. As she looked more closely, she saw that this dark gunge actually spread right over the joint where the wires were fixed on to the plastic. It was not really black, whatever it was, more a sort of very dark green, and whatever it was, it could only have got there off Salmon's nose. How long did it take to build up that weight of grease off someone's nose, she wondered.

For some reason this made her think of Salmon's bathroom, and suddenly she remembered noticing that the shaft of his electric toothbrush, and the place where the shaft joined the handle, had been covered in funny, bluish-grey stuff. Dried tooth foam?

She had merely thought it strange at the time. But now, quite suddenly, she did not want to think about it at all.

The taxi honked again.

—Sheina, said Salmon again. He did not say it with any great conviction, however, for he knew damn well that he could never get an erection after a gram and a half of cocaine in any case, that was the way it took him. And he could hardly say that he was really only looking for someone to ward off the terrors of the morning, and of all the mornings to come. No, no, no: you can hardly say that, can you? You have to at least pretend to be sexually infatuated. Which is kind of hard if your cock is definitely going to stay resolutely slack. So he just said —Sheina, more or less for form's sake, and placed his hand on her thigh. And Sheina, not being the kind of girl who is going to dish it out just for form's sake, thought again of Salmon's scummy toothbrush and his gunky specs, removed her hand in a pally way and said: —Got to go.

And she did.

So now they were both alone anyway, after all that fuss.

Las Madonnas del Cenicero

Jane, alone in Cardiff, rubbed her eyes, yawned, and looked grimly again at her bright little screen. Up and down she scrolled, scanning once again through her handout for the Option. It was too horrible. Yes, it had to be simple and *fun*, but she simply could not bear to do this to her beloved book . . .

A sound outside in the street made her look up blearily. A gaggle of drunken revellers was passing by. Jane could not resist getting up and looking out at them. At first, she glared at this display of Yoof. Then, realising that they were not really that young at all, she looked out wistfully instead.

In the street light she caught the gleam of woman's leg here and there. A man with big sideboards in a shiny leather coat was the obvious leader of the group (her ghastly Female Primate Radar detected this without her even knowing she had turned it on): he had a girl on each arm. One of them had a very low-cut dress on. The man was shouting something about artichokes and everyone was laughing with him. He was rather handsome. He was about her age. He did not look married. She recognised him from somewhere.

Jane looked at the gang of them and wondered what kind of place they were going to now, at 3 a.m.? What was the secret of their big, exciting lives?

Then she heard them all talking in Welsh. She felt foreign again: wherever they were going, it was nowhere she could go. Even if she knew where it was. Which she didn't.

She let her curtain fall dustily back into place, shutting out the night, and thought, *I suppose Life is like one of those parties you read about in New York: there aren't any invitations, you just have to know. If you know where and when it is, you're welcome. If you don't, no one's going to tell you. I suppose* (she added stoically) *that you just have to wait to be asked. Yes, and then* (less stoically) *when you finally get asked, you can't go anyway because you have got your kid that night. Oh, well.*

She looked back across the room at her laptop, with wary distaste, as if it was a small, unattractive and quite possibly hostile animal, lying there whirring away on her desk.

She had done what she could to make her bloody Option seem *fun*. But it was not easy. Jane's special subject was *Las Madonnas del Cenicero*, that little-known gothic romance from the early nineteenth century. She had chosen to study it for the following reasons:

1) You have to do a PhD to get a lectureship.

2) To do a PhD, you have to find something no one has yet written about.

So Jane had found a justly obscure work which no one had ever bothered to write a PhD on and had spent half of her twenties reading about it and making notes on it on filing cards. Her resulting PhD said things like:

> The very fact that there are absolutely no references to female sexuality in *Las Madonnas* clearly makes the point that the author is obsessed with female sexuality. All obsession, as Foucault shows, is rooted in fear. Therefore *Las Madonnas* demonstrates that the phallocentric rationalism of Dead White Male Western Thought is under siege (the siege motif recurs throughout

87

the text, as we have seen) from the subversive forces it seeks to banish from language itself.

Now, Jane had cunningly decided to do a sort of film version of *Las Madonnas*, by copying the style from a paperback edition of the screenplay for *Sense and Sensibility*, so she could show them how interesting it *really* was once you got through the sheer, bloody, endless, brain-irradiating *length* of it. She would show them bits of other films to illustrate what she meant. It would be a *fun* course. With not much marking for her to do.

That was the theory, anyway.

In practice, it was too horrible.

Jane sat down again and stared gloomily at the ludicrous bodice-ripping beginning to her pathetic screenplay thing. No, it was just *too* bloody awful.

Her hand slowly directed her mouse pointer towards the button on the screen which would delete the entire file. But at the last 'OK?' point she paused before clicking the screenplay into oblivion.

Why should she suffer alone? Wasn't that the whole point of resistyoof.co.uk?

Yes. Her comrades in the darkness.

Feeling better already, Jane logged on again, retrieved her ridiculous screenplay drivel and blipped it off, just so that Percival (and the other members of resistyoof.co.uk, of course) could see the sort of appalling thing that intelligent and sensitive and attractive female lecturers with firsts and PhDs coming out of their ears were reduced to these days.

She also, just while she was at it of course, added a little note, simply by the by and in passing, to the general effect that, yes, it might be fun to meet up sometime in the West End *or somewhere else.*

She clicked, and her message was gone.

Suppressing an inexplicable and entirely ridiculous murmur of excitement, Jane looked at the time: God, four in the morning. Still, it was partly a good thing that she would be knackered all day tomorrow: it meant that she would be able to go to bed early tomorrow, or rather, today, without feeling *too* guilty and depressed about wasting yet another precious Saturday night.

How many Saturday nights did she have left till she was forty? Hmmm. Best not to count. At least she was working. Well, sort of. OK, at least she had *done* something. She had communicated in some way or another with other human beings, even if they were only unknown or imaginary ones, and she felt better than if she had just watched TV alone or stood alone in some club for an hour feeling blushingly stupid or wanked half-heartedly alone in bed.

—No leeks for Dr Jane, said Jane, and laughed. Then she realised she must have drunk almost half the bottle of sherry, and felt ashamed.

Never mind, it was all OK.

Well, sort of.

Jane shut down her computer and headed for her lonely bed.

As she went along her little corridor to her little bedroom, she looked through little Bryn's door into his little room and saw his little mobile of planets, still spinning slowly in the convecting air. She paused and watched them again. She wondered why that man outside had been shouting about *bastard artichokes* in English when everything else he had said was in Welsh. Probably, Jane had been imagining it. She was quietly amused by the thought. Then, finding that she had arrived somehow at her own bedside, she undressed almost without regret, lay down exhausted and fell quickly into a dreamless sleep.

But her ethereal messages flew on, over the dark hills of Wales, and into the vastness of the international night.

Crossing the Andes

Paul Salmon could not sleep. Dawn had been up over Kentish Town for some two noisy hours now. It was too late to sleep: Salmon knew with horrid certainty that he was now doomed to wander about all day in lonely, polar desolation, quite unable to work, killing time until he could sleep, which (since he had taken enough coke to get half a dozen Bolivian peasants across a twenty-mile, snowbound, high-Andean pass, on foot, without food or water) would be at eleven o'clock tonight at the earliest.

He would invent missions. He would shop. He would lay in supplies of videos. Then it would be Sunday, and there was always the danger that he would get one of those nasty kickback hits of the stuff on Sunday night too, and be unable to sleep.

On Monday he had to have his Pitch for Alan Barony ready: he had hustled for this meeting for weeks.

You only get one chance.

Aha.

What?

Salmon lay, with the blood in his left arm pounding somewhat alarmingly and his brain wheeling crazily, but with a terrible clarity, through vast universes of frozen hopelessness. He had to find a new project. Now, while he was still hot and while Barony still listened to him. He had to make his pile right now, while it was there to be made, he had one chance to make that fabled lump sum that would catapult him into the realms of safety and warmth for ever.

Salvation.

Linen and Agas. God give me linen and Agas. And pure mornings.

It had to be *now*, before the Red Seas of his debts swallowed him up and the red veins on his nose swallowed his nose.

Use it, use the coke, use the buzz.

Pitch it, pitch it.

It had to have guns, it had to have sex, it had to have bombs.

But it had to be new. You had to fulfil the old formula in a new way. But how?

It had to cost Alan Barony less than £2.5 million. But it had to look like £10 million.

How, how, how?

Art!

Knee breeches!

Some two hours later, Salmon lay in a warm bath, floating through ice packs of isolation and despair. An hour after that, he sat on his lavatory, in case a good shit would calm his body. He was careful not to strain, in case his aorta exploded (Salmon did not have a very exact idea of what his aorta looked like, or even where precisely it was, but he could imagine it exploding only too well, in hideous, freeze-frame, digitally enhanced detail).

He picked up *Outlook* magazine, which somebody had left there as loo-reading. He read articles about the 'Free Market in China, Whither New Labour?' and 'The Human Genome' to try to stop himself thinking about whether he was shitting or not, so that he would be able to shit.

He had just about given up, both on his shit and on *Outlook*, when he saw the little article about resistyoof.co.uk once again. *It appears*, said the article, *that a group of respectable thirty-somethings has got together and declared war on Youth . . .*

Salmon read no further. His coke-riddled mind immediately span away: it could be the new *Fight Club*. Yes, a gang of thirty-somethings, using their dormant skills (one could be ex-army) to fight young criminals. *Death Wish* meets *Friends*. Could be, could be. Wow.

Salmon waddled over to his PC and logged on. He soon found resistyoof's website. He scanned its most recently posted messages. There was something about racing against young men in cars, then a wanky story about hamburgers. Then he read:

> I'm trying to get the sods interested in my Option on a much-ignored Spanish master-piece from 1828. I have to 'sell' it (!). And how do you 'sell' an important work of literature? Make it 'interesting' of course, make every subtle hint into an utterly blatant 'filmic' image, of course! For example, this is how the book starts (in my own translation):
>
> *In Mexico, during that troubled fifteenth year of the reign of Carlos XIII, the Baronesses of Cenicero, charming young heiresses to their late father's prosperous estate, renowned as far away as Castile itself for the excellence of its artichokes, had reason to be grateful for the unexpected arrival at their castle of the young Marques de Caceres: that bold youth's intervention saved them from the full rigours of an assault on their remote home by a band of disaffected soldiery – the result of which had otherwise been their certain ruin. Under these circumstances, it is doubtless no wonder that the*

young nobleman necessarily appeared to the sisters
as a paragon of all the manly virtues.

Now, this is what I have been forced to do
to 'sell' this work to a Yoof which is entirely
incapable of reading between lines. It all has
to be made literal. Here it is:

Salmon hardly read this, though, for at the very word
'Option' his mental ears, overcharged with chemical
electricity, had pricked up. He scrolled quickly down
the pages, until he stopped his mouse dead, his hand
trembling slightly, his mouth agape. There was no
doubt: it was a screenplay. Salmon allowed the wet
towel to unwind and fall from his waist; he settled his
big, warm, damp bum down upon his swivel chair; he
felt no discomfort: his radar was up. He read:

IRON NICK FILMS PRESENTS:

EXTERIOR. CASTLE IN SPAIN. DAY.
The seventeenth century. Burning sun. Among
huge fields of artichokes stands a Spanish colonial
church. An aristocratic Catholic funeral is tak-
ing place. The BARONESSES *(triplets, twenty-five,*
blonde, beautiful) lead the mourners.
    A horde of bloody, bandaged feet and boots
crush the artichoke crop. It is a gang of brutal
ARMY DESERTERS. *They fall on the* MOURNERS,
massacring them horribly. The artichokes are red
with blood. The BARONESSES *flee in a coach*
towards their castle. One by one, their SERVANTS
are cut down. The BARONESSES *just make it back*
to the castle and slam the great doors shut.
They breathe again. But the DESERTER LEADER

is already inside! He opens the doors and the
DESERTERS *rush in. The* DESERTER LEADER *rips
the* BARONESSES' *coats open, and closes in with
his men to rape them.*

KaBoom! his head explodes, splattering the
BARONESSES *with brains and blood. They scream
as* JUAN, MARQUES DE CACERES *(twenty-five,
dashing), enters on a white stallion, backlit, looking
like a god, his large many-barrelled muskets blaz-
ing. He massacres the* DESERTERS *single-handedly,
finally skewering the* DESERTER LEADER *through
the guts with his sword.*

JUAN

My ladies . . .

The BARONESSES *faint away before him. Stillness.*
JUAN's *face darkens as he realises he is quite
alone with them: only the dead are watching.
He unbuckles his belt: behind him, the skewered*
DESERTER LEADER *drips off the wall on to the
floor.* JUAN *does not even notice: with his boot,
he starts to slide back the black mourning dress
of the* FIRST BARONESS, *revealing her virginal
white stockings. We see from his face that* JUAN
is battling with inner demons . . .

TITLES: *LAS MADONNAS DEL CENICERO*

And of course they bloody loved it. See what
I mean? Yours in the trenches, DJ FEVA.

Salmon stared at the screen. On the back of his neck,
he could feel the hackles starting to rise. Feverishly, he
zipped back upwards to the start of the document.

Neglected masterpiece from 1828? So it was kosher historical literature: Art! But out of copyright: *public domain*. That meant about a hundred K off the film's above-the-line costs straight away. And not British. What was the title again? Ha, not mentioned, of course, not on the Internet! Too clever for that. Clever enough to have got the Option on the work, look, yeah, he talks about his *Option*. Trying to *sell* it, he says so. Cute: an Internet rumour campaign, like *Blair Witch*. Cool guy. Knows he has to aim for the Youth Market. Quite right, the sixteen to twenty-fours are all that matters. Who is this guy?

Salmon looked across at the little Personal Data box. All it said was 'DJ FEVA F 35'.

Hmmm. Girl, then. Always good for publicity, that. But if it's Public Domain how'd she get an Option on it? Ha, yeah, of course, she's registered the Intellectual Copyright on the Film Concept and her translation with that bloody new troublemaking EU body, fuck them, how does anyone expect us to compete with LA when they go around giving Writers fucking *inalienable moral rights*? Cunning lady . . . Yeah, see, like I said, the multi-barrelled musket! Knows her stuff all right . . . She's front-loaded the pre-title sequence: rape, shoot-out, posh totty all in three minutes . . . and a PG cert because she knew when to stop. Good, well done. Hmmm. Triplet sisters. Interesting concept. Identical sisters, of course. My God, he was firing on all cylinders now, he still had it! That's it, use the coke, *use* the coke. Cross the Andes, march through the snow. What a pitch. They could find three unknown triplets, now *that* would be sexy as hell. Or use computer-generated images from one actress – newsworthy or what? My God, even someone like Uma or Gwyneth would go for that! Either way, it was headline-grabber, a big-star triple-role vehicle . . . Or would it be better to go for *Massive New Talent Search, BASE METAL Producer asks: where are the triplets of my dreams?* How about those Irish singers, what were they called again, that family? Merchant Ivory meets *Gladiator*, bodices, men in knee breeches and boots (well, knee breeches and boots *made* Marcus Dale, don't knock knee breeches and boots): *lost masterpiece*, no, *notorious banned masterpiece brought back to life by BASE METAL team*. History the new sci-fi. And it's Hispanic, fucking A! – big help with the US box office, Hispanic and cool with the art-house geeks, too . . . who was the screenwriter again. Scroll up, scroll up . . . DJ Feva? Never heard of her. Cheap, then!

Cheap writer; not British; Historical; Public Domain. Hispanic. Christ. Salmon paused, exultant, not even noticing that he had taken his cock in his hand.

Saved!

PART TWO

Development

Differences in intra- and extracivilizational behavior stem from: 1) feelings of superiority (and occasionally inferiority) toward people who are perceived as being very different; 2) fear of and lack of trust in such people; 3) difficulty of communication with them as a result of differences in language and what is considered civil behavior; 4) lack of familiarity with the assumptions, motivations, social relationships, and social practices of other people.

Samuel P. Huntingdon
The Clash of Civilizations and the Remaking of World Order

Points of Net

—Mummy, said little Bryn for perhaps the third time.

—Mmm, darling? said Jane, trying to concentrate on her son, rather than on not thinking about phoning KewCPercival this morning. (They had just arrived at the bus stop for the school bus to Ysgol Mynydd Ynys-y-bwl on Monday morning.)

—*Bore da*, sang the other mothers, in Welsh, and

—Good morning, smiled Jane in English. (Naturally, it made her feel shamefaced to be speaking English; just as naturally, it also made her feel secretly outraged that she should be made to feel shamefaced about speaking English exactly two hours' drive away from Shepherd's bloody Bush.)

—Mummy! said little Bryn again.

—Sorry, darling, said Jane, quickly kneeling to bring her face level with his, —Sorry, I was just thinking about something. She looked into the small face, and was suddenly flooded by wonder: that this little human could think of her, Jane, as enough to ward off the whole world. She smiled. So did he.

—Cai was so naughty on *dydd Gwener*, what is it in *Saesneg*, oh yes, *Fri-day*, well, he was so naughty Miss Mor-gan said he would have to go to the *Eng-lish* school if he did it again. I won't be naughty, Mummy.

—Of course not, darling. But no one minds if you're a *bit* naughty, you know.

—Microbes are very small, aren't they?

—Microbes? Very, very small.

—But you *can* see them if you have a microskoke.

—Yes, you can see them with a microscope.

—Is anything really, really, really *invisible*?

—I don't think so. Atoms, perhaps.

—If I was invisible, I could do anything I wanted, couldn't I?

—You could.

—Then I could be *really* naughty in class and Miss Mor-gan wouldn't know, would she?

—Oho! laughed Jane, merrily but without committing herself absolutely. Bryn's eyes screwed up, twinkling, focusing distantly, as he considered the ultimate, the most joyous naughtiness conceivable to a boy just turned five.

—If I was invisible, I could *speak English in the classroom*! He rolled his eyes and grinned.

—Mmm, Jane tried to laugh along with him.

Some thirty seconds later she watched him struggle up the steps of the old school coach, then waved him off as the children departed to their unknown, and to Jane quite literally incomprehensible, world, in a cloud of D-reg diesel smoke.

She wondered for a moment why Bryn looked rather unhappy today, and why he was thinking about naughtiness, but for once her parental empathy was quickly drowned in her own personal excitement, and she only thought sadly about things like childhood and love and loss for a second or two, before striding across the road to where Dicky Emrys was waiting in his little Honda sports car to take them both to work.

—God, Mondays should be banned, groaned Dicky, as he drove away, —they're unnatural.

—Oh, I don't know, said Jane, vastly cheerful.

—How can you be like that, Janey? Monday morning always comes round about six hours too early, I'm *sure* they secretly put all the clocks in the world forward sometime on Sunday night. Ask anyone. Everyone *normal* feels like that: you're just a mad workaholic.

—Actually, I am a bit excited. I got a personal e-mail from the Barrister Called Percival.

—I thought you said that your stupid website didn't have chat rooms and things like any normal place?

—Exactly. He sent it in the open. With his phone number.

—His phone number? On an open site?

—I know.

—Bloody hell, he's keen. Well, that's very disappointing, I mean, that doesn't sound very *repressed* after all, does it?

—Not very.

—No offence, Janey, but you *sure* he meant you? If it was on an open website?

—Well, you see, I *suspected* he was talking to me before, but now I'm sure. He wrote my name, Dicky.

—How thrilling. So now the whole world knows you two are getting it together? God, it's like shagging in the middle of the virtual high street. How wonderful.

—We're not getting it together.

—Of course not, lovelygirl. Well? And?

—Anyway, who cares who knows, we're just ordinary people, why should anyone care what *we* do?

—*I* care. I think it's splendid. Go and shag him stupid. Well? And? Come on, come on, come on, we are all sitting comfortably in Mam's kitchen, the grate is stoked, it is still 1972, the wireless is tuned and *we all want a story.*

—He just said to phone him this morning.

—Just that?

—Well, the message just said: *OK, Let's Cut To The Chase: I Like The Way You Walk. Call Me First Thing Monday*, said Jane, with a gentle thrill.

—Nothing else?

—Nothing else.

—My God, how *dominant*. Well. London, I suppose?

—Of course. Where else are there any single men?

—*Real* London? I mean, Zones 1 and 2?

—Well, it's a central London number.

—I hope he left the prefix off. I always like that. It sort of shows *they* assume *you* assume its central. *So* mutually flattering.

—Yes, actually, said Jane, somewhat smugly.

—Oh well, London Lust it is then. I hope you've replied wittily?

—No, I thought I'd just phone, like he said. *Asked*, I mean. Oh God, should I have replied wittily already?

—Hmm. Perhaps not. Not on an open site, certainly. If he wants to play S, you're best off playing M right away: do exactly as he says.

—Right, said Jane, trying to fight off imprecise but lurid visions of what Percival might demand from her in the way of M. She looked out of the window.

—Funny. It all looks sort of 3D this morning, doesn't it? she said.

—What, love, you mean as if the green light were emanating not from the refractions and reflections of watery sunlight, but from within the wet Welsh hills themselves?

—Well, yes, actually. Something like that.

—On heat. I knew it.

—I am *not*!

Jane arrived in her office, however, with her heart undeniably beating from far more than the mere three flights of steps she had climbed to arrive at the Romance Languages and Media Studies Department. She pinned a sheet of paper on the outside of her office door, saying 'Back @ 10.15', sat down at her desk, and tried to work out exactly who she was going to be on the phone. How on earth could she make her voice sound as if it might be part of the wonderful, carefree, witty e-personality she had constructed in cyberspace?

At last, she plucked up her courage and, absurdly nervous, called the number Percival had left.

—Hello, croaked a voice.

—Hello, said Jane, trying to keep her voice slow and low, —this is, um, DJ Feva.

—OK, DJ lady, you ready to rumble?

Jane was shocked, more at the sound of Percival's voice than at his scarcely concealed sexual invitation. She had expected him to sound, well, *English*. The voice on the end of the line was English, yes, but not *English* English, more sort of half-London half-American. And much more wrecked, much more sort of, well, kind of, *dangerous* . . .

— . . . Ha ha, laughed Jane, trying to sound entertained rather than shocked, like a good citizen of the non-judgemental e-world.

—Because I'm ready, girl. I like your sound. I like the way you know what you want. We need to get together *pronto*.

—Yes, well . . . said Jane.

—So, where you at?

—Well, I just thought we could have a *talk*, you know.

—Time ticks by, lady. Others talk: I do.

—Oh, said Jane, feeling helplessly overwhelmed and horribly, embarrassingly excited. She had not been overwhelmed for a long time. Could this really be the same man who reported on his little triumphs against Yoof? On his Happy Meals and Aggressive

Compliance? What a *complex* man he must be, at once so understanding, so sensitive and yet so forthrightly sexual, so unashamed, so ready to *be in control* . . . —I mean, I suppose we could, sort of, you know, meet up . . .

—Fuck *meeting*, lady. We got to do this now.

—Now? said Jane, her excitement turning to horror, and yet not quite ceasing to be excitement. —What, you mean, *on the phone*?

—That's what they were invented for, Miz Feva. Let's go for it.

—OK, said Jane, weakly. She skittled across the floor on her gas-suspended chair to make sure that the door really was locked. She could not believe she was actually going to do phone-sex, for the first time in her life, in her own office, at ten in the morning . . .

— . . . So: tell me about *Las Madonnas del Cenicero*. I liked it. Especially the white stockings. Very sexy.

Jane let the earpiece of the phone slip a little away from her ear, disappointment and shame flooding her. So that was all Percival wanted. Not her. Not a real woman with real needs and longings. Just a female voice telling a cheap, soft-porn story which she had posted ironically on the website. Men.

—You *liked* it, did you? she said nastily.

—Possibly.

—*Turned you on*, did it? Especially the white stockings?

—The white stockings were good. But it all depends.

—Depends? Depends on what?

—Is it free?

—Free? For God's sake! shouted Jane, —I thought you were *serious*, but if all you want is *free stories*, I suggest you call one of those phone lines that specialise in . . .

— . . . Hey hey hey, said the voice, before Jane could hang up. —Do I sound like that?

—Well, yes, actually, said Jane, bitterly. —Or (she added hopefully) is this some kind of joke?

—Let's talk straight, shall we?

—Let's, said Jane.

—You haven't assigned it already?

—Assigned what?

—Don't play hard to get. The Option. Hel-lo?

—The Option? asked Jane, cautiously, feeling like some mariner who has firmly believed he has been heading west all night, only to see the sun rise directly in front of him. —Sorry, but this is . . . *Percival*, isn't it?

—*Percival?* Who the fuck are they? You haven't closed on the Option with *them*?

—What? No, no, no, look, I just . . .

— . . . Thank Christ. I mean, thank Christ for *your* sake, lady, not mine. Percival? Never heard of them. Hold on, did they do that heap of straight-to-video shit about King Arthur? No, that was Launcelot Films, right? Right. Percival? Look, lady, if *I* never heard of them, *no one* ever heard of them. Forget Percival. Talk to *me*.

—Um, OK, said Jane, utterly lost.

—The Option.

—Right, said Jane, feeling at least the distant prospect of firmer land.

—Is it still out there?

—Oh. Um, well, look, I'm sorry, this is all rather unexpected. Bit of a crossed wire. So, um, well, are you actually a *student*?

—You what? Jesus H. Christ, do I *sound* like some fucking film-school geek?

—No, no, I just mean –

—I produced *Suzi Got Whacked* and *Base* fucking *Metal*, lady. I can talk one-to-one with Alan Barony. You think Alan Barony talks one-to-one with fucking *film students*? You think Baz Andrews acts for fucking *film students*?

—What?

—Don't *what* me, girl, and don't try to play hardball with me. I want that Option, I want to make this film.

—Sorry?

—Girl, I want to make this happen for you and me, but I don't *need* this, you got that? I got a dozen projects I could get Green-Lighted yesterday. But I happen to like yours. Now: you want to write this, yeah?

—Well . . . began Jane, trying to suppress giddy visions of herself as A Writer. Only last week, the well-known (that is, well known in British universities) Spanish short-story writer Javier del Ferer had confirmed that he would visit Pontypool next term for an agreed fee: she could well recall the atmosphere of almost religious awe with which all Staff Members had greeted Professor Evans's gloating announcement. And now she had a chance to be *The Writer*, even if it was only the writer of a little documentary about university life . . . —Well, of course, yes, if I *could* . . .

—With me you can. Anyone else going to protect you like that? You need to work with someone who loves, but fucking *loves*, scripts, yeah?

—Of course, said Jane The Famous Documentary Writer.

—With me, that's what it's all about. The script, the script, the script. I will guide you. I will hold your hand. I will cover your back. Because of your script. Which I already love.

—Right, said Jane, checking the window to see if her office was still on earth.

—OK. I can go ten K if we close right now. And that's not an offer. That's *the* offer.

—*Ten thousand?*

—Twelve. And you get a guaranteed, I mean *cast-iron*, writer's credit: whatever happens, it has *your* name on it right after mine.

—Look, said Jane, feeling slightly wobbly, —I think we need to check a few points here, I mean . . .

— . . . And three percentage points of net, OK, OK.

—Net?

—Come on, lady, no one gets points of *gross*, not unless they got their name above the title and their face across at least one-third of the poster area. Twelve K up front, four points of net and a guaranteed writing credit. But this is off the market when I hang up. Fuck Percival, whoever they are. Talk to me, lady, clock's ticking. Well? We got a deal?

—Fine, said Jane, disbelieving.

—Call your lawyers, I'll call mine. Deal memo coming through in five, fax and e-mail, hard copy to follow. Give me your numbers.

—OK, said Jane, and gave him her numbers.

—Hey, where are you? You in the sticks? Where the fuck is that?

—Well, it's Wales, said Jane, a tad defensively.

—Wales? *Soft Money*, right?

—What?

—Oh, come on, you're obviously not bloody Welsh, I know why you've based yourself there, I'm not stupid. Only one reason anyone bases themselves in Wales. You can access Euro-funding, right?

—Well, we do get the odd trip to Europe, I suppose, and . . .

—Cannes? Berlin? Way to go. OK, let me think. If you're already based in Wales, this could be good. I like you, Fevalady, you deal straight but hard. I can make you happy. Keep your phone off the hook and your fax line free. See you on the ice.

—Ice? What ice? Asked Jane, but the phone was already dead.

Jane sat in her chair for a while, trying to work out if the world was still turning in the same direction as half an hour before. At length, she decided she had better go straight to Professor Evans with the news that a London film company wanted her to write a documentary about her Option course. She had a surprising amount of trouble making her knees work when she stood up.

A Writing Credit!

Salmon hung up and strode round the room in his dressing gown. OK, this was good, this was very good. A *writing* credit! Percentage points of *net*! It never failed. Suckers. Twelve grand for the Option *and* the Screenplay! Ha ha. God, he was good. Right. Time to start building the house of cards. This was what he was good at: this was what he *did*.

It was all going to turn out fine.

Jane knocked at the door of Professor Evans's office.

—Who the hell is it? shouted Evans, from inside.

—Jane, said Jane.

—Oh God, all right then.

Evans greeted Jane by plonking a vast heap of incomprehensible figures and columns in front of her. Evans was very good at virtual financial models and suchlike, whereas most academics, being experts in things no one else in the world cares a toss about, have traditionally been pretty well pleased with themselves for not knowing about stuff like virtual financial models and suchlike if they bit them up the arse, and trying to avoid them wherever possible. That is why, these days, Evans was Head of Department, and not them, and they had to do what he said, not the other way round.

—Well? said Evans. —You realise what this means? You don't, do you? You realise that thanks to those consummate bastards in Engineering, if I don't manage to get our First Year Beginners Language Modules rated at 1.2 per cent per head we stand to lose a total of £9,600 from top-up capitation next year? No, you bastard don't, do you? Of course not. None of you do. Too bloody posh by half, the lot of you. But *whose* job will be on the line if I don't sort this mess out for us? Not mine, is whose.

—Mmm, said Jane. And then she tried to seem dynamic. —Something's come up and I was wondering if maybe it might be quite a nice thing for me, I mean for *us*, to do. I was thinking that it might get *us* some quite nice publicity. Even if only one or two students more came to us because of it, maybe postgraduates, the fees might help *us* to balance out the –

—Because of *what*? said Evans, menacingly. Like most heads of most things in the world, he instinctively distrusted any initiative that did not, or at least did not seem to, come from himself.

—Well, I've just had a call from someone who wants to make a documentary about my Option course on *Las Madonnas del Cenicero*.

—Why the hell would they want to do that?

—I suppose they want to make a film about how you design a university course for a little-known work.

—Thrilling TV.

—Yes, well, they just called anyway, and I thought it

111

might be nice to get on the telly. I mean (she added hastily), it might be good to get the *University*, the *Department*, on telly. Good for student numbers, I thought. But perhaps not. They've offered, Jane added, sadly, for in the gathering frown lines on Evans's drink-beaten face she could already read the answer, —twelve thousand pounds for me to do it. And four points of net, whatever that is. And a writing credit.

Evans tapped his desk with a biro, several times, very slowly.

—The students would certainly want to shag you if you were getting them to appear on the telly. Hmmm. Let me think. I take it you have been communicating with this film company during university time? I assume you have been using university hardware on this project?

Jane became aware of the menacing subtext in Professor Evans's questions.

—Well, I mean, not exactly. No, actually. It was done on my own computer, in the evenings. You can check my e-mail. I have just made one call, the first. I can do it from home if you'd rather.

Evans looked at Jane with new respect.

—You would not have the sheer bastard brass face to deny that the Department *enabled* that work by allowing you to put forward your Option?

Jane swallowed boldy.

—Well, my Option isn't actually confirmed as *running* yet.

—It bastard well is now.

—Even if not enough of the students sign up?

—They will when they know it's going to be on the telly. And if they still don't, it will be gently intimated to them that the finals questions for this particular Option will be sitters. That pompous, posh

English twat Worple can do Business Language again this year. No offence, Jane.

—None taken. I'm not posh, remember.

—So you aren't.

—And I'm half Scots.

—There we are then.

There was a pause lit up by the secret comradeship of underhand plotting.

—Right, said Evans. —Sit down, girl, sit down. Well, well, well. See, the Vice-Chancellor is keen for us to seem at the cutting edge. Especially, he is keen on us getting on the telly at every opportunity. Hmmm. Right, here we are: that money comes to the Department, OK, and the Option course is described as *mine* and *I'm* the one that appears on the telly, teaching it.

—But I thought –

—Shut up and bastard listen, Janey. I tell people what to think round here. I'll tell you what this means to you. It means that you get to teach the Option you want to run this term and no Business Language Classes and no admin work. It also buys you paid study leave for three months next year in addition to your normal holidays and no one asks how come you got study leave in your first year or where you did it or what you studied or why the bastard hell you've got sod all to show for it except a deep tan, some idiotic souvenirs and several exotic sexually transmitted diseases. Deal?

—No.

—What? screamed Evans.

—*You* get to appear on the TV, but *I* get named as the writer of the programme, said Jane, amazed at herself.

—You cheeky cow. Bugger me, you really *aren't* posh, are you?

—No.
—OK, deal.
—Done.
—Good girl. Lunch, then?

Lunch

Lunch that day in the privatised canteen at BBC Wales, where in theory all ranks muck in together and in practice woe betide the wretched underling who dares to sit at, or in hearing distance of, the nice big table with the windows on two sides where Hugh Pritchard, Dai Jones-Hughes and Aled Morris-Thomas habitually gather to carve up their meat and their grants. Today, they were deep in discussion with their favourite young film-maker.

—It's the link between the centres that's the problem.

—We've got to stop giving an amnesty to fat bloody back-row forwards.

—I don't give a toss *how* big a fullback is so long as he can find the fucking touchline.

—Boys, we'll never be the best again until we believe we're the best! Until we stop our hearts sinking every time we are confronted at some posh lunch by a girl who knows how to eat a bloody artichoke. Mam is dead, long live the big world. And we got to get faster second-phase ball.

—Good man, Rich!

—That's the boy, Rich!

—Right then, said Aled Morris-Thomas. —So we just need a project. A hundred thousand from us, a hundred from you, Hugh bach, and I'll make sure that cynt Williams at HTV delivers at least fifty. Back-to-back English and Welsh, Owain will come in with the same from the Lottery and we'll double it with Euro funds. OK with you, Rich?

—If the script's right, said Rich Jenkins.

—Oh, boys, now, here's the thing: anyone here heard of a company called Pogo Pictures?

—I think so, said Pritchard. —They did *Suzi Got Whacked*, didn't they? Shit, apparently, but doing OK in Wigan. Why?

—I got a press-release fax today. Apparently they've got a Welsh film. Looking for a Welsh partner. And a Welsh director.

—Euro-money they'll be after, then.

The three of them nodded significantly.

—Catching on, they are in London, the bastards, said Aled Morris-Thomas. —What do you reckon, Richyboy?

Rich Jenkins did not hear at first. He had switched off from his companions the moment they turned to their financial plotting, and was, instead, wandering around a private vision: an angelic young rugby fly half weaving, backlit and in slow motion, around the pumps of a deserted petrol station at the head of a green valley, the rusted pumps frozen for ever in some prehistoric setting of pounds, shillings, pence and halfpence, and beyond them endless fields of artichokes . . .

He came back to earth at the third time of asking, found three glasses raised smilingly before his eyes, and, without overmuch concern as to the issue at stake, hastily joined in the new Official Welsh National Toast, which the Welsh Assembly had recently declared was to be used on all formal or semi-formal occasions, by all official, quasi-official, or merely positively inclined Bodies:

—There we are then.

—There we are then.

*   *   *

Lunch at Soho House:

—It's fucking Hispanic, Pete. You know what that means stateside? Big, is what it means. Barony will swallow it hook, line and sinker. And I'm already on to the Soft Money. Christ, I hate fennel. Since when exactly and why the hell do we have to have fucking *fennel* with everything?

—Right, Paul. Talking of lines, I thought I should let *you* know, before everyone else, you know, just in case you want some for a rainy day . . .

—. . . Yeah, I could use a livener, actually. You know, just to fire me up for the afternoon. Got some big calls to make . . .

Lunch in the Students' Union at Pontypool, where the Surfy and Sexy students sat in glorious isolation from the rest of their fellows, unapproachably cool and self-contained, devouring the ghastly canteen food without the least hesitation, seeming rather to enjoy the whole experience of slumming it here. In the holidays, they would return to their real world together.

—So shall we do Feverfew's film-course thingy?

—Miss Nineties Knicker Line.

—Ha ha ha.

—Yeah, man, I was just, like, sitting there waiting for her jeans to *implode* and disappear up the vortex of her fanny.

—Ugh.

—I think we should do it. It'll be piss. You can write, like, *any* sort of crap about that stuff. What they going to do? Like, *fail* us? And lose their fees? Re-ally.

—Ha ha ha.

Lunch in the one identifiable restaurant in Pontypool, Dr Jane Feverfew and Professor Evan Evans at a table underneath a fine display of pinned-up paper napkins signed by Neil Kinnock himself:

—Aled? (Professor Evan Evans spoke loudly to his mobile as he sucked unabashed on a mussel.) —Evan here. Look, I want to come and see you about some people called Pogo Pictures. Want to do a documentary about one of my courses. Could be a cut in it for you boys, I thought. Oh, heard of them already, have you? Oh, well then. Oh, you got Rich Jenkins with you, have you? Great boy, Rich. Rightyo, see you at the Neath game tomorrow. The S4C hospitality box, is it? Oh, HTV this time. Good, there we are.

—Your little chap's being brought up bilingual, isn't he? asked Evans, after a pause for thought during which he removed a small fragment of bivalve from one of his rear teeth.

—Yes, said Jane cautiously: she was not sure where Evans stood on the Language Issue, and she had already learned that it was always best, in Wales, to find this out before saying anything.

—Make sure you mention that, if you get involved with BBC Wales.

—Will it help?

—Can't hurt, girl. More wine?

Lunch in the Gallo-Cymric restaurant in Cardiff, paid for by the Head of Public Relations, BBC Wales (English Language Section) out of his own pocket. The Gog bastards finally had him where they wanted him: *Public Denigration of the Welsh Language in the Presence of a Potential Foreign Investor*. It might not be officially and legally a crime yet (not *yet*), but he was done for all the same. Unless he could hit them with something right away, right now. He poured more wine into

Serbian Media Delegate's glass, while carefully avoiding giving more than a splash to himself.

—You see, it *just so happens* that if we could find a Serbian-Welsh project right now, it could be very handy.

—Handy for you, said the Serbian Media Delegate.

—Well, yes. But for you as well. Look, I saw this fax today, there's some London company going wild about a Welsh script. How about shooting the locations in Serbia?

—It is a Serbian story?

—Who cares? It'd bring in plenty of hard currency. And you would arrange everything, naturally.

—I see. You pay me in hard currency, I arrange all local things?

—At whatever bloody exchange rate you can make stick. And here's a sweetener just from me.

He produced a fat envelope. Inside it nestled one thousand pounds in five-pound notes, money which he had withdrawn from his own building society account that very morning. It physically pained him to hand it over: but after all, what is a thousand quid compared to another twenty years' generously pensionable salary? As her hand reached out, he withdrew the envelope for a second.

—But every statement you make mentions me *by name*, OK? You approach Aled right away with the project, thanking me *in writing* for setting it up and praising me *in writing* for batting so well for Wales.

—Batting?

—Oh, for God's sake. *Fighting*.

—We have deal. Now I think we drink brandy. To your friend Dr Jaypeeah: long may he massacre the enemies of your nation.

*　　*　　*

Lunch (or at any rate, sandwiches) at Alan Barony Distribution Ltd, W1:

—Well, I suppose Salmon does keep the budget tight, said Barony.

—I think he's quite good, really, said Sheina.

—That boy who made that film about gangsters in Peckham three years ago was on the phone again, said Alice, the receptionist. —He wanted to know if the film was in profit yet. He seemed quite a nice boy. Should I call him back later?

—No. Have we booked the yacht for Cannes yet, Sheina?

—Yes. Should be rather fun.

—Are we moored near Hal Scharnhorst's yacht?

—Well, *quite* near.

—Oh. Oh, well. Yes, I suppose Salmon's all right. So long as he can find some Soft Money and bring the whole thing in for under two point five million. But I don't suppose he'll bring anything with Art in it.

—Are you *quite* sure about this Art thing, Alan?

—Well, not *Art* Art, of course: *MaxiPix* Art. You know.

—Oh, I see: you mean Art, but the sort of Art where the trailers can still be full of shoot-outs and we can get that Deep Male American Voice telling everyone what it's about?

—Exactly. Maybe *Art* isn't the word.

—Class?

—Very good, Sheina. Yes, we're officially looking for *Class*. Chekhov sort of stuff, you know.

—Big dresses and knee breeches?

—But under two point five million. Oh, and book an extra ticket on our flight to Nice, will you?

—Who for?

—She's called Kate, said Barony, frowning slightly,

as if he found his own voice mildly surprising. His gaze slid away across the W1 roofline. —I'll find out her other name later.

—Cattle? asked Sheina.

—No, actually, mused Barony, taken again unawares by himself. —Club.

—Coo. O-K.

Cut and Shut

After lunch, Jane found a twenty-page deal fax from Paul Salmon in her office. It was accompanied by what seemed to be a press-release fax stating that Cut & Shut Films Ltd, of Cardiff, Wales, had joined forces with Pogo Pictures Ltd of Poland St, W1, to enter Pre-Production on a film based on the long-banned Hispanic classic novel *Las Madonnas del Cenicero*, which was to be scripted by award-winning Welsh writer Jane Feverfew.

Drunk as she was, for she never drank at lunchtime and had gone Chardonnay-for-Chardonnay with Professor Evans, Jane realised at this point that Paul Salmon of Pogo Pictures Ltd did not, in fact, want to make a documentary about life at the cutting-edge University of Pontypool (Department of European Studies, Prof. E. Evans, Head of Dept). She immediately called London again, and Paul Salmon put her swiftly right.

—Damn right I've set up a new company, Jane. Your story, you and me, based in Wales, Soft-Money-friendly, fifty/fifty split of the back end. Cut & Shut. Cool title, eh? My own. Well? You ever hear of a writer getting that kind of deal? Ask around: you never did, you never will. And what does it cost you? Nothing. Your twelve K even stays ring-fenced, too, once we've got it.

—Oh. You mean I don't get the money yet?

—Hey, I got to *raise* it first.

—But I thought you said you couldn't raise the money for the Project before getting the Option?

—Of course not. And we can't pay you for the Option until we've raised the money for the Project, obviously.

—Oh. Right.

—And anyway we've got it, haven't we? Because you're going to assign it *to yourself* and me. Great, eh? Money for nothing, Jane. The moment you sign that, you are officially a Company Director.

—Golly. Me?

—Welcome to the locker room, partner.

—Um, right. So, how *do* you, I mean *we*, raise the money?

—That'll be a piece of piss now we've got a Welsh-based company, a Welsh-based female writer and Marcus Dale on board.

—*Marcus Dale?* squealed Jane, for she (like most women over thirty in the UK) could well recall staring up some two or three summers ago, in giggling disbelief, like prehistoric peasant girls worshipping at some phallic altar, at Marcus Dale's tight knee breeches, insanely enlarged on the silver screen.

—You OK with Marcus?

—God, yes. You serious?

—You approve?

—Me?

—See? You ever heard of a *writer* getting Principal Cast approval? Not on this planet you didn't. You and me, Jane, fifty/fifty. Obviously there'll be expenses, and distribution, and my fee at industry norms, we've all got to live, but as soon as we go into profit, fifty/fifty all the way. You got any idea how much that would be if we do just *half* as good as *Four Weddings*? Even *one*-fucking-*quarter* as good?

—Glurp, said Jane.

—Sorry?

—Just, um, well, yes, great.

—Sign away and fire it back, Jane: we have a movie to make. Right. I'll set up a meeting for us with the head of the Welsh Film Fund.

—Us?

—Well, of course you've got to come. The Director will be there too.

—Director?

—Rich Jenkins. He's Welsh, he's hot, he's kosher art house. You approve? Jane?

—Well, but, isn't that a bit . . .

— . . . Tough world out there, Jane. OK then. I'll try to get a four o'clock some day next week with the Welsh Film Fund.

—Well, OK, if you . . . Wait, no, no, I can't.

—Can't?

—I've got a child.

—A *what*?

—A child. He finishes school at three thirty.

—Oh shit.

—Um, can we, well, I mean, couldn't we make it some day at two o'clock instead?

—Two o'clock *in Cardiff*? You got *any* idea what time that means I have to get up?

—I'm really sorry, Paul, but I can't, I don't see how I . . .

— . . . OK, OK, who said this job wasn't work? I'll try for a two o'clock. Get your wetsuit on, girl.

—Wait. What are we going to say to the Welsh Film Fund, what are we . . . ?

But Salmon was already gone.

Jane scrabbled the long and unhandy fax up, fell over

it twice, and eventually read through it until she found the parts where she was to sign.

It was clear as day, really, and very simple to anyone (like Jane) who had a PhD (even when they were slightly drunk): Paul Salmon (hereafter PS) and Jane Feverfew (hereafter JF) were to be appointed Directors of Cut & Shut Films, with Company Secretary being one Sheina Hesmondhalgh, who would be awarded a salary to be agreed in good faith between PS and JF once the Project was Green-Lighted. In all business and creative matters, PS and JF were to confer and agree mutually; all Producer's Net Profits were to be divided on a fifty/fifty basis between them. It was foolproof. Just common sense, really. Lawyers? Who needs them?

Before she signed, however, Jane stopped and thought. Still filled with the warm delusion of eternal alcoholic cameraderie, Jane decided she had better show the fax to her new friend, Professor Evans, straight away, and ask his advice or at least let him know what was actually happening. It seemed only polite.

Bad decision.

—A film? If you think you can bastard well ponce about writing films *and* get paid twenty-three fucking grand to work for me, you got another think coming. The days when being a Lecturer was a part-time job for posh twats are dead and gone, girly. You think I'm going to sit here and rubber-stamp the state paying you twenty-three grand a year that could be going on hospitals and schools just so you can *write films*? Business Language Years One and Two it is for you, then.

—But that means that if the students *do* sign up for my new Option, my timetable will be much heavier than anyone else's, said Jane. —That's not very fair.

—Fair? Sod bastard *fair*. If you got the time to write sodding screenplays, I'm not working you hard enough, am I? One hundred per cent, you're paid for, and 100 per cent I'm going to get. I could have you washing my bastard car if I wanted, Miss bloody Poshypants.

—No, you couldn't, said Jane, feeling a strange wave of energy surge through her, the sort of burst she only usually got when ruining the days of adolescent drivers. —And by the way, I'm not posh, remember?

—What? (Evans was momentarily flat-footed.) —Well, maybe not, but I can still have you teaching the bastard Business Language Classes. And I want your Teaching Quality Assessment forms and your Research Selectivity Exercise forms and your Professional Development Plan in the office by Monday. *Writing!* What the hell has that got to do with teaching *literature*?

Jane walked off stiffly, if not very straight, down the corridor. The wine was cooking in her skull and her face was flushed with more than drink: it was burning with bitter shame at the thought of every time she had deferred to Professor Evans in the last three months; of the terrible jokes she had laughed at during the interview and had been laughing at ever since; of the pay cut she had taken; of the reasonable and nice Professor McGrimble at East Hackney University, of all the joys of London, of the nice educated journalist or barrister or whatever from Muswell End whom she would now never meet, of everything she had deserted and left for Wales and for Evans, that, that . . .

— . . . bullying little Welsh sod! said Jane loudly, to herself, once she was in her office. She spun vengefully round on her chair, and fell off it. She lay on her industrial carpet and thought of the horrors of her life to come here.

Somewhere in her mind, a quite particular horror was lurking just below the surface, like a fish in dark water. The forgotten-piece-of-toast syndrome again. God, her brain must be raddled with drink. What was it? What was this secret, guilty voice? She filed back cagily in her brain's hard disk, haunted by nameless dread, sifting through words and their associations: what thought had thrown that shadow over her mind?

Welsh sod?

Dafydd?

Leeks.

St David's Day.

Oh my God.

Oh no, no, no!

That was why Bryn had been so curiously quiet and withdrawn when she dropped him off at the bus that morning: she had forgotten all about packing his special clothes for the St David's Day parade. And he had been too brave to tell her. His mind had been circling around naughtiness and outsiderdom, but he had kept it all held in.

He would be sitting there now, tight-lipped with held-back tears, wishing he could be invisible, or at least microscokic, the only little boy in school without the clothes to dress up as a farm labourer from the twenties or a rugby player from the seventies. The only child without a leek to pin to his braces. Already, at five, he would have learned that Eden was closed off, that Mothers fail, that the world is a hostile, fragile place, where we have to stride about, lonely, in brittle, chilly armour . . .

. . . The leek was still under the seat in Jane's car.

She could imagine it clearly, lying there, unused. It would still be there when she went to her car now. Lurking in mute accusation. Festering. Radiating gamma rays of reproach out at her.

Bad mummy bad mummy bad bad drunken selfish mummy.

The other children at school would think Bryn was posh and English.

He would feel different.

He would be unpopular.

He would turn out like her.

Anything but that.

But perhaps there was still time?

The St David's Day procession was in the afternoon, Dafydd had said. Maybe she could still get there in time, with Bryn's special clothes? Could she make it to Cardiff, to the shops, and back out to Ynys-y-bwl again in time? What was the school's number again? Jane scrabbled to her knees, picked up her office phone and called Directory Enquiries.

—*Sorry, this number is barred*, said a motherly South Welsh voice on tape. Of course, the bloody university had bought in its own CD Phone Directory system, to save money for spending on new regalia and carpets for the Building Services Department. Jane called the internal number instead. It was, as always, engaged. She slammed down the phone, got out her mobile and dialled.

—Hoi, welcome to Orange Directories, how can oi help ya, Dr Feverfew? said a north Dublin voice, positively overflowing with that youthful, quasi-transatlantic helpfulness that is the worldwide hallmark of the Celtic Tiger.

—I'd like a number, said Jane, perhaps unnecessarily.

—No problemo, Doctor. And what name would it be please?

128

—It's in Wales, you see, she began apologetically. Already, her heart was beginning to sink in justified foreboding. She felt not entirely undrunk.

—Sure. Wales, UK. We can do that, I believe. What *name* please, Doctor? said the voice, slight impatience disguised with trained skill. Jane sighed.

—Ysgol Mynydd Ynys-y-bwl, she said, clearly, distinctly and (she thought) correctly.

—Uskal?

—I'll spell it.

—O-K. Fire away, Doctor.

—Y-S-G-O-L.

—Y?

—Why? Because it's Welsh.

—No, I mean *Y*. The letter. *Y* is the first letter in the word *Uskal*?

—Yes.

—Bizarre. But, hey: Y-S-G-O-L is it. And then?

—New word: *Mynydd*.

There was a small but palpable delay. When the Dublin voice returned, it was a degree or so less brimming with enthusiasm.

—*Munith*. OK, whatever. And how would we be spelling *Munith* today, Dr Feverfew?

—It's, um, M-Y, oh God, hold on, I think it's M-Y-N-Y-D-D.

—M-Y-N-*Y*?

—Yes. I think so.

—Ehhh, getting a bit light on the vowels here, aren't we, Doctor?

—Y is a vowel.

—Why is a vowel what?

—No, no, the letter *Y* *is* a vowel in Welsh.

—Well, Holy God. Where were we now? M-Y- . . .

—Just let me think. Yes, that's right. N-Y-D-D.

—NYPD?

—I'm sorry, this line is very bad.

—And it's after lunch, righ'?

—Sorry?

—My brother-in-law is a medical rep, Doctor, I heard all about those expense-account lunches for yous guys, don't you worry.

—Excuse me!

—Listen, no offence, but this call is being recorded, OK, Doctor? You want me to play it back to you? You sound nicely oiled up, I have to say.

—OK, I'm sorry, I did have a drink or two, but I'm sure I'm not slurring or –

—OK, OK, who'd blame a medical lady for taking a drink? Or two? Tough job. Now, let's calm this down and try again, shall we, *Doctor*?

—OK, thanks.

—No problemo. Right. Tell you what, we'll pass on that first word for now. Can we try the second word again? From the top, please, Doc.

—M-Y-N-Y-D-D, said Jane, clearly, blushing.

—O-K, whatever you say. Doctor's orders. And the third word was?

—Y-N-Y-S hyphen Y hyphen . . .

— . . . OK, hold on, hold on. Emm, look, let's try another tack, shall we. *What* is it? This place we're calling, I mean?

—It's my son's school.

—Oh, right, I get it: some kind of *faith school* right? Would that be Jewish by any chance, Dr Feverfew?

—No, look, it's nothing to do with that.

—Oh, Jesus, I'm sorry, I didn't cop on there. Ehh, will I look under *Special Schools*, so?

—My son is perfectly normal.

—Of course he is.

—It's a normal, local authority school. For normal children. OK? It just happens to be in Wales.

—OK. Fine. (The Dublin youth now spoke with massive self-control.) —So, might it help if you told me the name of this ordinary UK school, *in English*, maybe? Hello? Dr Feverfew?

—Look, I don't know it.

—Sorry?

—I don't know it.

—You don't know the name of your own son's school?

—In English, I mean. You see, I don't think it's *got* one.

—It hasn't got one?

—I don't think so.

—Let's get this straight. You're telling me this is an ordinary, state-funded, local authority school, for normal kids, in the good old U of K, but it has *no name in English*?

—Yes, yes, yes! cried Jane, knowing even as she spoke that it was (a) impossible in the rational world but (b) true in Wales. —Look, you, you wouldn't laugh if it was *Icelandic*, would you?

—*Icelandic*? I'm sorry, Doctor, we're getting nowhere. This is a free service and if you wish to abuse it after some big lunch with a medical rep or whatever –

—I'm not a bloody doctor!

—Oh, I see. I see. So you just *call* yourself Doctor? Ah, that's great. Sure, why not? If it makes life more of a laugh. So I tell you wha': I'll call *you* Doctor and you call *me* Monsignor, how's about that?

—Look, sorry, this is all going wrong. You're Irish, aren't you?

—Yes, our Call Centre is indeed located in the Greater Dublin area, *madam*. What of it? If you were intending any kind of racially motivated insulting language to my person or nation, *Ms* Feverfew, I should inform you that it is Orange policy to –

—If you're Irish, *you* should understand!

—Don't typecast us as drunks and fantasisers, Ms Feverfew. That's a plain insult.

—I'm not. I'm just saying that you lot must have bloody stupid Gaelic names over there as well, and –

—*Bloody stupid?* Whoa! Time out! Cultural abuse alert. OK, I'm terminating this one. I suggest you try again later, Ms Feverfew. I prescribe lots of black coffee. And if I were you, I'd ease up on this Doctor riff, you know what I mean? Impersonating medical personnel is one of the most common first signs of paranoid delusion. Call the Samaritans and keep away from the scalpels.

—What? Listen, you can't –

But he could, and did.

Jane sat back on her floor.

She got up, in order to find her keys, rush to her car, and race to the school. Then she realised she did not even have her car here. Then she realised she could not force Dicky to drive her. Then she realised they would never make it anyway.

It was too late.

She had to realise the truth which hurts any mother the most: there was nothing she could do for her child now. Nothing she could do to help her son. She could not save him.

Bad mummy.

Jane lay back on her floor, to consider her life.

She got up. She sat down. She lay down again.

She must have been mad to have ever agreed to come to live here.

Bastards.

Oh yes, it would have been different if it had been a *Welsh-language* film she wanted to make. Oh yes. That power-crazed bugger Evans wouldn't have dared stop her then, would he? No way. He would have just . . . hold on, hold on . . .

. . . Suddenly, Jane found that she was standing, red-eyed but grim-lipped. She sniffed, wiped her hand across her nose, and pulled her trousers up even tighter. A thoroughly devilish plot had arisen in a bubble of adrenalin that jumped, sour, into her chest.

—Right then, she said, out loud, —if that's the way *they* want it. Ha!

And she called Paul Salmon, to tell him to re-arrange the time of their proposed meeting with the Welsh Film Fund.

—Why? snapped he.

—Because I have a good idea for the meeting, said Jane.

—*You* have?

—We're partners, right?

—Of course, Jane, shit, but I've done this before, it's a *skill*, and you, well, with respect, Jane –

—Listen.

—What? OK.

Jane told him why she wanted him to rearrange the meeting. Salmon goggled audibly.

—Fuck me, my lady, you are *good* at this!

—Thanks, said Jane, bitterly.

—Oh, and don't forget to moniker our contract.

—Sure.

—Catch you on the Cresta Run, Ms Fever.

With a strange premonition that her life would never be the same again, Jane scribbled a signature on the deal memo, dated it, and faxed it back to Pogo Pictures. Then she walked out of her office, her determined boots ringing loud in the quiet corridor, slipped into the Departmental Office, and liberated a ream of paper, a printer refill, a pack of those little yellow stick-on notes and a great number of filing cards.

—Right, said Jane to herself. —And *sod* the bloody laundry basket.

In Good Faith

Enlivened and restored after his lunch and by his cocaine, Paul Salmon strolled elegantly back from Soho House to his little rented office in Berwick Street, ready to start work. God, he loved Mondays. And he was rather looking forward to meeting his New Writer now: she sounded like she had a bit of brain.

Of course, she had bought the crap about Points of Net and Credits, but they all did, first-time round. Good idea of hers, that, about the meeting with the Welsh Film Fund. Hmm. Maybe she would even genuinely be useful to him as a partner. *Useful*: the mere word tugged distantly at the deepest, darkest roots of Salmon's cock. Hey, she might even be OK-looking. Provincial girl in London, you never knew . . .

— . . . Well, sir?

Salmon found himself forced to pause by a pierced man who bounced out of nowhere to block his path, respectfully and yet insistently. Salmon did not at first recognise him as the Greenpeace seller of last week.

—What, friend?

—How are The Saviours?

—The which? demanded Salmon, trying to loosen the other's grip on his sleeve. Then he remembered the idea again (shit, *must* write this stuff down, forgot to get that Psion again!) and his Producering instincts took over even as he prised away the fingers and continued on his way. —Oh, yeah, great, going great, watch this space, we got a major development deal in the pipeline, check out the website, spread the word, see you on the ice, my man . . .

—What's the web address? gasped Skanky, desperately, as Salmon escaped him. Salmon stopped. He thought. Like any decent Producer, he had an unerring instinct for spotting the sort of young people who will work for nothing just to get a toehold in the slippery world.

—Hmmm. You any good with websites, my man? We had a bit of a problem yesterday, ours, you know, crashed, got infected, whatever. Gone. Tragedy.

—Websites, sir, they're what I do, I mean what I *want* to do, if only someone would give me a break, let me show what I can do, I always –

—You want to do one for us? For The Saviours?

—Me? gasped Skanky.

—No money upfront, you got to prove yourself. It's a hard world. But if this takes off the way I think, well, you're a made man too, my friend.

—I can do it!

—Get something down on disk, catch me again.

—Yes. Yes, sir. Where? When?

—Hey, I'm always around, winked Salmon, and was gone.

Skanky, web-designer elect to The Saviours, watched Salmon walk away: away, to his powerful life of mystery and fulfilment, to blonde dreadlocked girls in lowlit restaurants, to adventure and achievement that could transform lives merely by touching them. What had he spoken of? Pipelines, Ice and Major Development? Yes, Skanky understood. Alaska, must be. Machine-gunned whalers. Hard to the core. Yes. What had Lenin said? *The true revolutionary wears a tie and waistcoat*. Yes. Mr Salmon. Already, bright visions were flooding his mind. He looked down at the pile of Greenpeace brochures in his hand as if he were gazing at some distant, incomprehensible world. What was he doing with this wimp shit? He was in The Saviours now. He had A Life.

He looked around him at Old Compton Street, at the porn shops where he bought his porn and the corners where he bought his drugs and the booze shops where he bought his cider. His world. The streets that had ruined his life. The place where he had lost the heaven of his youthful innocence.

Satan's loveless lair.

When The Saviours came, all this would be cleansed.

In a Cardiff bar, meanwhile (it was actually quite a good imitation of an Islington bar), Dr Jane Feverfew and her Gay Posse were indulging in the (to Jane, at least) new delights of daytime drinking.

—Well, I think it's *lovely*, boys! Best news since Viagra.

—Me too! Well done, Jane! Our very own Valley Girl.

—Someone *doing* something at last!

—About time. Oh, look, there's that Antonio from the Italian deli, God, I could slice *his* Parma ham. Are you going to do it in Spain, Jane?

—I'm not really sure.

—Jane in Spain.

—The Jane in Spain falls mainly on her back.

—Thanks a bunch.

—We can all come over.

—I love that Marcus Dale. I'm sure he *is*.

—Of course he is. *Gorra* be.

—More tequila, Jane?

—To Jane.

—No, no, I can't, I've got to pick Bryn up. Christ, I must be mad, I nearly forgot.

—Tell your ex he's got to pick Bryn up.

—How can I do that?

—How? By telling him, lovely.

—But –

—Stop. Simple question, Janey: would your ex be able to make it to the school if he had to?

—Well, yes, but Bryn's expecting me, and he'll already be upset because of this bloody leeks business and –

—He'll learn to embrace the unexpected. Best training for the new world. You're drunk, love, just tell hubby that and sod him. You deserve some fun for once. Children don't want stability, lovely, that's what their parents want; children want to see the world. Make your life a caravanserai, not a potting shed, and he will be happy in ways you cannot imagine.

—But Dafydd will –

—He'll what? *Divorce* you?

So Jane called Dafydd and told him he had to pick Bryn up because she had got drunk with Professor Evans. She also informed him that for the next few months she might well need him to take Bryn for two nights a week instead of one night, to allow her to do more work in the evenings. Dafydd was too astonished even to argue.

—Coo, said Jane to herself, as she put the phone down. —Easy-peasy.

In his little office, Salmon snorted another line (just a little one, just a top-up to keep him tight and fighting) and began Producing in earnest. He still had an hour before his meeting with Alan Barony, so first he e-mailed Marcus Dale's agent.

Salmon headed his message *Without Prejudice*, and in it he stressed firmly, *For the Avoidance of Doubt* that the letter did *Not Constitute an Offer*: he also marked it *cc Alan Barony*, though he naturally had no intention of sending it there, of all places: his tactics were based on the principle that the more daring the lie, the less likely you are to be found out. Finally, he falsely day/timed the e-mail as having been sent earlier that morning, fired it off, gave it three minutes to travel the eighty yards to Marcus Dale's agent's office, then immediately followed up by phone.

—Mikey, Paul: what's with the Radio Silence, my man, you *trying* to fuck up Marcus's career or you just playing hard to get?

—Hey, Paul, I haven't even opened your e-mail yet, I only just fucking got it.

—Mikey, I sent it first fucking thing. I been fighting off the world, all day, ever since breakfast.

—I'm telling you, Paul, it only just came through.

—Don't tell me, don't tell me: you're *not on broadband* yet?

—Well, no.

—Got to be done, Mikey, Net's jamming solid. Shit, if we weren't friends already I'd have taken offence. What happens when ICM try to blip you a script from LA and you're jammed up because you were too fucking cheapskate to go broadband? ICM calls someone else, is what happens.

—OK, OK, point taken: tomorrow, we go broadband. But today: what's cooking, Paul?

—Mikey, you're not seriously going to put Marcus Dale *on stage* again?

—Paul, it's a long-term game plan.

—Yeah, yeah, yeah, we all know Marcus needs to get

back into knee breeches and boots, but why *the theatre*? You really want to live on 10 per cent of *theatre* wages, Mikey?

—Fifteen per cent, Paul, I take 15 per cent.

—Fifteen per cent of *theatre wages*? You can live on *that*?

—Marcus's not my *only* fucking client.

—Not yet he isn't.

—Fuck *you*, Paul.

—Hey, Mikey, they all came to you last year *because you had Marcus Dale*. This time next year they're all thinking: yeah, *but look what happened to Marcus Dale*.

—Marcus Dale is still a star! He's made the Sunday women's pages three times in the last six weeks, and twice they ran pictures.

—Mikey, Mikey, *I* know Marcus's still a star. *You* know it. The rest of the world just kinda *forgot*, yeah?

—Fuckwits.

—Which is why you want him back in knee breeches and boots. Just to *remind* them, right?

—Right.

—You want them to forget all that straight-to-tape shit he did in LA. You want them to think *Jane Eyre* again. You want them to remember *Fanny Hill*, right?

—They'll remember.

—Of course. The moment they seem him in knee breeches and boots again, they'll remember. It's what we Brits *do*. But I mean, Mikey: the *theatre* for Christ's sake!

—What you saying, Paul?

—I'm saying I can have him in front of the camera, *in knee breeches and boots*, on a white charger, with a sabre and a multibarrel musket in a month. We can have him in the papers, puffing it, in time for next weekend's Review sections.

—What, has Alan Barony given you a Green Light?

—Would I be talking to you? So call Alan, Mikey.

—Hey, Paul, no offence, but Alan Barony? Marcus is an *artiste*, fuck him. He's insisting on doing *Art*. I can *try*, but –

—Trust me, Mikey, so is Alan.

—So is Alan *what*?

—Insisting on doing Art.

—Alan? Art? *Alan*?

—Yep.

—Really? Fuck. What happened?

—Fuck knows. Mid-life crisis or something, must be: guy sees Time's Winged Chariot coming up in the mirror, guy starts thinking, guy decides he wants to have more than just 'He was loaded' carved on his headstone. Look at Bill Gates.

—Wow. So, who you got slated to direct?

—Totally kosher art-house guy from Wales. Won shedloads of awards. Loves actors. This is going to be big, Mikey. Big for Britain, anyway. And classy.

—OK, now you fucking listen, Paul. This has to be an offer, OK? I'm not using up my influence over my client just so he has to go stand in a queue. *If* I talk to him, *if* he says yes, the part's *his*, yeah?

—Mikey, whose else would it be? This has *Marcus Dale* written all over it.

—And we can't defer any of the wages.

—LA was *that* tough, huh?

—You want me to put the fucking phone down, Paul?

—Hey, hey, Mikey: who said anything about deferrals? Ten grand a week.

—Twenty.

—Fifteen, and we tell the world twenty, and Marcus's guaranteed his face at least 75 per cent bigger on the posters than anyone else's. Clock's ticking, Mikey. Lot of pretty new boys in town.

—Deal. I'll talk to Marcus. Leave him to me. Oh, yeah, shit, and what about the script? You got a script I can show him? You know the *talent*, Paul, they're all the same, they always want to look at the fucking *script*.

—Yeah. Mikey, no offence to your pay days, but the day we can fire all the fucking actors on earth and do it all in computer-generated images will be the day I buy champagne for everyone in town.

—Keep wishing, fuckface.

—OK, tell you what, Mikey, let me get the writer to tweak it a bit specially for Marcus, yeah? What kind of stuff is Marcus into, scriptwise?

—Oh, just the usual shit.

—Method-acting ego-trip stuff, yeah?

—Yeah. Get your scribbler to put in crap like 'he does blahblahblah *like the superb athlete he is*', yeah? Marcus really likes that stuff.

—Sure, sure, I know, I know the schtick: 'As he blows away the bad guys *we see that he is clearly a man of deep thought and sensitivity*', yeah?

—Paul, you're a pro.

—It takes one to know one, Mikey. I'll sort it myself. Oh, and listen: you know that Welsh grandmother of Marcus's?

—Marcus has got a Welsh grandmother?

—He has now. Her name was Granny Soft Money, Mikey.

—Oh. Oh yeah. Now I think about it, I knew her well.

—I thought you did. Memo coming through, Mikey. Hey: surf's up!

—See, Lucinda, with Marcus on board we absolutely *need* a Female Lead who can, you know, *absorb* Marcus's full power, which is *some* power, and throw it back *right in his face*. This one has to fucking *crackle*, Lucinda. And Marega needs to get off the telly and on to the big screen. This is her big one. Marega is the only game in town for me: I'm not calling anyone else.

—Paul, darling, I'll get her right away. When can we see the script?

—Real soon. Tell you what, just thinking about Marega in the Female Lead gives me an idea for a couple of tweaks. Let me get the writer to customise it. This is how we're going to treat her, Lucinda: like the big-screen star she will be. Tell her from me, this is what takes her over the watershed. After this, Marega will not have to be nice to *anyone*.

—Cool!

—*Bore da*, good morning, Cymru-Wales Film Fund.

—Am I speaking with Owayne Hughes-Evans?

Salmon's plump finger marked the paragraph headed 'Wales' in the *Euro-Art-House-Funding Nexus Handbook*. His phone nestled between his multiple chins and in his other hand he grasped the *Guidelines For Funding Applications* issued by the Cymru-Wales Film Board. He had ringed one particular paragraph in red ink:

> The Cymru-Wales Film Fund, following recent experiences common across the UK Lottery Funded Sector (i.e. the non-distribution and hence failure to achieve meaningful box-office penetration of any films ever financed by any of the UK Lottery Boards) intends henceforth to target support at Film Projects which, while maintaining a distinctively Welsh character and improving the Quality of Life of the

people of Wales, with proper regard for issues of the Welsh Language, Race, Gender and Disability, nevertheless have a realistic likelihood of gaining at least a limited public cinematic distribution. Projects meeting this criterion should be submitted in the first instance to OWAIN HUGHES-EVANS, Distribution Supervisor.

—*Owine*, actually, said Owain Hughes-Evans, smugly.

—See! *Owine*, of course it is, that's how little I understand about Wales, how little *anyone* in bloody London understands about Wales, and yet here I am, Owine, about to meet Alan bloody Barony with this *fabulous Welsh script* in my hand.

—A Welsh script?

—Owine, I'm really sorry to disturb you, I know you're busy, I just need your advice. My name's Paul Salmon, by the way.

—Alan Barony? The Distributor? Well, well. A *Welsh* script you say?

—Welsh, and yet *European* too. It's incredible, Owine, I just got it, the Writer's some girl nobody ever heard of from Pontypool, and suddenly, wham! she comes out with this.

—A girl from Ponty, eh? And it has a specifically Welsh angle, does it?

—*Specifically* Welsh? Owine, it *is* Welsh. Would I be calling you if it wasn't?

—Oho, wait a sec, you must be the boy Aled at the Beeb was talking about. Said he had some press release or something.

—Yes, that's us, Owine. The Writer and I, we've started our own company, her and me, here in Wales, you know, wing and a prayer, but hell, this material is so good, what else could I do? I mean, London is fine, London is rolling in money, Alan Barony will back us all the way, Marcus Dale is lined up, because of his Welsh granny I think, partly –

—Marcus Dale has a Welsh grandmother?

—You didn't know?

—No.

—He loved her deeply. And Marega Angelina's screaming at me for the Female Lead, so London money I can get by the cartload, but it's *a question of principle*, you see. This is a *Welsh* film. This material *needs* a Welsh director. I was thinking about Richard Jenkins. I've admired his work for so long.

—Rich? Good boy, Rich. Knew his dad's brother-in-law. Well, of course, if we can help in any way. Alan Barony, you say? Marcus Dale? Marega Angelina?

—We'd love to come down and meet you.

—Well, yes, of course.

—This week?

—Well, I don't see why not. Of course, we'd have to see the script before we agree to anything.

—Good God, Owine, of course. But our girl in Ponty, she's very sensitive, very shy, a real artist, I had to practically drag the script out of her hands, she wants to meet Rich Jenkins first. You could have a Treatment by the end of the week. We could meet Friday.

—Hmmm. Tell you what, I'll call Rich and see if he's about. And I could have a word with Dai Jones-Hughes at S4C, meantime.

—Could you? That would be wonderful. If we could *possibly* meet later in the afternoon, I've got lunch with Paramount that day, and . . .

—Eugenie, listen, I know it's kind of bad form, I hate going behind someone's back, and Marega Angelina is a lovely girl, I wouldn't know how to tell her she wasn't getting the part, not after *what she's done* to get it, but your Roberta is the girl we really want for this.

—Paul, you're *lying*. You're not telling me that Marega actually –

—Hey, Eugenie, what's the difference between an actress and a whore? Whores don't kiss.

—Paul, this is absolutely *outrageous*. I'm going to hang up *right now*.

—Whoa! I'm kidding, you know me, Eugenie, would I break the rules?

—I should bloody well hope not. So Marega *didn't*?

—No, no, no, of course not. Hey, look, if a producer asks a girl to *be nice*, and she plays along, she gets the part, fair and square, yeah?

—Absolutely.

—We all know that. Shit, if I let Marega be nice to get the part and then blew her away, where would we all be?

—Quite. Really, Paul, you've made me go all *cold* just thinking about it. A whole international edifice of *trust* destroyed in one afternoon. No girl would ever be nice to a producer ever again.

—I know. They'd take out a contract on me in LA.

—I'd take one out myself. Anyway, so that's OK then, so long as Marega *didn't*.

—You going to call Roberta then?

—OK, but you better bloody *promise* me that if Roberta says yes, Marega gets handed the Humane Killer.

—Eugenie, what kind of idiot would prefer Marega to Roberta?

—That wasn't a promise, Paul.

—Hey, you know as well as me: in this business, if you have to *promise*, it isn't going to happen. All that counts is the maths: Roberta is hotter than Marega, the rest is bullshit.

—And Roberta does *not* have to *be nice* any more, OK? At least, not in Britain.

—Shit, no, Eugenie. Roberta's crossed the watershed, this side of the river.

—Good. And we'll want fifteen a week.

—You know Alan. I could maybe go eight.

—We'll talk numbers tomorrow. Leave Roberta to me. Shit, I forgot; she'll want to see the bloody *script*, of course.

—End of the week do you?

—Fine. Oh, and is Fatty posh-able this afternoon, do you think? That always helps, with Roberta. Come to think of it, I could do with one myself.

—No, I think he's in Brighton until tonight.

—Oh, bugger.

—I can sub you a line if you need one.

—Oh, Paul, *could* you? A friend in need.

—Meet you down in the sushi bar in two minutes.

—On my way. My hero.

—It's just what we want, Marcus, and *you're* the one *they* want.

—Alan Barony's financing?

—Alan Barony *and* the Welsh Film Fund. Hey, I know, Barony's not *strictly* art house, but he's hands-off, Marcus, and he gets the stuff out there. It's a European classic, Marcus, with an Art-House Director. Very actor-centred. This could be your *Jean de Florette*. Barony's talking two hundred screens, and if MaxiPix take it up stateside, bingo, all is forgiven and forgotten and we're as hot as we were two years ago. Salmon's offering ten K a week. Lot more than the Equity basic

147

rate, which is all you'll get in the theatre. And who goes to the theatre?

—The broadsheet reviewers?

—What, and they *don't* go to see *Jean de Florette*?

—Ten?

—I think, *I think*, I can get you more. Leave it to me.

—I'd have to see the script, of course.

—Good God, Marcus, of course. It's your *career* we're talking about. *See* the script? Hell, we'll take the script apart. They want you that bad you can *rewrite* the script.

—Oh, I don't know, I feel an actor should *trust* the script. Trust it with his *life*. Which one is, really, in a way. The script is all we have as we go over the top, into the drumfire of the limelight. Of course, *he* also needs to be trusted, in his turn. In a sense, he is *always right*.

—He?

—The actor.

—Hey, Marcus, shit, what can I say? You are not just an actor. I tell them every time: you think this guy is just a goddam *Arab pedigree racehorse with a golden voice* or something? This guy is a fucking *philosopher*.

—An actor should be something of a racehorse, too, of course.

—Marcus, of course, *exactly*, that's just what I'm saying. Oh, yeah, look, and I wanted to talk to you about your grandmother . . .

Dai Jones-Hughes, Aled Morris-Thomas and Hugh Pritchard processed along the new concrete paving slabs beside the River Taff, hard beside the Millennium Stadium that stands, unreal, like some vast space-craft moored for a brief goodwill visit to earth, amid the resplendent consumptional facilities of Europe's Youngest Capital. Having feasted on Szechuan lobsters, they now proceeded, mildly drunk and in their own good company, to the HTV Wales box at the Cardiff ground for the match with Swansea.

—It's bloody perfect, Dai.

—I dunno, Aled.

—Look, for quarter of a million our side plus the Serbians plus the Euro-Match-Funding from Owain, we get this bastard English git to finance Rich's first feature. *We* get the first TV screening in Wales *and* a premiere in Cardiff and a cut of the world rights. Couldn't do it for twice that ourselves.

—Hmm. But what's this Ponty girl's film *about*?

—Well, we dunno, yet, do we?

—To be honest, boys, I was hoping to use this Serbian money to do something about Patagonia.

—Well, yes, *Patagonia*, his companions intoned respectfully.

—See, I was thinking we could shoot Serbia as Patagonia.

—Rich Jenkins buy that, will he?

—Good as gold, Rich is.

—Tony: lose the black-and-white sequences.

—*Lose* them? But, Alan – . . .

—Trust me, Tony. I want this movie to win. I'm paying for it. I'm going to put up sixty-four-sheet posters for it. Posters the size of houses. You're going to be in all the papers. And we need to make money.

—Yes, but, Alan, without the black-and-white sequences, we lose all of the, well, of the *Art*, Alan.

Alan Barony looked at his Director with distaste. He could scarcely believe that he had Green-Lighted £1.85 million for this idiot last year, largely on the basis that his accountant had liked the underlying novel. He pressed a button on his desk and spoke to his intercom.

—Is Paul Salmon out there already, Sheina? Hello, Sheina?

—Oh yes. (*Sniff!*) —Sorry, Alan, just had a bit of a sneeze. Yes, he's out here now.

—Send him in, will you?

—Will do.

—Alan, please, I really think we *need* those sequences, it's absolutely –

—Tony, you know Paul Salmon. Paul, come in, come in.

—Alan, hey, the man! Hiya, Tony, you good?

—Fine.

—Paul, I want you to explain to Tony about Art.

—You making *Art*, Tony?

—Tony's got these black-and-white sequences, Paul.

—Don't tell me, Tony: children with satchels, leaves blowing in the wind, right?

—Well, yes, actually, but everyone loves them, and –

—Shall I tell him, Alan?

—Tell him, Paul.

—Tony, tell me something I've never really understood: why exactly does everyone who ever went to film school think they have to show the whole world that they once saw a few fucking French movies that were shot sometime last millennium and never made a penny at the box office even though they were only up against two terrestrial channels on TV sets with screens as big as a sheet of crap-house paper? Huh? That's *clever*? Or maybe they once went to see some Euro-funded fucking lecture about a bunch of spoilt rich kids from Denmark who think they *invented* jumpy camerawork, crap lighting and self-indulgent actors? That's *clever*? No. I'll tell you what *clever* is, Tony. *Clever* is getting the stuff *you* want to say *seen*. By *people*. By *lots* of people.

—He's right, Tony.

—Alan, please, I *need* those black-and-white sequences.

—Listen to Paul, Tony, he's been to L.A.

—Tony, listen to me. What the hell is so good about making a movie no one except your mummy wants to see? Any six-year-old with a video camera can make a movie no one except his mummy wants to see. You want your movies to be *seen*?

—Yes, of course, but –

—This is the real world, Tony. You want to live in the real world? Or you want to crawl for the rest of your life to some bunch of queers and women that never made a movie in their lives but can give you a few poxy ten grand if you say all the nice, right stuff in your application and get ready to lick ass? Who do you trust, Tony? A bunch of grant-funding Euro-queers, or a guy like Alan? A guy that makes movies and gets them out there. Hal Scharnhorst's right-hand man this side of the pond. A guy who lives by his wits on the seat of his pants?

—Sorry, Paul?

—I mix my metaphors, Alan, but hey, Tony: *Black and White*? That is the *one* thing that could stop Singapore Cable Channel 17 buying this movie. From what I hear down the grapevine, you got just enough fucks and bangs to sell to Singapore, but those people, when they see Black and White they don't think *Art*, they think: *cheap old shit*. They want Kodacolor for their bucks.

—Agfacolor, Paul.

—Agfa, of course, Alan. Hey, Agfa is just as good, really. Good enough for Singapore Cable, anyway. Tony, look. I want to talk about the future. Your future. Let's think about it. Come with me. OK, so here's a hotshot Art-House guy, the kind of young gun film-head that sets himself up as some kind of guru of Deep Thought and all that crap. Clever guy. Knows a lot. Hey, you know what: he's so clever he *actually saw a few old French films once*. Whew! OK, so now let's fast-forward and take a look at this guy when he hits fifty-five.

Scenario One: he stayed up his own arse, he made no money, he's drunk and fat and still hitched to the schoolteacher or actress who liked his little short films when he was twenty-five and married him before he was used-to-be-kinda-famous-in-the-Art-House because who else but a schoolteacher or an actress would be stupid enough to pay the rent for some idiot that says he *wants to be an Art-House film-maker*? And every year he fills in his nice, right-on applications to get his few poxy grand from the queers and beards and Euro-commies. Great life.

Scenario Two: same guy, same fifty-five, but *this* time he got wise when he was your age, *our* age, Tony, and *toned down* his Art-House tendencies, Tony, that's all Alan's asking, this guy *toned it down*, got wise, cut the B&W shit, made some money and now, Lo and Behold! he's one of these guys that no one is allowed to say bad stuff about *ever*, even if their shtick bores everyone stupid. He even gets to put in his swirling leaves and his schoolkids with satchels nowadays. Hey, here he comes, fifty-five and looking good and, Wow! who's that walking along with him? A fifty-five-year-old ex-actress or still-schoolteacher? Nope. Correct: it's a *twenty-five-year-old actress and model*. Yes, the guru of Deep Thought has found his regulation-issue arm-candy at long last and he's a happy man and he's telling everyone what a fabulous and true love it is. Your Art will shine through, Tony, believe me. You don't have to worry about the Art, you worry about making money. You worry about the future.

152

—Now, come on, Tony, lose that black-and-white stuff and we have a movie. Sheina, I think Tony's ready to go now, take him to the cutting room, will you?

—This way, Tony, darling.

—Um, OK, Alan, I'll, um, yeah, right, bye, Paul . . .

—Bye, Tony.

—Paul. That was very good. You sounded so . . . American.

—All true, Alan.

—I know, I know. But even so, Paul, don't you ever think, not *ever*, that it would be nice to make, just once –

—Of course, Alan. I want what you want. I want the Holy Grail: *reverse crossover*.

—My God, yes. Reverse crossover.

—Clean up at the box office *and* ooze quality.

—*Class*.

—Much better, Alan. *Class*. Yes. Alan, look, I, this is so weird, I, hell, I don't believe this myself.

—Well? I'm a bit rushed, Paul, so . . .

—Right. Alan, I got this fabulous new script, Marcus Dale is hot to do it and –

—Budget?

—Got to be three million, Alan. It's historical.

—Sorry, Paul: two point five or nothing.

—Alan, history *costs*.

—Better go somewhere else then, Paul.

—Alan, wait. I've got 750 K of Soft Money lined up and ready to roll.

—You have?

—Would I be talking three million if I didn't? Your exposure is two point five mil tops. You can't lose and you know it.

—Where's the Soft Money from?

—The Welsh Lottery, BBC Wales, S4C, Europe. Idiots.

—What, is it a *Welsh* film?

—Good God, no. But *they* think it is.

—Well done. Genre?

—Knee breeches and big dresses.

—Mmm.

—History is still hot, Alan. And this is a European classic, *out of copyright*.

—A European classic? You mean . . . not British?

—Absolutely kosher. Alan, this has got everything to win at the box office. Marcus Dale in the lead, Roberta Flood or Marega Angelina CGI'd as three identical triplets, who cares which? They're both hot with the sixteen- to twenty-four-year-old boys and either of them'll get her kecks off like a good girl for the plug in *FHM*. And you know you can trust me on the pyrotechnics. But we *could* win prizes too. It'd look good in Cannes, Alan. It's got . . . yeah, *class*.

—Cannes? Could we do it by then?

—I got the Script, I got the Stars, I got the Director, I got the Soft Money.

—What director?

—Some Welshman with a dozen Cymru-Wales Oscwrs.

—I don't like the sound of that, Paul.

—You don't have to, Alan. Taffy Art House brings the Soft Money in and flatters the fucking talent. Once the cheques are cashed and the cast are signed up, we engineer some dispute or other and take Mr Leekface round the back of the shop where we keep the big meat-grinder. Then we hire some good old-fashioned do-what-the-fuck-we-tell-you director who has major alimony to pay and a big gap on his year planner.

—Yes, I see.

—There's a button on your desk, Alan, and it says 'Green Light'. You press it, I run out into the street and

I start hiring. We can be turning over in a month. Get you a rough cut by Cannes, no bother. With Class. And with the tax breaks, you know you can't lose.

—How much have you promised Marcus Dale?

—*Promised* him? How could I *promise* him anything before I talk to you, Alan?

—Paul, how much have you promised him?

—Well, he wants twenty-five a week.

—Twenty-five? That's out of the question.

—So I told him. I'm sure I can beat him down to, say, eighteen.

—Identical triplets?

—In white stockings. Great, isn't it?

Barony paused. He looked at Salmon with suspicion. He was quite sure he had never mentioned white stockings to Salmon while out drinking with him for the simple reason that he knew he would never have mentioned it to anyone unless he had been drinking with them, and he never drank with anyone, let alone Salmon.

—White stockings? What do you mean? So what?

—Everyone likes girls in white stockings, Alan. Even poofs.

—Oh. You think so?

—I know so. You show me a man who doesn't like girls in white stockings, I'll show you a man who can't afford a girl who looks good in white stockings.

—Really? Right. Oh, well then. Hmm. Ha! OK, send me the script. You have *got* a script, Paul?

—Would I be sitting here without a script?

—Paul, I sometimes wonder. How much have you promised *him*?

—Who?

—Your writer.

155

—Oh, the writer. Oh, *she* gets twelve K for the rights and the script.

—Cheap. Well done.

—Plus I've assigned her 50 per cent of net profit.

—What net profit? You think I'm stupid? You think I'm going to fund and distribute a movie and leave any *net* for anyone? Am I a charity?

—Alan, Alan, Alan, I know all that. May I take a piece of paper? And a pen? Thank you. Let's see. I know that when you press that button, Alan Barony goes to the UK board of MaxiPix holdings, which is Alan Barony, and MaxiPix (UK) OKs a two point five million loan to Alan Barony Distribution at, what, 17.5 per cent?

—Seventeen point five per cent? You're joking. Times are hard. Wars and rumours of wars. Cash is King. Trust no one. I demand 20 per cent even from myself.

—Right. Then Alan Barony Distribution lends Alan Barony Films Ltd the same two point five million which is now three million at 25 per cent, and then you, I mean Alan Barony Films Ltd lends the three million which is now three point six million to us, Cut & Shut Films, to shoot the movie, at 25 per cent.

—Twenty-two point five per cent. I like you, Paul. You deliver.

—Alan, what can I say? Meanwhile, you personally, Alan Barony, Executive Producer of the movie, obviously have to go to Cannes and shit, exclusively on *Las Madonnas* business of course, you have to buy out your time with MaxiPix, who obviously have you over a barrel, so they can work a sixty/forty box-office split with Alan Barony Holdings, who work on sixty/forty of what's left after MaxiPix's sixty/forty before it goes to Alan Barony Films Ltd, who naturally have to foot the huge bill for Prints & Advertising through Alan Barony Film Labs and Alan Barony Marketing, and then Alan Barony Distribution will have to have its cut, obviously, and, well, I'd say that if we come in for three million budget and take worldwide box of, say nine million, the movie should end up owing you and Hal Scharnhorst about four million.

—Paul, I always knew you were good. So you'll be putting *your* fee in as a line in the budget, right? Payable on First Day of Principal Photography?

—Of course.

—In other words we shaft the writer.

—Hey, it's her first movie. Everyone gets shafted their first movie. Come to think of it, the writer gets shafted *every* movie. Even *I* got shafted, my first movie. By you, Alan.

—Good God, Paul, I do believe you feel *guilty* about her.

—Guilty? No way. She's some bluestocking, some lady professor, she gets forty K or whatever a year for talking bollocks to a few rich kids for a few hours a week for a few weeks a year. Then she goes off to Mummy and Daddy's place in Tuscany for her five-month summer holiday. You call that getting shafted? If that's getting shafted, you can part my ass right here.

—Guilty, I knew it.

—It's a hard world.

—So: how much are you putting yourself down for, Paul?

—My days of being shafted are over, Alan. I just passed the being-shafted baton on.

—One hundred K.

—Jackie Mornington paid me a hundred K on *Base Metal*, Alan.

—Oh, did he?

—Yes.

—Oh, well.

—I need 150 K this time.

—A hundred and twenty K and you can hire your car and your office to the production. Better for my tax.

—Throughout pre- and post-production?

—OK.

—What about my secretary's wages?

—I didn't know you had a secretary, Paul.

—I haven't. But I still got to pay her.

—All right. But you only get sixty K on First Day of Principal Photography. The rest is on completion.

—Done.

—And if the Soft Money or Marcus Dale back out, so do I.

—Marcus isn't going anywhere, Alan. I know how much he owes his dealer. If Marcus backs out of this, he reverses right off the cliff.

—So where's the script? We do *need* a script, Paul.

—The script is there. But let me kick the writer up the arse, give it a final polish. That was so true, what you said about Art, Alan, I just want to have a final look at it in that light, yeah? Make sure the Art *doesn't show*. Just the *Class*. End of the week?

—All right. You sure you won't have a sandwich?

—Hey, Alan, why not? Fennel, great.

Early evening, and in his father's house in Cardiff, little Bryn Feverfew-Williams lay dreaming. In his dream, he found himself in a large bathroom, with his favourite toy monkey. It was time to change the monkey's nappy. Bryn realised he himself needed to go to the toilet, and put the monkey down on the floor. He pulled down his trousers all by himself. But when he sat down on the toilet seat, he looked up and saw that his monkey was growing. Growing and growing.

Now it was taller than a grown-up and looking down at him, grinning.

—No, said the monkey, in Welsh, —*I'm* going to change *your* nappy!

Bryn woke up yelping for his mummy. His daddy came. It was nearly as good.

Night in Cardiff. Jane, oblivious to the mighty workings of Soho and the troubles of her son, oblivious indeed to everything, lay snoring gently in her little bedroom in her little house, with the covers pulled up almost over her head.

In the dark house, downstairs in her little study, her desk was now ordered with unwonted and mathematical precision for the new life of Work & Triumph that was to start tomorrow. She had set it up with a slightly manic and very drunken burst of energy when she had got in (Dicky and the boys had gone on to a place called Club Z; they had been loud in their invitations to come with them, and this time Jane had looked briefly into the doorway; but the clientele all looked rather like council park gardeners in string vests and leather trousers, and the place smelled of disinfectant, so she had decided to go home alone, once again). On the right of her desk, the in-tray for the Business Language Option, with its dedicated out-tray nestling, snug and as yet empty, beneath it. To the left, her work for the Second Year Option Course on *Las Madonnas del Cenicero* occupied an identical pair of trays. Before her chair, her laptop stood booted up and ready for her commands; beyond it, on the wall, where her eyes would come to rest if they ever deviated treacherously from their Work, was a large banner she had made that very night, red paint on a white sheet, which read (in Spanish, for she had taken the quotation from Miguel de Unamuno):

We have arrived at the irreconcilable conflict
    between Thought
and Life: ¡Let us, then, mythologise!

Upstairs, her laundry lay around in straggling heaps.
She had not logged on to resistyoof.co.uk today.
In Bryn's bedroom the luminous mobile of the solar
system revolved, unnoticed, in the incalculable currents
of air that swirled gently above the empty little bed.

PART THREE

Green Light

A woman's difficulty is that she has a much wider choice of men to provide her with genes than she does of long-term partners. She could probably persuade many men of her choice to give her their genes – it only takes a few minutes of sex, after all. Her options for a long-term partner, though, are much more limited.

Robin Baker, Sperm Wars

Replace All

Like all men who take any share of the care of their children, Dafydd, Jane's ex-to-be, had a notable blind spot when it came to maths. This was all the more remarkable since he was also the kind of man (that is, the male kind) who was liable to indulge in completely pointless maths at any given opportunity, such as working out how many mpg his car did, as if *knowing it* made any difference; it seemed that he had (like most men) an almost religious belief in the power of lists and facts, and derived some kind of strange pleasure, or inner peace, from them.

Except when it came to childcare.

When it came to childcare, Dafydd's maths inexplicably deserted him. He was absolutely sure that one night a week and every other weekend was *practically* a fifty/fifty split; he was thus genuinely convinced that Jane's new plan, where he would actually have his son for two weekday nights instead of one, meant that he was now to all intents and purposes a single parent.

So when the phone rang in Jane's office on Tuesday morning, she answered it crisply, or at least as crisply as her hangover would allow, assuming vaguely that it would be Dafydd trying to wriggle out of picking Bryn up, or possibly Professor Evan Evans harassing her vengefully: either of them were fitting candidates for her New Crispness. But it was neither: it was Paul Salmon.

*   *   *

—Um, wow, said Jane, not very crisply at all, when Salmon had outlined to her the state of his various and complex negotiations.

—So, I'll be up your end of the world *this* Friday, meeting's arranged with the Welsh Film Fund, I'll need a full draft script by then. Make sure you describe the hero's heroicness and the heroine's beauty in great detail, will you? And for God's sake keep the white stockings in, write them in wherever you can.

—By the end of *this* week? said Jane, very uncrisply: rather faintly, indeed.

—You cool with that? Jane, I had to promise it on the spot, you are only ever hot for fifteen minutes. This is ours.

—Just a, a . . . *draft*, right?

—I'm relying on you, Jane. Better than that: *you're* relying on you. Don't think of it as a *week*, or *days*, think of how many *hours* of work you can fit in. You can do it.

—But I've got teaching, I've –

—*Teaching?*

—Yes, I know, but –

—Jane. You heard of the Big Break? This is yours. It's what people cut their right arm off for. Our Company, Jane. Take the week off sick.

—Sick? The whole week? But I can't.

—Better: take two weeks off sick, I need you to meet possible cast and OK the director. You know how many writers get to audition the cast and OK the director, Jane?

—No.

—None.

—Oh.

—There's geeks pay for film school for three years and then flip burgers for another ten years while they wait for this, Jane. And where are they now? Still smelling of old fat and burnt onions, is where.

—Two whole weeks?

—Jane, what did the trade union guys get transported to Australia *for*? So you could take a fortnight off sick if you really need it without getting the boot. You'll even get paid, won't you? And you really need it.

—Do I?

—Jane, I love your stuff, I'm with you all the way, but it's a hard world out there, and no one gets more than one shot. Well, not unless they're related to Scorsese. Most people never even *get* the shot. Everyone wants to see the script. Town is buzzing. But the clock is always ticking. Windows close. It happens.

—Oh my God, what can I do?

—I'll tell you what you do. This week, you don't sleep, you work; next week, you come to London, meet and greet and party; after that, you can go back to teaching and sleeping. Life's a long game, Jane.

—I suppose I could lie to my doctor, I –

—Who's lying? Just tell him you're stressed to fuck and you need this. You pay tax, don't you? You pay national insurance? You pay the penny, so take the bun.

—Paul, look, it's not that easy. I've got a young child. I can't just drop him like for a whole week. And I certainly can't leave him for a whole week and then come to parties in London. Even though it would be nice . . .

— . . . So leave the kid with hubby.

—I'm divorced. Well, nearly.

—You got friends? You got family?

—Well, yes, of course. I mean, no, not really. Not here. Look, I can't. He's only five, we've only just moved here, he's still not settled in, it would be –

165

—Whoa, Jane Jane Jane. Don't hide behind your kid.

—What?

—OK, so tell me: what do you remember from when you were five? Well? You remember individual *weeks*? Jane, we have to be real here. If it's your turn to be hit by the 767 tomorrow, what would he remember about you in twenty years' time? Hel-lo? This isn't bad shit, Jane, it's just *real* shit. If he doesn't see you for two weeks age five, you know how much that is going to matter? Not. Not a bit. What is going to matter is *who he sees every day until he's eighteen*. Who's he going to see, Jane? Sixth birthday, seventh birthday, eighth birthday . . . teenager? Every day. Is he going to see a boring fucking teacher who once had a shot but didn't have the guts to take it, so she still takes orders from some little asshole with a beard? Will he see you as the woman who devoted her sad non-life to him and now kind of would prefer his girlfriends *not* to meet? Huh? Or? Or is your son, age sixteen, going to see his cool fucking mum, Writer, Producer, Maker of Deals, the one they all want to shake the hand of, the one whose phone never stops? And when he takes the call by the poolside, he doesn't hear some whingeing idiot in a tweed jacket moaning on about fucking timetables and exams, he hears LA saying: Oh, hi, can we speak with Jane Feverfew *please*?

—Look . . . said Jane weakly.

—You *do* this, you have a slightly pissed-off boss and a kid who's going to cry maybe a couple of hours. You *miss* this, you get to regret it at 3 a.m. every night for the next fifty years or however many days you got, whichever happens to be the longer.

—All right, said Jane.

—I'll send you the books by courier.

—What books?

—The bibles.

—Bibles?

—You know, Syd Field, Robert McKee, all that shit.

—What are they?

—The books that tell you how to write a screenplay. Just do what the boys tell you, you can't go wrong. It's not rocket science and it's not even Art. I'll send a few notes of my own, too. Just follow the Yellow Brick Road, Jane, and you are a made lady. Oh, and one other thing.

—What? said Jane, very faintly indeed.

—The story has to be Welsh.

—Welsh?

—It gets made as Welsh or it doesn't get made, Jane. You choose.

—But it's nothing to do with Wales.

—A good story is universal, Jane.

—Yes, but Paul, *this* story is set in eighteenth-century South America.

—Yeah, yeah, yeah, I know. Shit, huh? We got to think of something.

—But it's impossible.

—Hey, Jane: the Concept is *my* job. Meanwhile, I assume you got a 'Replace All' function on your word processing package?

—Yes, but –

—So press the button and change the hero's name from *Juan* into *Rhys*. At least then it'll *look* Welsh for the time being.

—But, well, I mean, I wish we could have *discussed* this first, Paul, I just mean –

—Nothing to discuss, Jane. The Hard Money follows the Soft Money and this time around the Soft Money says it's got to be something to do with Wales.

—Paul, I can't do this.

—This is serious, lady, it *has* to be Welsh. Money talks, even Soft Welsh Money. I didn't make the rules. If South America has to go, it's *hasta la vista* South fucking America. Look, let me think, let's say our hero's Welsh, he got his heart broken, no, his girl was killed by evil English landlords, that's good, evil English landlords play really good in Hollywood. And Wales, I bet. OK, so he flees the redcoats and ends up in Mexico, and –

—Stop! Stop. Paul.

—Jane, we can't stop. We're in too deep.

—No, no, I mean: wait. Oh my God.

—Oh your God what?

—I think I've got it.

—You have?

—Paul: look, have you ever heard of a place called Patagonia?

When Salmon had hung up in order to speedily fax a one-page Patagonian scenario to Owain Hughes-Evans, Jane sat down on her chair and blinked several times. Half-consciously, she logged on to resistyoof.co.uk. She did not know why she was doing so, but suddenly it seemed the only place she wanted to be. Speedily, she posted a message on the noticeboard. It was a very short message, and one which she knew was utterly at odds with the entire ethos of resistyoof.co.uk. But she did not care. Her message merely said:

DJFEVA:— R U there?

To her surprise (surprise mixed with a strange and not entirely comfortable feeling of Fate), she found a message popping up straight back at her. It said:

KewCPERCIVAL:— Do you mean me?

DJFEVA:— Yes, actually.

MCWARRIOR:— Hi, everybody.

KewCPERCIVAL:— Who are you?

MCWARRIOR:— Hey, just another old fart. It means Middle-Class Warrior, you see?

DJFEVA:— Could you go away please?

MCWARRIOR:— What? This is a public chat room.

KewCPERCIVAL:— I agree, go away.

MCWARRIOR:— This is contrary to all established principles of resistyoof.co.uk. ·

KewCPERCIVAL:— Oh bugger off.

DJFEVA:— Seconded.

KewCPERCIVAL:— Right. Hello again properly.

DJFEVA:— I just wanted to talk about maybe meeting up in the West End. Like you said. A gang of us, obviously. It's just that I think I might be there anyway quite a lot next week.

KewCPERCIVAL:— Right. Look, let me give you my own e-mail will you?

DJFEVA:— But then everyone else will get it too.

There was a tiny pause before his reply came through:

KewCPERCIVAL:— So? Who's going to pester a forty-year-old divorced barrister with a five-year-old son?

Jane stared at the screen, letting this information seep quietly in. Thank God video links had not been perfected yet. Thank God that even in a supposedly real-time chat, e-mail gives you time to breathe.

And thank God even more that keypads are not like those electric pianos that can feel and transmit how hard, or how tenderly, you hit the keys. Happily disguised by the neutrality of the typed word, she wrote back:

> Well, I don't think anyone much would pester a thirty-five-year-old divorced lecturer with a five-year-old son either.

There was a slight but undeniably significant delay, long enough at any rate for Jane to wonder what KewCPercival was thinking of her cunningly revealed information, before his reply came through.

> Right john.a.percival@hotmail.com
> Thanks. My name's Jane, by the way.
> That's nice.
> Actually, sort of a female version of John, historically speaking.
> Really?

Jane had a sudden feeling that things were getting out of hand, so she lied.

> Bugger, kid crying, got to rush.
> Write?
> I will.
> Bye then.
> Why don't you two just go ahead and grope each other on-site? I'm going to report you two for breach of resistyoof.co.uk etiquette.
> Oh get stuffed you silly old sod.
> Bye for now, Jx.

Jane logged swiftly off, discomfited, taken aback by her own careless x. She blinked again, several times. She considered the information given out and the information received.

So he was divorced after all.

With a son Bryn's age.

To her horror, she found herself trying to imagine what his child looked like. She should *not* have put that x in . . .

Her phone rang.

—Miz Feva, what you doing with an engaged phone line?

—I was just, um, on the Net. Looking something up.

—Fuck the Net, girl, you are a genius. They *love* the Patagonian angle. Well? You happy?

—Yes, yes, of course.

—So get working. We got a movie to make. All I need from you is one hundred pages of Patagonian sex and violence. We can rewrite afterwards. Just give me that, Jane, and you know that villa in Tuscany you always wanted? You can have it. And don't forget the white stockings. Waves are building, Jane: let's get to work.

—Boys, I think we're on to something here. A *Patagonian* script, they got, apparently.

—Aye, Owain said. I never knew Marcus Dale had a Welsh nan.

—Nor me. Still.

—If we can bring bloody Tongans over here to play for us, I don't see why Marcus Dale shouldn't have a Welsh nan if he wants one.

—Fair's fair. Ours now, he is. We just bought a new Welshman, boys.

—Good.

—Funny. They think *they're* getting our money for nothing. But it's *them* that have to toe the line.

—Serve them bastard right. I mean, when *we* used to win every year, did *we* ever say we were too good for the Five Nations?

—Six now, Dai.

—Aye, changing world, it is. Fair play to it.

—Fair play to the world, boys.

—There we are.

Strange: a lot of people find it very hard to say that *they* need to do something, but very easy to say that their *work* needs them to do it, as if Work were somehow more important than Life. They find it easier to say *I must, for my work* than *I need to, for my life*. For example, if someone wants to leave their wife or husband, they will often handily get a job at the other end of the country, somewhere they know their wife or husband would hate, because so long as the Job demands it, it is OK and then it all becomes the other person's fault. It is also notable that people accept physical collapse much more easily than mental decrepitude as reason for not doing something: if you tell your boss that you really really really need to take two weeks off because you have a Chance and if you do not take it, you will never forgive yourself, he will show you to the door and hand you your cards; but wave a doctor's note for the flu, and all will be well. Finally, every amicably warring parent knows that if you can cunningly present your demands as being all for the good of Little Muggins, you will have your ex on the back foot right away.

These were the very tactics that Jane used on Professor Evans and Dafydd.

First, she went and told her doctor that she could not sleep and was drinking too much, so he gave her a sick note for two weeks off work. Evans was unimpressed, but even he was powerless in the face of officially vouchsafed medical necessity. Second, Jane told Dafydd that she had A Job which demanded her absolute dedication for a week here in Cardiff and her absence for another few days in London. Over the next two weeks, she would thus only be able to see Bryn for about as long as the average Executive Father sees his child, i.e. not very much at all.

—But, Janey, you can't.

—I've got to, Daf. It's *work*.

—Oh. University work?

—Film work.

—What?

—I'm making a film.

—What film?

—A film the Welsh Film Fund is going to support.

—A Welsh film?

—It's about Patagonia, actually.

—Bloody hell.

—Which I don't suppose will do Bryn's future here any harm, will it? Sorry? Daf, I thought that was why we moved here in the first place? To give Bryn a home and all that? Hello?

—Well yes, but –

—So this should keep him well in with the whatsits, the *Gogs*, shouldn't it? Help him find a good job here, in Wales, shouldn't it?

—Two weeks? What am I supposed to do?

—Visit Auntie Blodwen a lot. I hear she makes good chips.

Jane put down the phone and stared out of the window at the hills beyond: fifty different shades of green. And then she sat down and she did what she had always done best, or rather, the thing she had always done when she had nothing else to get up for (*but then*, she told herself, *maybe that is the only clue to what we were actually put on earth do to?*): Jane worked.

All week, she worked.

Chain-smoking again after years of Being Good, and with *Make It Obvious* her watchword, she hammered out her screenplay in the style of her Option proposal. Her first new scene concerned a chapter in the book which began thus: '*The three sisters spent many long nights, each in her own room, disturbed by the memory of that encounter.*' Now, how would she make the possible secret implications of that scene clear to a brainless student? She pondered. At last, and with a curious smile, she began to type:

INT. THREE ADJOINING BEDROOMS IN THE CASTLE. NIGHT.
Rrrrrustle! Each of the sisters tosses and turns in her crisply sheeted four-poster. Outside, moonlight plays spookily on the artichoke fields. Each in her own room, as if impossibly sharing a dream, they unconsciously throw off the sheets and . . .

. . . and Jane worked on. The tendons in her wrist ached; her back complained; her lungs burned. But whenever she grew close to giving up, she would look out of her window and remind herself where she was: Wales. She would think of escape: London. If she failed: this hopeless, grey reality. If she succeeded: that unknowably bright future.

It was enough, every time. Then she would lean back, in her chair, make herself dizzy with thoughts of infinite possibilities, and let her new mantra form itself on her lips as she lit up yet again, curling round the thick, creamy smoke, dark with a kind of insightful laughter.

—So much for the cheerleaders.

And then she would go back to work, eyes red with exhaustion, but lit with an inner fire which was half a lifetime old.

Goats and Agas

Paul Salmon, having made it to London in his twenties, rarely left Town unless it was to go abroad or for weekends at someone's cottage in Cornwall. And so, on the Friday, as he trundled on the delayed 10.00 from Paddington, past Swindon and on into what passes for countryside in England, he was anxious to ensure his lines of supply.

—OK, Pete, give me the guy's number.

—You won't be disappointed, Paul. I'll tell him you're coming. Hell, I'm just starting up in Cardiff, wouldn't mess things up by letting one of my best mates down, would I? It'll be as good as you get in W1, guaranteed.

—I trust you, Pete.

—Things going good?

—Great. This writer-girl has worked her tits off to get her break, of course.

—How do you find them, Paul?

—Pete, how do you find your best customers? Instinct.

—I suppose.

—No, but she's good. Most scribblers got nothing but work-rate and ambition, but this one, she's got a brain too. I'm going to let her run this meeting.

—Hey, Paul, introduce me when you bring her up.

—Let me get the straw out of her hair and the cowshit off her boots first.

—You're the man, Paul. I'll set it up for you in Cardiff.

—Cheers, Pete.

*　　*　　*

The pallid late-afternoon sun warmed the dome of the Millennium Stadium, where Wales had lost 49–6 to Eastern Tonga the day before. In crumpled newspaper wraps, chips stewed in last night's grease and headlines, inviting seagulls. At the station, Jane, exhausted but elated, waited to meet Paul Salmon. She had described herself (ironically, she thought) as looking like a Lady Doctor. He had described himself as tall and blond.

She spotted him immediately as he strode through the ticket barrier. She had two full seconds with which to take him in before he was upon her, air-kissing her cheek. He was tall, indeed. Rather more bald than she had expected, and with a chin or two more than strictly necessary in a man, but his skin looked a wonderful, healthy pink, and she had not seen such fine blond hair (what there was left of it, anyway) since moving to Wales. As his cheek brushed hers (it was the first time she had air-kissed since leaving London, and she almost got it wrong), the scent of jasmine washed pleasingly about them. Salmon looked at her with open admiration.

—We meet at last, Miz Fever. Hey, wow, you look great. (*See? Heh heh. Look, you meet some drop-dead actress, the last thing you do is say how great she looks, idiot. She gets that a thousand times a day. No: you tell her she's clever, stupid. Spin it around: does this Dr Jane Feverfew want to hear she's clever? Nope. Why? She knows she's clever. She's been clever all her life. And she knows that Clever is no good for girls. For a man, maybe: a guy can be fat and bald – if he is clever and witty, he might still get lucky with the good-looking girls; but a fat girl with shit hair doesn't get the good-looking guys, however clever and witty she is. The good-looking girls get them too. Tough world.*)
—Hey, they don't let you loose on eighteen-year-old

177

guys, do they? They must think they've died and gone to heaven when *you* tell them off, said he, smiling and nodding with open, easy, metropolitan sophistication.

—Yeah, like, really, said Jane, turning a mild pink.

—Well, they got our Selling Document, I just checked. Good work, Jane.

—I don't understand: why didn't we send them the whole script? I nearly bloody killed myself to do it by this morning –

—That's why we call them *dead*lines, Jane –

—Ha bloody ha. And then you go and tell me *not* to send it yet. Why?

—Jane, it's a delicate business. We need to see *who* the scripts are going to before we lock it off. Leave that to me. *This* meeting is your gig, Jane. I'm taking a back seat on this one. You ready for war?

—I think so.

—Don't *think so*. Think *yes*.

—OK. Yes.

—Right. Remind us, you're officially from Pontypool, right?

—I was born there, then my father died in the mines, my mother remarried a Scotsman so we moved away to Scotland when I was a baby. But now I have come back to my roots. To live near my Great-Uncle Gwyn, who has never moved.

—Great-Uncle Gwyn is great, where did you think him up?

—I didn't. He's real. He's just not mine.

—You're good. Well, shall we go get our nuke?

—I feel sort of, you know, a bit *bad* about this bit, Paul.

—It's a hard world, Jane.

Shit, not bad, actually. Bit shy. Take her anywhere. And

178

take her anywhere, probably, heh heh, these intellectuals are always the wildest, underneath. Bum a bit big. But nice tits. Kid. So? She'd be so fu-uucking grateful: take her on, kid and all. What do uni lecturers earn? Got to be forty K. Not great. But: forty K rain or shine. That's the difference. Rain or shine. Credibility. Gratefulness. Never ask why I'm away, because I'm nice to her kid. Maybe have a kid ourselves. Why not? Place in the country. Plenty of trips to town, for me! Business calls, must be off, sweetheart, see you Friday, bye, kids. Great. Long holidays, lecturers get: cover the summer hols with the kids no bother. Adoration. And posh. Listen to her. Definitely. Mummy and Daddy pop their clogs one fine day, nice big tip, little studio flat somewhere in W1 to go with the place in the country. Why not? Give it a bash, anyway. Looks like a little girl, sometimes: excited as hell. Shy. Why not? Give Sheina a rocket up the arse, anyway: always like you more if you're shagging someone else. Funny, really: they sort of lose all sense of their own good looks, you could be shagging a real dog and all they can see is another woman. A rival. But this is no dog. No. She's got a bit of class. Alan's going to like her. Take her anywhere. Why not? Bring her to the Groucho, give her a line or two and watch her go. Quite pretty, really. Goats and Agas . . .

At the Arts Council of Wales (Lottery Film Fund), the light slanted through the vertical window blinds and came to rest upon the Draft Application for Funding for *Las Madonnas Del Cenicero*, which lay upon the large, expensive desk of Owain Hughes-Evans. Hughes-Evans, Dai Jones-Hughes and Aled Morris-Thomas broke off their conversation (they were discussing the new Floating Opera House in Cardiff Bay) to greet their favoured son as he entered the room

179

boldly, easily at home in this office after ten years of entirely successful meetings conducted here.

—Rich, mun, come in come in, first to arrive, you are.

—Owain, all right? Dai, Aled. How's your Mari?

—Oh, duw, fine. How's your Mali?

—Producing *Pobl y* bastard *Cwm* for her sins.

—Pays the rent. So, Rich, what you reckon?

—Well, I dunno, boys, I mean, what's the point, eh? We build the best bloody stadium in the world just so that everyone else can kick us all round it.

—No, no, Rich: the film, I mean. Serbia?

—Oh. Oh, right, yeah.

—Patagonia shot in Serbia. What you reckon, Richy-boy?

—Well, fuck boys, what is Patagonia but a non-existent place of the mind? A phantasm of our own *need* for it to exist, for *Wales* to exist somewhere but in bastard Wales? What is Patagonia? A place no one has ever been to except those who went determined to see what they knew they wanted to find; a dreamland for a dreamless nation; a barren patch on most people's maps, but a vast land of milk and honey and hope for we on this small side of Severn, a simple –

—Eh, good on you, Rich, so: Serbia do you then? Shoot something there, could you?

—Aye, why not?

—Rich, you do *want* to do a Feature Film, do you?

—Well, bloody hell, I dunno, boys, I got this two-hand play to finish for the Eisteddfod, see, about this bloke that kills lambs.

—It's a great chance *for Wales*, Rich.

—Put us out there in the big world, boy.

—But do we need the big world, Dai?

—Rich, mun, we can't live on the Eisteddfod for ever.

—I know boys, but –

—Look, have a read, Rich.

—Oh, got a script, have we?

—No, but they say it's all there. We got this just in, Richyboy. Here it is. See what you think.

Rich Jenkins took Jane's single-page Selling Document from Owain Hughes-Jones with unwilling interest. He strode with thudding boots to the window, and read cautiously, as if watching out for traps. Then he blinked. He looked up with a mixture of suspicion and hope.

—You read this, boys?

—No, Rich: just in, it is.

—Something wrong, Rich?

—You OK, Rich?

—Boys, I dunno. Listen to this. *'High in the Patagonian pampas, surrounded by great fields of artichokes,'* fuck, I can see it now, we're low down, sun in the lens, dust on the pampas, a Welsh chapel sitting in white-hot South American sun, like a lost traveller, surrounded by endless artichokes, Rhys comes riding up and –

—Oh, here's our Lady Writer now. And our London boy. Shhh now, Rich, boy, don't seem *too* bloody keen. Welcome to Wales, Mr Salmon; and welcome to Cardiff, Jane, girl: How's Ponty these days, love?

—Hello, said Salmon. He was good at doing shy and self-effacing when he had to. He could blush falsely on demand, and did so now.

—All right? sang Jane Feverfew (Dr), Princess of Darkness, Writer, Associate Producer, Director of Cut & Shut Films Ltd and manipulator of men, in a slight yet distinct impersonation of a Pontypool accent (she had been practising all day). She strode boldly yet shyly forward. Her trousers were especially tight today, her hair newly blonded-up and her lips a particularly devastating shade of red. But her real trump card, her weapon of mass destruction, walked on small feet by her side, holding two of her fingers in his little, nervous hand. (A last flash of guilt swept across Jane's consciousness, but she said to herself: *He'll never know. And if that's their game, it's their fault. It's his future. He's why I'm here anyway.*)

—Oh, and who's this little man?

—This is Bryn, I'm *so* sorry, but it was the only time I could make, see, we've come straight from school haven't we, Brynnie bach? And we're going to see Great-Uncle Gwyn later, isn't it?

—Yes, Mam.

—Yes. Straight from Ysgol Mynydd Ynys-y-bwl, said Jane, quietly, easily, practicisedly, perfectly, distinctly, Pontypoolishly and quite as if by-the-by. With grim pleasure, she saw her linguistic/cultural cruise missile fly slow and true to its multiple targets:

—Oho! said Rich Jenkins.

—Oho! said Owain Hughes-Evans.

—Oho! said Dai Jones-Hughes and Aled Morris-Thomas.

For the next five minutes Jane listened to Bryn chattering proudly away in Welsh to them all. As she listened, or rather, as she watched and heard the rise and fall of familiar yet unknown sounds, she nodded indulgently, and occasionally raised her shoulders to one of the men by way of helpless, light-hearted apology for her sweet little son's chattering, thereby incidentally giving the impression that she had at least a vague idea of what was going on. At last:

—Duw duw, said she, and scooped him, glowing with pride, into her arms.

—*Welshwelshwelshwelshwelsh, Mam*, she heard her little son say, his eyes bright as they gazed earnestly into her own eyes, and:

—Ah, yeah, she nodded, wisely, lyingly, and:

—Well, well, said Owain Hughes-Evans and, turning to Salmon at last:

—Alan Barony on then, is he?

Salmon looked Hughes-Evans straight in the eye. There is a time to lie and a time to be bold, so he said:

—He's on if you lot are. Simple. You have to fire first.

—What you reckon, boys?

—There we are then. Rich?

—Have to see the script first, won't I?

—Well, of *course*, Rich.

—It'll be in the post Monday. Let me call Alan Barony. You'll have his memo back in five.

—Well, pints, then, is it boys?

—Let me call Dafydd. My husband. Childcare.

—Mam, does the fat pinky man speak Welsh too?

—No, *cariad*.

—He looks like Captain Underpants, doesn't he, Mam?

—Come here and give me a kiss. A big, big kiss.

Jane and Salmon went to a lot of bars in Cardiff with Rich Jenkins and Owain Hughes-Evans and Aled Morris-Thomas and Dai Jones-Hughes. As the drink flowed, the men about her slowly grew more and more aware of the physical fact that she was a woman, and Jane found herself becoming somewhat the centre of their competing attention. It was not unpleasant. They pulled out the stops and treated her to a blow-by-blow account of the rugby Grand Slam decider between

Wales and France on Saturday 18 March 1978. Jenkins could remember it almost as well as the older men, though he, being the same age as Jane, had been only twelve at the time.

For some reason, this reminded Jane of something she had quite forgotten: that when she was a little girl in Edinburgh, her father had taken her to watch rugby matches. She began explaining her memories of sitting on her father's shoulders and being called *Wee Janey* by smiling, red-faced men. Before the males about her had time to be too bored by this unexpectedly personal angle, she mentioned, without thinking about it, that on one of these occasions, her father and his friends had tried to explain to her that she had just watched one of the greatest things she would ever see.

—Some man in a red jumper sort of skidded through the mud right in front of us and it was a really important score. At least, I think it must have been, she said, hurriedly reaching for her wine glass, for she realised that she had already well exceeded the allotted time for any female to say anything. But when she looked up, she found the men about her not wearing masks of polite indulgence but gazing at her with the deepest interest.

—What year?
—Must have been '73.
—No, '71, boys.
—How old you say you were, Janey?
—Murrayfield?
—Must have been Gareth.
—You seen Gareth Edwards score a try!
—You remember it!
—Boys, more wine. Bubbly.

Eventually the older men went off to eat Chinese food at Barry John's restaurant and Salmon nipped off to visit a friend of a London friend and did not come back, so Jane and Rich Jenkins kept on drinking together and by the end of the evening it seemed to Jane that she now knew everyone in Cardiff.

She made quite sure everyone knew about her alleged babyhood and exaggerated Scottishness. It seemed to help. Sometime in the evening they stopped to eat in a small restaurant which seemed entirely full of Welsh-speaking people. Jane had that curious feeling that sometimes comes on holiday when you forsake the beach with its happily international folk, head inland, and suddenly realise that you are in a place where your own, known world is a very long way off, and utterly meaningless. Foreign again. And yet, tonight, it seemed somehow different: exciting, exotic, a window on to an unknown life, the sort of foreign that makes you want to get to know it.

As the wine warmed her face, Jane noted with utterly inappropriate pleasure that Rich Jenkins was devouring large portions of white bread and butter, not to mention wine and cigarettes, without a care in the world. They grew familiar. At one point, she asked him why he was so excited about the artichoke angle.

—Don't you know the story about Burton?

—No.

—Well, there he is, right, just made his name, London in about 1947, rationing, dark suits, pies and mash. And Burton gets invited to some posh house with some posh girl, and he's doing fine, everyone wants to meet this handsome Welsh boyo from nowhere, posh totty lined up wall-to-wall, posh London queers licking their lips, chateau wine passing about, and Burton in seventh heaven, right?

—Right, said Jane hastily, after a short pause in which she realised she had stopped listening to his story, and was just watching it while staring into his eyes, if you can watch a story.

—Right, and so then what d'you reckon happens?

—Um, what?

—They go and serve bastard artichokes. Whole artichokes in little silver bowls, with posh dips. Dips! Artichokes! Burton's never even heard of bastard artichokes. He's seen a photo of a pineapple on a can once or twice, but that's the closest. He scans the table, desperate for some sign of what to do with the fucking thing, but these are posh twats, they would rather die than start before their guest of honour. Burton stonewalls, but at last the hostess, Lady Poshpants or whatever, says: *Mr Burton, do tuck in.* And he has to start eating the bastard thing.

—What happened?

—No one knows. He never said. To the end of his days he could never speak about it. You wouldn't understand, maybe. I reckon *you* know how to eat an artichoke, right?

—No, actually, said Jane. —I've never had one, at a table, like that, I mean.

—Oh. I thought you were posh.

—I'm not. Really I'm not.

—Oh.

There was a curious silence. Jane thought the unthinkable. Then a girl dressed like a hooker on holiday came up and started chatting jealously to Jenkins in Welsh; as she spoke, his phone rang and he said, into it:

—Babe, all right? Aye, fucking great, *welshwelshwelshwelsh* not too bad *welshwelshwelsh*, well, no hardly, babe, *welshwelshwelshwelshwelsh* rightyo, half an hour, see you, babe.

And then he had to go home to his girlfriend. Of course he did. He had a life. And like everyone who has

186

a life, he naturally assumed that Jane did as well, so he thought nothing of leaving her there. Jane, defending this healthy image of herself, said good night merrily and watched him walk rollingly away.

Then she sighed, but not in despair. True, she was half drunk again and had been left alone again. But tonight, somehow, it did not seem so bad. She had been drinking with a quite attractive and interesting and clearly heterosexual man, at least. She had been definitely fancied, if only in passing and if only by middle-aged men and if only because of the wine. She had made some connection, however feeble, with some people. She had linked her life briefly with other lives. Not much, but something.

As she was walking home, she passed a video shop and saw in the window, amid the best-sellers, a tape called *Great Welsh Seventies Rugby Victories Over England*. Insanely, she wished the shop was open, so she could buy it. She continued homewards, wondering at her own lunacy. But through the tramp of her feet and the wine in her head, she heard a voice, a male Scottish voice from some lost, misty time of her past: *It's J.J. to J.P.R., and ohhhh myyyy, the choirs will be singing till dawn in Cardiff tonight . . .*

—What? asked Jane to Jane, out loud, happily mystified.

Then, as she passed the stone beasts that clamber up the walls of Cardiff Castle, a text message came through. It said: *great play feva. C U @ groucho monday 4pm. waters lovely.*

Suddenly, her strange, interlinked thoughts of prehistoric rugby matches, her own past and a possible future in Wales after all were banished. She stopped and smiled inwardly at the message. A wave of futurity burst softly inside her ears. She looked a stone lion straight in its marble eye.

—I am back in the world, she said softly. —London, here we come.

The Undisputed Capital of Northern Europe

—Christ, Janey, I love London! The undisputed capital of Northern Europe, my God, how can anyone live in Britland and *not* want to live here? What the hell are we doing, living in Wales? At least I got the excuse that I was born there, but you, lovely? You once lived *here* and now you can even *consider* living in *Wales*?

Jane and Dicky Emrys were sitting on the train, approaching London. Jane found herself washed over by the strange, expectant melancholy of homecoming. She watched the concrete walls of Westbourne Park trundle by, their graffiti completely unchanged since her student years, which she had spent going up and down the Metropolitan Line from grotty shared flats in Shepherd's Bush to the spacious but friendless corridors of University College.

—Oh, I didn't live *in London*, said Jane, explaining to herself as much as to Dicky, —I mean, I *did*. But I didn't.

—Very clear, lovely.

—I was a student here. I had a grant and I only survived on it by sneaking cheap lunches at the hospital. The only good my hips have ever done me. I never *did* anything that people come to London to do. Before me and Daf got married, I had a horrible bedsit in Shepherd's Bush and a few quiet friends. After we got married, I was pregnant and then we had Bryn and we had no money and never, ever went out into town. I don't think I've ever been inside a black cab in my life.

—You and most of the people who live in London, lovely. Well, at least you're coming back in triumph. Promise me three things?

—What?

—One: take a taxi and *don't look at the meter*. Promise?

—All right, all right.

—Two: call me at eight. I'll be in the Admiral Duncan, talking in a high voice about my mam and doing Dylan Thomas impersonations. It never fails, in London.

—I'll call at eight. Promise.

—And last but not least: for God's sake *gloat* a bit, Janeylove. I know the Romans used to put that bloke in the chariot with Caesar when he had a Triumph, so he could whisper 'Remember, Caesar, you too are human', well, if it'd been me, I'd have said: Look, just *fuck off*, will you, buttyboy, it's *my* bastard triumph. Honest, Janey, I never saw someone take so little pleasure in success.

—I'm knackered, Dicky. I haven't slept all week. And I'm worried about Bryn. I hardly saw him last week, and –

—Um, Janey: you had him all weekend, as I recall. Correct me if I heard wrong earlier, but I thought you said you took him to the park, you played football with him, you baked cakes with him, you cuddled him and read to him and made Sunday lunch for five adults and eight children and they all played for hours and –

—Well, yes, but –

—Look: either go home *right now* or stop it.

—OK, laughed Jane.

—And *start gloating*.

Some five minutes of gloating later, Jane Feverfew, Film Writer and Director of Cut & Shut Films Ltd, strode tall from off the train, kissed her Gay Friend goodbye in a thoroughly London manner and, with a distinct thrill of wickedness, headed steadfastly for the taxi rank, ignoring a lifetime's training:

—And I am *not* going to keep looking at the meter, said she, firmly.

Waiting for the cab, she found herself amid a swelling orchestra of men talking into mobiles, cab-rank attendants shouting directions and taxi drivers screaming abuse at building workers in vans. Perhaps she was still only half awake, she thought, or perhaps it was the recession? Something had changed in the atmosphere.

Jane listened, looked, sniffed even, to try to find out what exactly seemed to have altered in London during the four months since she had last been here. Why did it feel so strange?

Smell: fumes, of course; the whiff of burnt diesel at the back of her nostrils; surprising how clear after being away for a while: had she really brought little Bryn up in *this* for nearly four years?

See: greyer faces than she had remembered; that old familiar, but now somehow forgotten, hurrying step and fixed stare.

Listen: a strange sort of background noise; it seemed to undercut everything everyone was saying or shouting; a hum of London which she had never noticed before.

It was the listening that made Jane think the most. What on earth was this weird underground hum? It felt wrong; it felt unpleasant. It seemed at once to radiate aggression, a complete satisfaction with its own stupidity, and a lurking well of self-pity.

A football commentator?

An England match?

England.

With a jolt, Jane realised exactly what she was hearing, and why: she had not been out of Wales for four months; in that time she had been unable to get *proper* Channel 4; she had spoken only rarely and briefly on the phone to her London friends. And now she was shocked to find herself besieged all around by the thin-lipped, nasal, grinning whinge of Estuarine English.

—Muswell End, said Jane, to the cab driver, slightly shaken, feeling inexplicably foreign, and instinctively camouflaging her otherness by falling back into that snapping, metallic whine herself.

—Oh for Gawd's sake, sighed he, but allowed Jane to get in.

Jane sat back happily. More than happily. In her very own cab, black and fat as a gondola, she felt like a female Nero, wildly throwing money to the wind. It was OK, it was fine: all against tax, Paul had said. Quite right. She needed to readjust. She was no longer merely a struggling provincial lecturer. This was her new world: she was going to have some *fun* at last. She was rather looking forward to meeting him. In the Groucho Club! She felt famous just thinking about it.

Her jeans felt good and tight today.

—Just here will do fine, please, I'll, er, I've got to go to the chemist, said Jane at Muswell Broadway, some three-quarters of an hour later, quite unable, tax or not, to face the moment when the meter reached £40 (she had been watching it with nervous disbelief ever since £30). She nevertheless rounded the fare up from £38.60 to £40, at which deadly insult the driver paused in disbelief, stopped writing out the receipt and stuck it half finished through the window as he pulled away.

Jane thought she caught the words —Tight Welsh cow, but since the driver could not *really* have thought she was Welsh, she decided she must be imagining it. She then proceeded, past the splendid ranks of ludicrously expensive children's clothes shops and ridiculous delicatessens, to her friends' house.

Her friends were the sort of people who had moved here because the area was full of People Like Us. They call them PLUs, as if it were just a joke, and not actually the reason they had moved here. These People Like Them did the kind of jobs which, thirty years ago, would certainly have allowed them to live within Zones 1 and 2 of the tube: now they were eloquent about how easy the travel really was from halfway to Zone 4. The way these PLUs knew each other was mainly because when they said 'the paper' they all meant a certain daily which had been founded to champion the rights of northern trade unionists in the nineteenth century and which nowadays consisted largely of reviews of restaurants that said things like:

> *Style*: Not quite the right word. *Service*: Nazi Minimalist. *Fellow Eaters*: Mobile Phonies, My Little Ponies. *Genre*: Grand Bay Fusion Lost The Plot. *Quality*: Come back, Waitrose Cook-Chill, all is forgiven. *Price*: £75 per head with grotty Chilean Merlot. *High Point*: Cool Murals. *Low Point*: Cold Plates. *Value*: 9/10. *Verdict*: Sorry, got to be done.

The remainder of *The Paper* was given up to articles about the moral difficulties of being rich but liberal and middle-aged but still young at heart, pictures of designers or architects, and a TV guide which spent two-thirds of its available space giving readers a scene-by-scene account of exactly what was going to happen in today's episodes of three or four US comedy-drama series. The main reason Jane's friends and the PLUs lived in London generally was that they had no choice because all their jobs were in London; and the main reason they had all come to live in Muswell End particularly was to save their children from the horrible fate of sometimes having to play with black people's children; but since they could never admit these things, or even think them, they had invented all sorts of strange and wonderful reasons to explain why London in general and Muswell End in particular were fabulous places to live.

Jane embraced her friends warmly and spoke briefly of how fantastic it was to be back in London at last and how she missed it and how she was *really* not worried about Bryn not being able to read Harry Potter at five (—He actually has to *speak Welsh*? My God, that's *ridiculous*, said her friend, who in earlier years had spent much time on Troops Out marches). They agreed that it was rather galling to have paid £500,000 for a terraced twenties house in a Good Catchment Area, only to find that the critical mass of rich but liberal PLUs had sneakily decided that there really was *no alternative*, after all, even here, to private education, so that the formerly Good State School was simply *no longer really good enough* for their child. Jane agreed that nothing in the third millennium could please her more than the thought of going out to a new Australian restaurant in Crouch Hill later on. Her friend was gratifyingly jealous of her new Writing and Producing career. They began to plan Jane's new flat in Muswell End. They spoke of the legendary Single Man of Muswell End, whom her friend actually knew quite well and could invite round any time.

Jane found, however, that the Single Man of Muswell

End no longer seemed so interesting. She also discovered that she did not want to hang around and see her friend's child and hear him read the Bible. (Her friends had made a sudden and very public rediscovery of their Cultural Roots in the C of E in order to ensure little Marmaduke's place at the formerly Good State School, and were still keeping this up religiously, just in case they could not get him into one of the many £10,000-a-year private schools in Muswell End.) So she unilaterally put her appointment at the Groucho (*ah, the thrill of just saying the name!*) forward by two hours and hurried upstairs to make her bed, drop off her overnight bag and shower. She then used her friends' computer to send a hotmail to Percival, telling him that she was In Town Tonight On Film Business (giving, she thought, the clear impression that it was no great shakes for her to be In Town Tonight On Film Business) and boldly giving him her mobile number casually (*ag! the nerves*) in case he just happened to fancy dinner tonight or lunch tomorrow.

She had naturally planned to take a taxi back to town, but for some reason, just e-mailing Percival made her incapable of looking another £40 fare in the face, so she said goodbye to her friends and went down to the tube station at East Finchley (which was where her friends actually lived) to get the Northern Line down to Soho.

She had forgotten about the tube.

It was not that the tube was insanely crowded, dangerously airless and disgustingly filthy: all these details simply fitted back into place as part of nature. What she had forgotten about was the horror of sitting (or rather, standing most of the way) in touching-and-smelling range of a dozen other higher primates, astronomically complicated machines designed for the sole purpose of communicating one to another, but whose prime, or only, concern today seemed to be to avoid any possible look, movement or sound that might conceivably be mistaken for an attempt to communicate.

Jane closed her eyes, and tried once more to gloat: after all, she was back in *London* . . .

Highlights

In the little office of Pogo Pictures in W1, Paul Salmon rubbed his nose and checked that he had put the seven copies of *Las Madonnas del Cenicero* (as edited and polished by himself) into the right envelopes. He did not want to have a mix-up in so vital a Producing matter.

First, he checked the three envelopes addressed to the Welsh Film Fund, BBC Wales and S4C. These three copies of the screenplay were identical: Salmon had made a special front page for them, on which the name of Rich Jenkins and Jane's Cardiff address featured prominently; he had gone through them with his trusty yellow highlighter, marking all the places where the Patagonian-ness of the script was to be noted. Satisfied, he sealed them and franked them.

Next, he re-examined the envelope which would be opened by Marcus Dale's agent. This time, he had highlighted every speech assigned to, every action undertaken by, and every mention made of Marcus Dale's character, in the certain knowledge that Marcus Dale, being an actor, would not read a single other word in the screenplay.

Marega Angelina's agent was to receive a parallel version, just as richly marked, with especially broad highlighting on those places in the directions which made it abundantly clear that Ms Angelina only had to undress several times for the very best artistic reasons and was still Acting at these points, *not* just being photographed in triplicate without her clothes on.

Baz Andrews's version, on the contrary, contained as few highlights as possible, in order to stress the extremely minimal effort Andrews would have to make in order to earn his £8,000 per week for six weeks as Lead Support.

The next one up was Alan Barony's script, in which Salmon had highlighted every instance of sex, violence or otherwise unBritish behaviour; they added up hearteningly; to this version, he attached a budget proving conclusively that the film could be made for under £3,000,000, especially if they paid the crew, the art department and the writer only when the film was officially into profit, i.e. never.

Finally, he made sure that he still had on his desk the version he would show to Jane Feverfew today: this script was exactly as Jane had e-mailed it to Salmon the previous Friday, and Salmon's highlighting took the form, in this case, merely of large question marks in the margin at every point where he had, in fact, already deleted or changed Jane's lines in all the other versions. Well, you had to make writers *feel* they were part of the process.

Satisfied, Salmon surveyed his desk and chopped himself a well-deserved line.

He was good.

The Big World

—Save the world, madam? said a voice in Jane's ear, and she awoke from her tube reverie to find that she had arrived in Old Compton Street, and was having a Greenpeace brochure flapped in her face by a youngish man with more piercings than would have been thought facially possible or medically advisable a mere ten years ago, and wilder eyes than most civilisations in history would have thought safe to allow out on the streets.

But, shamed by her own recent and superior musings on the sad lack of communication between humans in London, she stopped, smiled brightly, and said she would take a brochure with her to fill in at home.

—The Saviours are coming. Check out the website soon, lady, muttered the man, mysteriously.

—All right, said Jane brightly, and hurried on.

Skanky returned to his wanderings. Outside the vast burgermeister fast-food restaurant, a lorry was disgorging endless gallons of cooking oil into some unseen, subterranean chamber. Skanky observed it. The sight unnerved him, for some reason. He had not had a hit of cider or drugs today. He turned into one of the many little alleys which thousands pass each day but few enter, in the hope of finding out where his dealer might be. From the cellar at the back of a Chinese restaurant, he saw a large brown cockroach scuttle for shade. Further down the alley, on the steps that led down to the kitchens of Jean-Paul Le Marche's restaurant, he saw chickens lined up to defrost, each thawing down into the other. Skanky shivered. In the strange theatre of his head, he saw the endless cellars and sewers of Soho, awash with half-burnt cooking oil and congealing fat, seething with roaches and rats, measureless caverns flooded with the detritus of half-devoured animals and meaty human shit.

One day.

One day.

When Mr Salmon gave the word.

There was no lack of communicating going on in the Groucho. On the contrary, there was nothing else going on at all.

As Jane entered shyly, hastily turning off her phone in obedience to the notice in reception and wishing for the millionth time in her life that she was five foot seven instead of five foot ten, she could immediately feel the tendrils and tentacles of atavistic human awareness filling the club, as if she had been scanned by a gentle yet insistent electricity the moment she stepped through the door. It was a feeling she had once known before, but could not place: yes, that was it: once, she had gone to audition for a large and demanding role in the College Theatre Society. She had walked into the room, seen through unfocused eyes the massed ranks of beautiful fellow auditioners, and fled. That was the feeling: the suspicion, no, the certain knowledge, that Judgement is being made, that the secret Court is in sitting. It reminded her of walking through unseen filaments of airborne spiderwebs on an October morning: a brush of nothingness that nevertheless brings a blush to the cheek, a tingle to the stomach and a curious new alertness to the tightness of one's jeans around the crotch.

But this time, Jane had a *right* to be here: she was A Screenwriter.

—Fifty Points of Net, she murmured to herself, and strode towards the bar, tenner already in hand, throat already tasting drink, eyes already bright.

At last.

—Sorry, madam, you can't *pay for drinks* here, said the ridiculously handsome barman, smiling at Jane as if at a rather amusingly gauche visitor from some distant, provincial star. Jane's overheated confidence did an instant Hindenburg. Blushing a fiery, English red, she explained the position.

—Mmm. Yes, I see. The trouble *is*, you see, Mr Salmon meets *lots* of people here, and I'm afraid he recently left *strict* instructions that *no one* was to put drinks on his tab unless he was actually *in* the club. And you can't *pay*, you see.

—Oh, well, said Jane bravely, feeling the unseen eyes of the whole bar on her bum, —I'll just, well, pop back later then.

—Oh, hold *on* then, said the barman, with excessively youthful world-weariness. After some minutes of discussion with an equally good-looking colleague, during which Jane had ample time to wonder what on earth she was actually doing here, he conceded that one drink could be put on Mr Salmon's tab. Before asking what drink Jane wanted, he commenced to make a Sea Breeze. Jane, strongly aware of the fragility of her position, and unsure if this might be some sort of Tradition or something, dared not say that she did not much like vodka.

—You haven't been here before, have you, luv, whispered the barman, as if suddenly spurred to sympathy by Jane's unearthly hopelessness.

—No, actually.

—Down from Wales?

—Yes, but how did you . . . ?

— . . . Well, just make sure he offers you the job *before* you're *nice* to him, that's all.

—Oh, I've already got it.

—Been nice to him already, eh?

—Well, he seems very, um . . .

—Oh God, yes. Mr Salmon is very . . . So, is it a good part?

—Part? I'm sorry?

—Oh, aren't you an actress?

—No, laughed Jane, proud beyond measure.

—Oh, sorry, they're casting some new TV thing upstairs, I thought you must be up for the Motherly Doctor part.

—No, said Jane, mortified beyond imagination.

—They *say* it's a good part, said the barman, suddenly wistful. —Really *dangerous*.

But Jane had rediscovered haughtiness somewhere inside herself, and smiled condescendingly as she said: —Actually, I'm, you know: A *Writer*.

The barman was pleasingly stunned.

—A *writer*?

—Yes. I'm, you know, doing a film with Paul.

—You should have said.

—Well, you know, ha ha, I didn't want to seem –

—You're a *screenwriter*?

—Yes, actually.

—Oh, God, Mr Salmon really *won't* be pleased. Putting drinks for *screenwriters* on his tab? He'll think I've been helping *myself*. God, you could have *told* me, luv.

—Oh.

—Good trousers, said a voice beside her. —Ironic, right?

202

Jane turned and found a young man dressed in a stripy retro-seventies roll-neck sweater and the most enormous glasses she had ever seen.

—Sorry?

—Nice look. Very kitsch. Who put it together for you?

—It's not a *look*, it's *the way I am*, snapped Jane, finally tired of being ashamed of herself.

—Nice line, nodded the Young Man, admiringly. —Yours?

—Have it, snapped Jane.

—Thanks, said he, surprised, and, having looked at Jane for several long seconds, left for his table, where he joined a very short and very drunken man who had a brush of red hair and even more enormous glasses, and who was dressed in a dinner jacket and baggy shorts. The stripy-roll-neck man said something to the short-trousered man and the two pairs of oversized specs turned slowly upon Jane and her trousers. To her shock, Jane realised that she was now staring at, and was being stared back at by, no mere human being, but by Kay Gee, the pop star famous for wearing hats. She had been reading about his latest hat *only last weekend*, on the lav, in the colour sections of *The Paper*.

Swiftly, she turned her gaze away, but now she had recognised Kay Gee, there was no escape: it was as if she had suddenly learned how to see the world about her. All at once, the bar of the Groucho (Oh my God, she was *actually here*!) jumped into focus. With horror, Jane realised that she knew who almost everyone here was. There was that weathergirl, my God, talk about setting out your stall, and wasn't that the TV archaeologist, yes, and beside him that silly old style guru queen, whatsisname, and Marina whateveritwas, the Pergola Goddess they called her, and . . .

It was like a rainy Sunday morning in her kitchen come horribly to life, all these dazzling people leaping from glossy page to real life simply in order to mock her crass lack of famousness. Quickly, she drained her horrid drink and grabbed her friendly handbag. What the hell was she doing here anyway? This was nothing to do with her. She could still make the 4 p.m. Cardiff train from Paddington, if she ran: she would be home by seven, she could call Dafydd now and say she would take Bryn tonight, after all. He would gladly bring Bryn round, the bastard, and by eight she would be reading her beloved son his stories; by nine he would be asleep and she would be lying next to him on his bed, underneath the mobile of the solar system they had put up together, hearing his small, clean, soft breath, watching the planets spin lazily, feeling oblivion drifting slowly over her . . .

. . . Or else she could run to an internet café and e-mail Percival again. My God, he might be phoning her right now! Did she dare turn her phone on? Impossible. But what if he called? He might even now be within an hour of her. They might be able to have dinner before she went home, even. Maybe he would be having his kid tonight, though? So what? She could eat with him and his kid. Much better! *That* was her world. Her child was part of her. *He* was her world, the fruit of her womb, not this: not famous people with big glasses and barmen like gigolos. Why had she not given her phone number to Percival before? What was she playing at? Where would she find a taxi? She needed to get to Paddington fast, she had to get out of here, she . . .

— . . . Hey, Feverlady! Welcome to my humble club. George, two Sea Breezes, stiff.

—Coming up, Mr Salmon.

—You OK, Miz Fever?

—Um, yes, fine, but I was just –

—Great. I got a few ideas for the Script, he said, loudly, his hand resting for an instant, as if by accident, on the swell of her bum. —Marcus Dale is screaming for it. Alan Barony has his finger hovering right there over button 'a', we are almost rock and roll, Lady Jane.

Jane detected a frisson of hidden interest amid the tables they passed, the unmistakable change in the studied attitudes, the instant of doubt which said that she might after all, be Someone. Now the gazes which, just moments before, had seemed to be sucking all life from out of her, turned to warm rays of energy-giving force. Soft waves of acknowledgement flooded in about her. Suddenly, unexpectedly, Jane found herself sitting back happily in a deep chair, another Sea Breeze in hand, lighting up a cigarette and forming her words with the smoke.

—So, how's the, um, *package* looking?

—Looking good.

—Cool.

—Who's that with Paul? That big woman with the ridiculous trousers. *I've* never seen her before.

—It's his new Writer, that's all.

—A Writer? Oh God, have we *got* to join them?

—We'd better. Paul wants us to schmooze her. We're supposed to wait until he waves us over.

—But is he posh?

—He'd bloody better be, I'm gagging.

—Mmmm.

Jane stared in slight disbelief at the script on the table before her. She flicked slowly through the pages, seeing big yellow question marks on almost every scene. She felt cold with horror at the thought of how much more work it would need. She wanted to burst into tears.

—It's not a question of *losing* the original novel, Jane, just making it *cinematic*. I mean, what's the point of your script if no one sees it? Cinema is a very literal art form, that's all: if someone's billed as Good, we got to see them doing Good Stuff. If they're meant to be attractive, it's got to be someone we all want to fuck. If they're Bad, they do Bad Stuff. Got to play in downtown Delhi. So we got to lose that big scene at the dinner party, for example.

—Yes, but Paul, that's the scene where the actual problem of the story is revealed. It's the heart of the script. You said everything depends on the script. You said everyone wants to see it. You said –

—Jane, you got to understand, this is called the *Film* business, not the *Script* business, right? They all want to see *a* script, of course, we got to have *a* script, we can't make a movie without *a* script, but who ever made a movie *because of the script*? Windows, needs, chances, that's what makes movies. The script is part of it. But it's all process, Jane.

—So I just throw this away?

—No, no, no, we just need a bit more work. I mean, where did you find that scene where the three triplets are all wanking off in their separate bedrooms? Does it *say* that in the book?

—Oh God, sorry, I knew that was ridiculous, but I thought –

—You kidding? Best scene in the script. The sit-down scene, the talk-about scene, the oh-yeah-that's-the-movie-about scene.

—The what?

—Look, you remember that movie a few years back

about the two American teenagers who go on a rampage with guns and kill loads of people?

—Oh yes, you mean, um, what was it called –?

—Who cares what it was called? That's the point. You *remember* it, see? This is going to be *that movie with the three identical triplets wanking*. Get it?

—Oh. Right.

—Marega Angelina loves that scene.

—I thought you said we were getting Roberta Flood?

—Shhh! Never mention Roberta Flood again. We never even *heard* of Roberta Flood. Marega was always our first choice, OK? Always. Everyone we get was always our first choice, you understand?

—OK.

—Right. So: Marega loves that scene. Everyone loves that scene. We need more of that stuff. You are going to be *so in demand* after this, Jane, I tell you. We just got to cut a lot of the chat. The lines are just spaces for the actors to do their shtick. So, the big dinner-party scene has to go.

—Oh. Right. So, I suppose, we have to reveal the conflict at the heart of the book somehow else, you mean?

—Yeah, and something has to *happen*. I was thinking, how about the Priest fucks the Orange-Girl.

—Oh. Right. Um, you mean, OK, so, the Priest's desire to improve the human condition of the poor is, sort of, metaphorically expressed as a physical attraction for the little Orange-Girl? In short, she represents the entire oppressed poor of Mexico . . .

—Patagonia, Jane, Patagonia . . .

—Yes, sorry, Patagonia, in the eighteenth century, all their innocence, their distrust of religion and yet their deep-seated reverence for traditional forms of belief, for the Church, for priesthood, for –

207

—Right. And I know this great little actress, perfect for the part, gets her kit off and spreads them at the drop of the word Motivation. I'm joking, Jane. You're absolutely right. She's a metaphor for, whatever, for all that stuff you said. You're clever.

—Thanks a bunch.

—As well as a knockout, I mean. Hey, Sheina, c'm here and meet the new face of British Screenwriting.

—Paul, hel-lo.

—Jane: Sheina, Miranda. Great Writer, superb Development Executives.

—*Fabulous* trousers, darling. Oh, hi, Max.

—Hi, girls, said the young man with the stripy roll-neck, as he passed on his way to the Gents. —Hi, Miss No-Look.

—Hi, said Jane.

—Oh, do you *know Max*, Jane? Oh, well, then. Imagine: Sheina said you were just *a Writer*. How funny.

—Miranda, did Sheina also tell you that Jane's on *fifty points of net*?

—Fifty? Golly, what *fun*, darling.

So then they all drank lots more Sea Breezes and then went and ate sort of Thai-ish food, and then they waited about for quite a long time for someone called Fatty in the Coach and Horses, but Fatty never turned up, everyone seemed in quite a bad mood about it for a little while, and while they waited, Jane called her old friends in Muswell End and told them her meeting had gone on really late and could they leave a key by the door for her.

When she was calling them she found there was no message from Percival, but that all seemed pretty unimportant right now anyway, for all around Jane the vortex of W1 spun and whirled, gay and straight, as she bestrode in vodka-fuelled triumph the very streets she had so often trudged alone, heading for the Cheapest Chinese Food In Town to take a break from her researches at the British Museum.

Jane had always been poor. But it had never mattered until she came to London: she had never truly realised before the existence of a planet where the inhabitants casually spend on lunch what the state deems fit to support a single mother for a week. And so she had spent her London years taking buses and walking about with carrier bags and sometimes she had passed by in the rain and happened to stare in at the bright Soho windows and secret Soho clubs and beautiful Soho people, not *jealous*, exactly, no, not *even* jealous, more like some Third-World peasant glued in his hut to a TV show about LA teenagers: far too distant for jealousy, simply . . . *wistful* for a life that could never, conceivably, be hers . . .

And now it was.

Ha!

By now, they had been to a very small and hot place called the Colony Room and said hello to lots of people, but no one knew where Fatty was, whoever he was, someone pretty important, obviously, and they were drinking glasses of Chablis in the French House, surrounded by people whose faces and voices had been gently bombarded into Jane's brain, by *The Paper* and Radio 4 ever since childhood.

She could feel herself getting posher by the second and could do, *wanted* to do, nothing about it. Here she stood, with her Producer and her new friend Sheina and her new friend Miranda, and they were all laughing at Jane's stories about Bryn's Welsh school and Dafydd's Welsh relatives and Professor Evans's Welshness and so on.

—How wonderful, darling! It all sounds just *too* authentic.

—We must come to Wales one day if it's *that* awful. You'll probably win a Cymru-Wales Oscwr anyway.

—It must be pretty difficult *not* to, surely, Jane, darling?

—Ha ha ha!

—We can all come down and see them *being Welsh*.

—A *Cymru-Wales Oscwr*, how extra*ordinary*.

—This is *too* wonderful. A *Welsh school*. You should write a column. In fact, you *must*.

—Of course you must.

—It would be perfect.

—Great fucking exposure, too, Jane. Think about it.

—Can't Emma fix Jane up with a column?

—It would be wonderful.

—Hey, girls, don't steal my Writer from me just yet!

—Ha ha ha.

—Oh dear, I'm so sorry, said Jane, for she had sort of unbalanced herself on her heels while she was laughing, and had spilt a few drops from the whisky glass of an elderly woman beside her who Jane did not actually recognise, but whose carriage, clothes and daring make-up suggested clearly that she was famous.
—You must let me get you another.

—Large Bell's No Ice, said the Obviously Famous Lady with practised speed. —And he'll have a Sea Breeze, won't you, darling, she added to a tall and handsome youth of perhaps twenty to whom she had been talking.

—Mmm, said he.

—Of course, said Jane, turning away quickly to hide her annoyance. Oh well, after all, what was a drink? She must train herself to be less *petty*. —Here you are, she said merrily, when the drinks arrived. —Whisky. And a Sea Breeze for your son.

—I beg your pardon?

—Your grandson?

The Unknown But Undoubtedly Famous Lady looked at Jane with more amusement than contempt.

—My God, you silly little Welsh shop girl.

After that, Jane was very glad when they all went to Soho House. As Salmon skipped heavily up the steps in front of them with Sheina, to sign them in under someone else's name, Jane and Miranda stopped on the dog-leg of the staircase in order to leave off their coats with the beautiful Romanian girl in the little coatery.

—You know, I think we're all going to have a lot of *fun* with this project, Jane, darling.

—Yes, it might be quite a laugh, said Jane. She felt tired and depressed. She quite wanted to see her old friends in Muswell End again now. She wished Percival had called.

—Sorry? Oh yes, I see. A laugh. Well, yes, that too, of course. Darling, look here, I've been meaning to ask, I don't suppose you're *posh*, are you?

Jane stopped dead, coat in hand.

She felt a curious wave of relief. Especially after what had just happened in the French House. Serve herself right, she thought, robustly. She would just have to tell the truth: it was better, after all. What was so bloody good about being posh anyway? Rich Jenkins had not been posh. Amid the hateful braying of the English Posh, another noise she had quite forgotten, Jane could almost hear the remembered, imagined, deep tones of Rich Jenkins. Silly bitches. She had always hated herself for sounding posh and now she hated herself even more for having tried to sound even posher and now, well, now it was high time to be honest. And if these posh bloody cows didn't like her anyway, so bloody what. She would get the next train back home.

Home?

With a jolt, Jane realised something very unpleasant indeed: that she did not really have one.

She had a place where she happened to own (or rather, where the mortgage company happened to own) a house, and that place was Wales, but Wales could hardly be home, could it? After all, she had spent the last hour or so laughing at Wales, and how can somewhere be home if you think it is funny? Thinking somewhere is funny is what strangers do: they may think it is funny stupid or funny fascinating or funny noteworthy or funny captivating or any other kind of funny. But if it is *any* kind of funny it cannot be home because home is not funny or weird or interesting or stimulating, it is simply home: it simply *is*. And Jane realised that she had nowhere like that.

And never had.

Tra-laa.

—Tzank you I tek your coat?

—Oh yes, of course, sorry.

So actually, Jane had nowhere to go. She could go to Paddington and sit on a bright-lit train when she just wanted to go to sleep, and end up back alone in the place she happened to have a house. Or she could stay here and talk to people like this posh cow. She found the thought of arriving back to her so-called home, at 10 p.m., with no one there and nothing to do and being hung-over, filled her with something uncomfortably close to fear. So she decided to stay. But she also decided to put the record straight once and for all, so as she handed over her coat she replied to Miranda, her social defences already up and charged.

—No, sorry, I'm afraid I'm *not* posh.

—Oh. Oh well. Oh bugger.

—Sorry. Does it matter *that* much?

—No, no, of course not, darling, we'll have a *wonderful* evening anyway, won't we? Do say we will, darling.

—*You* are, I suppose? Posh, I mean.

—Me? 'Fraid not, darling.

—Really?

—I bloody well wish I was, though.

—Do you?

—Not half. What, don't *you*?

—Well, yes, I suppose I must do.

—No point denying it, is there, darling?

—No, not really.

Jane recovered from her amazement and felt deep shame at her pre-emptive judgement of Miranda. She warmed to her fellow sufferer with corresponding, apologetic speed; her blush was an invitation to further confidences: Miranda was obviously *just* like her, really. At last, someone she could talk to.

—Actually, said Jane, cautiously, —the thing is I just *can't help it.*

—I *know*, darling. Especially when you walk into this bloody club, eh?

—Yes, or that Groucho place, for example.

—Mmmm. Sort of *Pavlovian reaction*, I suppose. It gets me every time. As soon as I walk in that door, I can feel my whole *body* changing. Ghastly, really, isn't it?

—Yes. Actually, you know, I hate myself when I do it.

—Jane, darling, *I know.*

—I really wish I could stop it.

—I wish I'd never bloody *started*, darling.

—I can't even remember when I *did* start. When I was about thirteen, I suppose.

—Really, darling? Thirteen? Golly, Jane, that's good going. I must have been fifteen at least when I first did it.

—I suppose we'll never be able to stop now.

—Well, as long as we can *keep it in check*, darling, that's the thing.

—I suppose so. And I often think, well, a lot of other people do it as well, really.

—Absolutely *everyone*, darling. You're so right. We mustn't get all guilty about it, must we?

—I don't suppose there's much we can do about it anyway, is there?

—Exactly. What can we do? Better just get a stiff drink to see us through, eh?

—Lets.

Jane and her new friend Miranda passed up the stairs, by the receptionist's desk, and on towards the bar in warm companionship.

—It's ridiculous, isn't it? said Jane. —I mean, I just sort of *assumed* you were posh.

—Yes, said Miranda, rather bitterly, —people do just *assume*.

—I know exactly what you mean.

—Do you, Jane, darling?

—God, yes. Everyone in Wales just assumes *I'm* posh all the time.

—It's so *unfair*, isn't it?

—It certainly is.

—I mean, it's not as if it *shows*, is it?

—I suppose it's just the way we talk.

—Oh my God, do you think it's our *nasal passages*, darling? Don't say that.

—No, no, I think it's more in the throat, really, you know: *far back* and all that.

—Do you think so? The throat? You think it gets

that far back? God. I always thought you only had to worry about your nose. I suppose (Miranda's voice sank several decibels, so that it was now pitched almost at normal human volume) —I suppose we should really *try doing it the LA way*, don't you think?

—The what?

—Well, I mean to say, darling, all the actresses over there do it *that way*, don't they?

—What way?

—Oh, come on, darling, you make me feel quite scummy. You know as well as I do it works just as well *that* way. After all, the whatevertheyare, *membranes down there*, must be much tougher than the ones up your nose. Obvious, really. Or your throat, come to that. And it doesn't matter nearly so much if it all starts *falling to pieces* a bit down there, does it? Not exactly *pleasant*, I don't suppose, but it wouldn't *show*, would it? Not like *nostrils*, ugh!

—Oh.

—Oh God, darling, God, no, I'm not suggesting we go and do that *right now*. How silly you are, that was so sweet, darling. Assuming we can *get* some, that is. Not exactly sociable, is it, I mean, it may work in theory, but you can hardly imagine us having a nice pally chat in the loo while we stick our fingers up our fundaments, can you? Anyway, I've got nails on. I just meant for *home consumption*, you know. Reduce the effect on the nostrils, at least, if one did it that way just once in a while, in the privacy of one's own bathroom, don't you think? Are you all right, darling? You look quite ill. Oh, I'm so sorry, it's all my fault, isn't it, I should never have started talking about the bloody stuff until we're sorted, should I? So stupid of me. Talk about breach of etiquette. And now we'll just spend the rest of the bloody evening waiting for

215

it, won't we, and it will be all my fault. Quick, let's get another drink to take our minds off it. Oh, thank God, look, here's Fatty at last. I hate the way they *make you wait*, don't you? You *must* meet Fatty, darling, he's vile. But terribly handy. Come along. Oh, and have you got some money on you, darling? I completely forgot to go to the cocaine-voucher machine, silly of me, I'll pop out later on.

—I think I'll just go to the lav. The loo, I mean, actually. For a pee.

—Oh. Oh, right. I see. For a pee. Right. See you later then, darling. (*Hold out on me, would you? Little Welsh bitch!*)

Wannabee

In the Arts and Features section of *The Paper* in London's Docklands, the Section Editor scrolled boredly over his page. He was often bored, what with the endless designers and architects and photogenic cooks.

—Hello, said he, picking up his phone.

—Joe, it's me, said the Head of Public Relations at BBC Wales (English Language Section).

—Hello, you, how's Wales? Still devolving?

—Slowly but surely. Hey, Joe, you put the paper to bed tonight?

—Not quite. What, you got some Welsh scandal?

—More of a *story*.

—Oh. Oh well. What kind?

—Academic Plucked From Obscurity to World of Film.

—Wannabe stuff? I don't know . . .

—Look: How many boring bloody academics read your paper, Joe?

—All of them, I should think.

—And how many of them wish they were Film Writers?

—All of them?

—Exactly. This is just what your bloody readership wants.

—Mmm. I suppose so. OK, fire it through, I'll see if it's any good.

—And, Joe. I never asked this before but I need it now. If you use it, name-check me?

—What, you in trouble?

—Big.
—I'll try.
—Cheers, Joe.

At Home

Jane stood outside Soho House, watching the people and the night and the neon, waiting for Dicky Emrys (mobile phones were not allowed inside the club, it said so clearly, and although everyone else was ignoring this on the grounds that every call they had to make or take was of life-changing importance, Jane was too shy to do so in case she got thrown out). Not that she wanted to be inside anyway. As she waited, several young men came scuttling up to her by turns, asking if she was looking for A Score or for Some Trade. Jane shook her head to everything, dumbly, as if saying No to the world itself.

Percival had left a message for her, which she had just received. His voice had sounded nice. Deep, and English, and as if it was the voice of a man who knew what he wanted. He could not come into town tonight, but he could meet her for lunch tomorrow. His voice was the first she had heard all day which had said *meet for lunch* rather than *do lunch*. It already sounded Victorian to her. But good. She replied to his voicemail, trying to sound undrunk, relaxed and deep-voiced, saying that she would very much like to meet him for lunch tomorrow. She could not resist naming the Groucho as the place they were to meet.

With a flush of satisfaction, she stashed her phone and waited for Dicky Emrys. OK then, she would get Dicky into Soho House, then she would go home. OK, OK, not *home*, just to bed. To sleep. They could do what they wanted with the bloody stupid film script, they could stuff it up their arses together with their cocaine. Tomorrow she was going to meet Percival and have lunch and talk about children and then she would go back to her lovely son and . . .

— . . .Why do you wait outside the Chapel of Lost Souls? said a voice in her ear. It was the pierced man from earlier in the evening.

—Excuse me, said Jane frostily.

—I see a troubled mind, lady.

—Go away.

—What you doing here, lady? What are any of us doing here?

—I'm waiting for a man. Get lost.

—Lost? We're all lost, man. Pray for the planes to rain down, lady; pray for the revenge of Gaia on the White Tribe who have despoiled her; when oak trees grow from the ruins of Canary Wharf, then we shall know Home again. Then we shall know love. The Saviours are coming. Check out the website.

—Thank you, sweetie-pie. Now go home and get a wash, will you, said Dicky Emrys, shoving the pierced man aside with built-up arms. —You'll never get any trade like that, lovelyboy, not even the roughest. Now: how are we lovelygirl? Ready for fun and games?

—I'm not sure about this, Dicky, I think the girls I'm with are going to take cocaine.

—Oh, goodie, can we have some too?

—Dicky!

—What?

—But –

—Oh, for God's sake, Janeylove, what do you think me and the boys do when we leave you and go a-prowling? Drink Horlicks?

—What *do* you do, actually?

—Ask not, lest ye be told.

—Oh. Yes, well, OK, but I mean, Dicky, this one girl, I think she must be an *addict* or something, she was talking about putting cocaine up her bum. At least, I *think* she was. She can't have been, can she?

—Oho, advanced stuff, eh? Well, you *must* get me in then.

—But I don't want to *go* back in.

—Don't be so bloody silly, Jane. You're a Writer now. And a sort of Producer too, really. You're *allowed* to have fun now.

—Am I? asked Jane, but Dicky was already dragging her up the stairs.

At the receptionist's desk, Jane oversaw him getting in on Paul Salmon's friend's guest list, and watched him plunge, gaily and gayly, into the unknown crowd about him (—Oh duw, this is one of those places my mam always warned me about, trilled he, bright in his red Hawaiian shirt, already the happy magnet of attention among the surfeited metropolitan chatterers in their charcoal, black and grey). She was truly about to leave him to it with a sad, yes, a wistful smile, and walk off into the night, and start the long trek back to whatever she had instead of a home.

Except that just then a mane of dark hair swept stridingly by her, attached to a tall, black-clad body and framing a lean, black-eyed, cheekboned face. For a moment, a fine-veined, olive-skinned hand rested on her shoulder, gently easing her out of the way, and a breeze of citrus and sandalwood wafted across her cheek. A half-known voice purred: —Paul my man, and Jane, turning in fluttering disbelief, saw Marcus Dale embrace Paul Salmon. She stared, fascinated.

—Hey, Marcus, welcome back in the water, London needs you baby. Meet our Writer. Jane: Marcus Dale.

—Glrunrk, said Jane, hideously, wonderfully, ecstatically aware of the little social clearing which had mysteriously opened up, of its own accord, in front of her, amid the no longer purely self-regarding drinkers, in the space between herself and Marcus Dale. He stepped forward, lithe, as if into automatic limelight, and took her hand, *her hand*, with glorious condescension.

—Maestra, said he, and kissed Jane's hand, —Without *your* words, what are *we*?

—Ha ha ha, said Jane, suddenly brainless, helplessly smiling. Then Salmon whispered something into Marcus Dale's ear and Marcus Dale sort of blinked, then looked at Jane as if he had not really seen her before at all.

—Oh. You're *on points* too? Oh, well, then. Hi, Jane. Good to meet. Love the script. It's really . . . dangerous. I really want us to talk about it. Got a few ideas.

—Glruk, said Jane.

—Sea Breezes, said Salmon.

—Glug. I mean, *cool*, said Jane.

—Staying now, are we? whispered Dicky in her ear as he passed by with one of his new friends.

They were.

It is a great shame, these days, to have the wrong biorhythms. Jane's biorhythms were, whether by birth or by culture, of the period before all-night clubbing became the latest habit of the world. She had spent her undergraduate days in the last years before the invention, or at least, the popularisation among quiet undergraduates, of raves; she had stayed up all night on perhaps two or three occasions in her entire twenties.

Everyone at Soho House, however, many of whom seemed older than she herself, were all bright-eyed and bushy-tailed as the clock above the bar passed 1 a.m.

Everyone was happy and successful, all their plans were sure-fire certainties, all their futures bright. Jane, though, felt tired, even sitting beside Marcus Dale. Tired, frumpy, and provincial.

—You OK, Jane? asked Paul Salmon.

—Oh, yes, thanks, said Jane bravely.

—Fancy a quick trip to the downstairs loo?

—Sorry?

—Fancy a livener?

—What, you mean . . . ? Are you, what did Miranda say, *posh*?

—Well, said Salmon, with a broad, warm, open smile, —I thought we might celebrate tonight. Not every day your film gets practically Green-Lit. Well? Look around you, Jane. Almost everyone here's done a line or two in their time, you see anyone dying of it? Hey, I'm easy, if it's there I might do it now and again, if it's not, who cares? Take it or leave it, that's my motto, owe to nobody, depend on nothing. But it might be a laugh. Just a livener. In a way, it's our duty, you know: we can hardly leave Marcus here, can we, not tonight? Not before Marega comes along. And I'm feeling a bit tired, I must admit, ooops, sorry, excuse me, I got a bit of a cold, itchy nose, you know. So what do you reckon? You coming downstairs? Why not?

Jane looked at her drink for a second.

She had been very good for a very long time.

She had spent many endless summer evenings, in her twenties, penniless and PhD-ing, looking out of the little windows of horrible rented flats, wondering what the Exciting People were doing and where they were going in their two-tone Beetles and their camper vans. She had never Done Thailand or stood in the back of an open-topped car and waved her arms to crunching rhythms or set Trafalgar Square on fire in a riot or anything of the sort. She had been good. She had said no, no, no. She had made a child, a fine, healthy child, eight pounds five ounces at birth and everything in the right place; she had breastfed him for a whole year, then stuffed him with little pots of organic pap; she had put her entire life on hold for him; she had *gone to Wales* for the good of him.

Wales.

The very word seemed to decide her.

She had been a good girl, she had worked hard, she had delayed her gratification all her life. And what had she got out of it?

Wales.

Loneliness.

She looked once more about her, at all these people chattering away so warmly, so brightly, having so much fun, being so very, very unlonely.

London.

People.

—Cool, said she. —Why not?

They got up: Jane felt that every eye was upon her, that they all *knew*. It was not entirely disagreeable: that's me in the spotlight. At last.

Wickedness.

Immediate Gratification.

As Salmon led her to a flight of winding steps, Jane realised that the Victorians had been quite right about staircases. To the Victorians, staircases were social minefields of Tits and Bums: it was strictly forbidden for a man to go *up* a staircase behind a woman (in case he found his eyes level with her bum) or *down* one in front of her (in case he turned and found his eyes level with her tits). Thus, in order to avoid having the back of Salmon's head level with her tits, she nipped into the doorway before him and skipped girlishly towards the bowels of Soho House, her tits and bum safe from his gaze.

Down, down, down.

Behind them and above them the chatter died. Their steps rang out on the stone. Their merry words seemed forced. They passed the half-closed door which led to the infernal places of the kitchen: from within, miasmas of hot olive oil and seared fennel drifted about them. Then they were through and into cooler regions where their footsteps clumped louder still. At last, they came to the small wooden door to the small lavatory right at the bottom of the stairs. Jane went in first, and finding there was hardly room for one person, let alone two, squashed herself backwards towards the wall as Salmon followed her in through the wooden door and shut it with a practised swing of his large buttocks. This left Jane feeling rather like some shuddering virgin in a melodrama, pressing vainly away from her stalker, with nowhere to go.

—Tea for two then, said Salmon merrily. Now, his plain, simple happiness made Jane feel like an idiot. She watched as he took out a little glossy envelope and unfolded it: inside, nestling on the photographic lap of a tasteful, bony model, lay a small heap of bright, clean, white powder. Nothing scummy or low life. No spoons or papers or needles. Salmon searched in his wallet, produced a plastic card and shoved some of the powder off the paper and on to the wooden top of the little toilet-roll cupboard. The card was a Greenpeace membership card.

—*Well, well*, thought Jane. —*So much for the macho show. He's really a softie.*

Salmon, looking up at her, noticed where she was looking, and seemed to blush. He waved the Greenpeace card vaguely, as if he was himself surprised and embarrassed to see it.

—Oh, well, you know, got to do our bit, haven't we. No man is an island. Generations yet unborn. Whales and tigers, you know. Well, let's see what happens with this stuff, shall we?

What happened first was that Jane felt something quite extraordinary:

Normal.

Within three minutes of taking Salmon's cocaine (she had spent the first two minutes shitting) Jane had breasted the topmost of the winding stairs and emerged blinking into the chattery light of the Soho House bar again; she then reoccupied her place at the sociable table, sliding her bum neatly in betwixt Paul Salmon and Marcus Dale not as the tired, doubtful, distant Dr Jane Feverfew of ten minutes ago, but as the incandescent doppelgänger of Dr Jane Feverfew; Jane Feverfew squared; DJ Feva to the power of two.

Jane had become what she always felt she could have been.

So *this* was what normal people felt like, normal people who find their own lives obvious, their happiness ordinary, their contentment self-evident. She felt as though the shining tanks of liberation had entered her ruined, dusty, repressed city and she had flung off her purdah to greet them with face lifted to the sun at last. Her Sea Breeze (which, ten minutes before, had seemed cloying, dull and musty) now slid down like bubbling mountain water; her cigarette (whose predecessor had seemed a pointless, sad offence to her throat) released its smoke in a cool and perfumed cloud which seemed to flow out again, like daylight, straight between her ribs; her life (which, just now, had felt like a lost and aimless blundering through a dark, tangled, thorny forest) now appeared to her as simple progression from a confused past to a sunlit future.

So *this* was life.

This was the warm normality which she had never known.

The arrival of an Actress at their table (which, ten minutes before, would have had Jane shuffling nervously around to see if she was in the way of this impossibly tall, inhumanly slim and inconceivably blonde person) now merely resulted in New Jane joining happily in with the round of air-kissing and shoving her handbag unceremoniously to the floor to make way for her new friend.

—What a *wonderful* script, darling, said Marega Angelina (for she it was). —And Paul tells me you're *on points*? That's *so* good. Writers are treated so badly. And yet, without the Writer, what are we poor –

—No, no, the script is merely a constellation of spaces where *your* work can grow, said Jane, to her own surprise. She assumed she must have heard someone saying something like this earlier. It sounded good, she thought, blowing a thick cloud of cigarette smoke almost vertically upwards.

—It has to be a *creative partnership*, nodded Marega Angelina. Jane thought she had never met anyone so beautiful and soulful in her life. —Jane, darling, I don't suppose you're *posh*, are you?

—No, said New Jane blithely, —but Paul is.

—Oh *good*.

—Paul, darling, Marega *needs* you.

—Marega, baby, of course.

—Thanks *so much*, Jane. See you in a minute. Don't you *dare* go away.

Tra-laa.

*　　*　　*

Ms in-the-swim supernormal DJ Feva next spoke seriously and in eye-sinking depth to Marcus Dale about the Actor's Life in general and Marcus Dale's upcoming projects in particular. She replied to his profound yet charming insights with a merry and witty expostulation concerning her divorce. He appeared amused by her tales; she felt amazed by his revelations; they both, in fact, seemed amused and amazed by everything.

Jane, thoroughly amused and a little amazed, noted that she had recently developed an extraordinary capacity to listen to things she would normally have found utterly boring, and to narrate things, in her turn, which she would ordinarily have felt to be utterly pointless. Moreover, everyone around the table seemed to be in the same happy state: they chattered and listened and smiled with gleaming (ever-more gleaming) teeth: everyone was happy; all tales ended up well; each person shone with mighty futurity.

Then she noted that she was, quite suddenly, feeling rather tired and, well, sort of *grey*, and that everyone else suddenly seemed to be shouting very loudly about nothing and listening to no one else.

Jane did not like this at all.

She had been far too alone far too much since Bryn had been born. Now she was not only no longer alone, but sitting with exactly the sort of people she had always wanted, secretly, oh so secretly, to sit with. For half an hour, she had felt beautiful and bright. And normal. Now, life seemed unbearably flat.

—Bugger this, said Jane stoutly to herself: for once, her thoughts translated themselves immediately into deeds (as recommended by many Romantic poets through the ages), and scarcely had she thought this, than she found herself beside Miranda at the bar and

—Darling, she said, —you *must* introduce me to Fatty right now, and then we can go and powder our noses, can't we?

—Well, of *course*, Jane, darling.

So then Jane went and met Fatty and after a decent interval in which they spoke of points and suchlike, he asked her if she happened to want some cocaine and she said yes please why not and gave him more money than she usually spent on food for Bryn and her in a week, even though she always bought him organic things, and then she went down to the basement loo, down down down again, with her new friend Miranda, who had, by now, quite stopped worrying about stupid things like her nose collapsing, and they had a fine old pally chat about how wonderful Paul Salmon was and so forth.

The next thing that happened was that several hours appeared to pass very quickly indeed.

At some time or other, Jane found that the person in the striped jumper, Max, whom she had met earlier in the Groucho, had come in to Soho House and they chatted away with one another as if they had known one another for years and then a friend of Max's who had even bigger glasses than Max's joined them and *he* said that Boring People hated Art because of course Art and Crime were the two jobs where what you got for your work appeared to be nothing to do with the amount of time you put into it because of course the Boring People did not understand that to the Artist, his whole life was part of his work, and Jane quoted a South American Romantic poet who had said much the same thing: she said it in Spanish and everyone seemed terrifically impressed. Max's friend said he wanted her to write it down for him for his next piece of Art and Jane she said that she did not know much about Art but she thought all that Installation Art stuff was balls wasn't it, and everyone laughed because it turned out that the man she was talking to was actually the famous installation artist Dorian Height, creator of the most expensive beer mats in the world and father of the earth-shaking new range of venetian blinds at B&Q. Everyone thought Jane was being wildly ironic, even if they were not quite sure exactly how, since of course no one in the world, and certainly not anyone in the world who was allowed to come to Soho House, could possibly not know that they were sitting next to Dorian Height when they were sitting next to Dorian Height. So suddenly Jane found she had a reputation as a wit and lots of people started asking her to come with them when they went out, and so Jane had several funny little giggly, girly sessions cramped into warm loos with her New Friends, holding each other's hair up out of the way as they sniffed their cocaine, and then Jane and Max and Dorian decided to start a company to make LCD screens to put in the back windows of cars, to say insulting things, and Paul Salmon drew up a Heads of Agreement on the back of a menu and they all signed it merrily and then Salmon told everyone about *The Saviours* and everyone wanted to be in it or design it or direct it or make the clothes for it and several people said of course Jane should write it and she said Cool and told everyone about a new idea for a screenplay she had just had, about an ordinary waitress in a diner (Jane had never said 'diner' before in her life and it made her feel very cool to say it) who is stalked by a famous man because he falls in love with her because she is so ordinary, which everyone liked a lot, especially Marega Angelina, who said she would make Hal Scharnhorst let her Co-Produce it and be the Female Lead in it and Marcus Dale said that if Marega played the Female Lead he would play the Male Lead for nothing and everyone laughed and Jane quietly asked Marega if she had ever fucked Marcus (Jane very rarely used the word 'fuck' outside her lectures; that made her feel very cool too) and Marega turned to Jane with eyes that were all pupils and whispered *not yet* into Jane's ear in a very deep and lovely voice and Jane thought Marega was the most wonderful woman she had ever met and Miranda said she would make Richard Branson lend them his private island to have a party on when *Las Madonnas* was finished and then everyone went to the loos again except Marega Angelina because she had picked up a text message and had to go to the Savoy because Hal Scharnhorst had suddenly flown over to London for the first time since 11 September and he was very stressed by it and wanted her to come to his suite.

—He's *terribly loyal*, said Marega, as she stubbed out her cigarette and donned her fur.

—Go get that Co-Producership, Marega, said Paul Salmon as he air-kissed her goodbye.

—Bye-bye, darling, said Jane, who was actually rather shocked, as she air-kissed her goodbye.

Happily, though, she was quite sure that her ridiculous, provincial shock would not show, because she had recently discovered that the muscles in her face were no longer capable of making any shape except that of a wide and toothy smile. But no one seemed to notice so that was OK. Then Jane had another great idea, which was to make a modern version of Dicken's *Bleak House*.

—Out of copyright! said Salmon. —Good thinking.

—Well, if Emma whatsit can make so much money by doing Jane Austen, I don't see why we shouldn't do Dickens. We could call it *Bleak*.

—Yeah, or *House*.

—Cool. Or *Bleak House*.

—Brilliant, Jane. I see it: We make the little crossing-sweeper into a little rent boy and –

—Yes, and we do the bit with the fog as if it was . . .

Jane kept bumping into Dicky on her toings and froings to the toilets. At some stage or other, she was standing and waiting for the one right at the top, by the terrace, (she had forgotten how to find Paul Salmon's semi-secret downstairs place) and Dicky was nearby, talking to a tall, severe-looking man in a strange, glittering suit and rimless titanium spectacles.

—Ye-es, said this man (Jane thought she vaguely recognised him from *The Paper*), —I suppose that I first realised that I was gay when I read Foucault's analysis of power relations. I realised then that established norms of sexuality simply *have* to be challenged, or rather, inevitably *will* be challenged, in the era when procreation and sex have, for the first time in human, or indeed animal, history, been definitively separated. The human adventure really *is* just beginning, and I suppose I felt that I simply had to be part of the bold, brave attack, not spend my life on the wretched pallisades of a crumbling Empire.

—There's lovely. *I* realised I was gay when I realised I liked sticking things up my bum.

—Well, yes, that too, of course.

Whether it was having overheard this conversation or not, or whether it was the memory of Marega Angelina's soft breath on her ear, Jane did not know, but the final thing that happened was that Jane, who had not had sex for nearly a year, and had almost forgotten what it was like, could suddenly think of nothing else.

Sex.

Sex sex sex sex sex.

Jane became acutely aware of the tight seam of her jeans between her legs; she dwelt shamelessly on the firm swell of Marcus Dale's little bum when he went to the bar to get more Sea Breezes; and when Paul Salmon leaned across the table, to speak gloatingly and confidentially of their pre-ordained success, she found herself, while nodding wisely and looking into his big, black pupils with her now-fixed smile, actually thinking of nothing but a large, strong, olive-skinned cock sliding . . .

— . . . For God's sake, said Normal Jane to herself, merrily. But it was no good. She did not feel very normal any more. Instead, she felt her legs swinging apart, absurdly, beneath the table; it was as if there were a warm floodlight aimed between them. All her life, she had thought that D.H. Lawrence was an idiot; suddenly, she could see what he meant.

—Mmmm, said she to whatever whoever was saying.

—Top up? said Salmon.

—Cool.

Once again they descended the cold, stone steps. This time, Jane did not bother about who went first. She watched her feet and tried not to think about how Salmon's cock was exactly a foot behind her head. Instead, she tried to think about how she had seen steps like these in ruined castles, worn down by centuries of feet. Bare lovers' feet, perhaps? *Stone steps worn by lovers' feet, though bare?*

—Eh? said Salmon

—Nothing, said Jane.

Then she told Salmon about her latest *latest* idea for film, which was for a comedy about an American

233

hitman who specialises in drive-by shootings and then gets hired to do a job in England and realises that he can't do drive-by shootings in a car with a manual gearbox.

—Great! laughed Salmon. (—*Bloody hell, she's pretty good, too, she throws the ideas out, all right.*)

Jane tried to stop her sexual hackles rising at the sound of this deep, confident, male laughter behind her. It was hard work. And now they were squeezing again into the little toilet. Jane fished quickly for her cocaine in the ticket pocket of her jeans: as she did so, she pulled in her tummy; she could feel the line of her own knickers with her finger as she dug into the tight little denim slot. She caught Salmon looking at the seam of her jeans, and he caught her catching him looking and he held up his hands as if in surrender and as she gave him the little envelope of cocaine he produced his Greenpeace card again, with a smile, and smoothly divided the last of the powder. As she saw the glossy paper being scraped clean, revealing the face of some TV chef or other, Jane could already feel herself wanting to ask where there was more. But somehow what happened next was: as soon as they had finished standing still for a moment and breathing heavily, as if they had just run several hundred yards quite fast, as the cocaine reached their brains, they somehow ended up banging their teeth together and kissing hard.

The last time Jane had had sex had been with Dafydd, shortly before they decided to break up. And so, quite naturally, she had not kissed hard for longer than she had not had sex, since married people do not kiss hard even when they have sex.

Jane had thus entirely forgotten what it was like to feel her own mouth open wide, jaw-wrenchingly wide, smashed up wetly against another wide-open mouth, and to feel her tongue wrestling with someone else's tongue. She was taken utterly by surprise by the sensation of having a man's big hands crush her breasts. She felt his hand and his fingers inside her knickers, and herself suddenly wet, with all the amazed discovery of the first time ever. Panting with disbelief, she reached her hand down to grab his cock through his trousers. It was slack and small, but she longed to feel it grow.

—Hey, Jane, um, listen, whoa, I mean, shit, you OK?

—Oh my God, what am I doing?

—It's OK, it's OK.

—Oh God, I'm so sorry.

—Jane, it's OK.

—Is it?

—Jane, it's just, I really . . . like you, you know, it's just, I wouldn't want, if this thing between us, it mustn't be, not like this . . .

— . . . Oh, Paul. Hold me? (*A man. A real man. A big man like a barn door to hold me. A man who can say 'no, not like this'. A man who wants more than a quick fuck.*)

—Yeah, I'll hold you, Jane. (*Phew! Fucking coke, man, why does it do that to me? So fucking unfair, Baz Andrews can shag all night on the stuff. Or so he says, lying bastard.*)

Jane clung for a while to Salmon, like a shipwrecked sailor clinging to the rock that has just sunk his boat, then some other people started shouting from outside.

—Oh, really, come on in there, place is closing any minute now, you doing a *shit* in there or something, you antisocial bastards? So Jane and Salmon dropped each other and readjusted their clothes and squeezed past the three new people who wanted to get in.

—Oh, Paul, it's you.

235

—Hi, Max. Is Fatty still upstairs?

—Hello, Jane, *you'll* come back to Dorian's, won't you? Fatty? Yes, but he's just going.

—Shit, better rush.

—Bye, Max.

—Bye, Jane.

Jane went swiftly up the stairs, holding her arm out behind her so Salmon could hold her hand. They stopped and banged their teeth against each other's teeth again for a little while halfway up, and Salmon rubbed his knee between Jane's legs and she thought that for the first time in her life she truly knew what a cat feels like when you scratch its chin and then more people interrupted them, and they laughed and went on. Upstairs, they just caught Fatty in time.

—Split one? said Salmon merrily

—Cool, said Jane, —I'll just get my bag. Or rather, she tried to say that, but actually she said: —*Kchhhool, I'll zhust ghet my bug*, because something rather strange was happening.

The nice feeling that had come from the cocaine first time and had lasted a good half-hour had, this time, only lasted as long as it had taken to snog Salmon and climb the stairs; the nasty feeling of ragged nerves and universal isolation had come back almost immediately, and much more strongly.

Also, she could no longer speak.

As she waited, dumbly grinning, for her coat, she looked down the stairs and watched as Sheina and Miranda and Marcus and various others were bossed about unceremoniously in front of the door to the club by a large Nigerian man with scars who was organising horrible unlicenced cabs. Her mouth felt almost frighteningly dry, her nose burned and her head felt sort of hollowed-out and sandblasted from

236

within. Worse, she felt horribly, catastrophically alone. Worst of all, she could think of nothing that would stop it except more cocaine right now. She felt her fingers tap her jeans for the little envelope that she actually knew had been all used up.

—Sorted. My place? said Salmon in her ear. Jane grabbed his arm thankfully.

—Yes. Yes please.

The cab ride seemed to take approximately a thousand years, and by the time they got to Kentish Town in their battered armada of Toyotas and Protons, all of which smelled vile and none of whose drivers knew anything about where anywhere was, everyone was utterly gagging for another line, naturally, so they all went straight into Salmon's kitchen.

Jane stood and watched as Salmon made up a dozen lines. She took hers with a sort of fatalistic acceptance. This time, it did not do anything nice at all, unless stopping the horrible feelings could be called nice, which presumably it could, and then she suddenly felt as if something had sucked all the blood and energy from her body: when she saw Salmon's bedroom door open as she passed it, her only thought was to sneak in quickly before someone else bagged it, because surely everyone would want it soon?

No sooner had she lain down than Salmon appeared, looming above her. Without ceremony, he stroked her between the legs of her jeans as he looked down at her. Jane did nothing, because she could not think of anything to do.

—Sorry about earlier, he said.

—No, I'm sorry, she said.

—I really like you, you see.

—Do you?

—You need to sleep, don't you?

—Mmmm, nodded Jane.

—I'll bring you some water.

—Thank you.

So then Jane lay and thought how wonderful it was, in this big wide wandering world, to have found a man who not only loved her script but wanted to do things like bring her glasses of water. It had been a very long time since she had been looked after by anyone. When he came back with water, he even tucked her up and kissed her on the head. As he left the room, Jane let her head loll sideways, at last, and closed her eyes, at last, and breathed out long and slow and deep.

At that moment, she realised with terror that she would never, ever sleep again.

Some kind of ghastly internal arc lights came on inside her head, flooding the space behind her eyelids. She closed her eyes desperately and then realised they were already closed. She opened them and realised she was lying on a strange bed in a strange house. She could not move her tongue and dived for the glass of water beside the bed. When she had finished it, her mouth was still parched. She could feel a strange sort of buzzing in her temples, like a nest of wasps just out of conscious hearing range. When she opened her eyes, she wanted to lie down and die of exhaustion on the spot; but when she lay down and closed them, the blinding lights fizzed on again and her limbs could not stay still. The bed was strewn with hot sand, surely?

The bed.

Jane had always liked the feeling of sleeping in her friends' beds. How wonderful, to go to sleep surrounded by someone else's life, knowing that you will wake up surrounded still by someone else's freshly ironed, spring-cleaned life. But not this bed. It had to be the cocaine, of course, the sheets were perfectly, well, nearly perfectly clean. The room was pleasant. But for some reason, a voice in Jane's ear told her she had to get out.

Home.

No home.

Friends' house. Yes.

Escape. Flee.

Jane edged unsteadily out of the bedroom, carrying her shoes. Silently, she peered down the corridor, and could see Salmon, Sheina, Miranda and their friends, all leaning over the kitchen table, sniffing away: they looked like vampires at a feast, gathering to suck the blood of some poor child.

Poor child.

Bryn.

Bryn!

Devastating guilt burst into Jane's flash-fried brain. In an instant, she was out of the flat and some minutes later found herself wandering around in front of Waitrose on the Holloway Road. Some time later still, she found herself getting out of a black cab, mouth glued shut, head swirling, trying to mutter thanks to the driver who, by some miracle, had strayed this far north. Somehow, she survived the journey to Muswell End. Unable to speak, she overtipped wildly instead, and fled into the house, remembering at the last moment to be as quiet as possible.

Incredibly, horribly, her friends' child was already stirring as she crept and padded up the stairs; unbelievably, impossibly, it was dawn already.

Jane lay in bed, heart belting against her chest, planning the lifetime of penance that would start as soon as she got back to Wales tomorrow.

If only Bryn did not die tonight.

If only she was spared this night.

She had been good for a long time.

Now and at the hour of our death.

As the sun came up into her room, as the normal people in the house and outside in the street, the blessed ones, resumed their daylight lives, Jane said to herself (quoting a little-known Spanish poet):

The sick man cries: Day! Day! Now may I sleep!
And presses closed his hot and fevered eyes.

and fell at last into a curious half-slumber, from which she suddenly opened her eyes after half an hour, totally exhausted, hideously awake, racked, bleached and desiccated, but with some confidence that she would, in fact, live long enough to make amends.

That would be her life from now on: amends.

She would teach her Business Language Classes with joy; she would never turn on the video again when Bryn was with her; she would play with him joyfully, lit through with gratitude, all the hours he was awake, then carry him to bed and tuck him to sleep and sing him to rest and watch him snoring gently and then do her washing and rejoice each day in the cloudless heaven of True Normality.

—I have seen the Chapel of Lost Souls, said Jane to herself, out loud, and was surprised to find that she had said it in a sort of Welsh accent.

Paddington.

Wales.

Back.

Yes, back: home is only home when you have gone away and come back.

Home.

She would never move again.

She arose, and went down the stairs through the

thankfully empty house. On the kitchen table was a note. Jane picked it up, wondering exactly what words her Old Friends had chosen to express the fact that they would not mind if they never saw her again after this appalling behaviour.

The note said: 'WAY TO GO. SEE YOU LATER?'

Jane put it down, confused. More London irony, she supposed. What was so good about bloody irony anyway? They had called her trousers ironic. Posh metropolitan bastards. Renewed horror swept over Jane as she discovered that she had a mercilessly total recall of the previous night. She wanted to put her head in a bag. No, a burkha. That was it.

Yes. She would wander Pontypool in a sheet for ever, looking out at the world through a little mesh grille. She would live on a mountain with Bryn. She would learn Welsh and get back with Dafydd and have three more children straight away before she got too old. She would never allow thoughts of Lost Possibilities to disturb her, ever again. Dafydd would read the *Western Mail* out loud and they would sit in the quiet Pontypool evenings, as the fifty greens of the fading light played across the distant valleys, listening to her children playing in Welsh, and at night, when all were asleep, she would sit, alone with The Lord and with her memories of Sin, and record the glorious morality of her life in bulletins to resistyoof.co.uk . . .

Percival.

Oh God.

She sat trembling at her friends' breakfast table, mobile quickly in hand. She was supposed to meet Percival for lunch *today*.

Impossible! If he saw her like this, he would run a mile. Her eyes filled with tears at the thought of his nice messages, his solid, English normality, his gentle humour. She would have to lie; she would meet him another time, in two weeks, three weeks, when she had exercised and saunaed ten times, and slept a hundred hours, and eaten several bucketloads of organic fruit and caught up with her work and loved Bryn enough. But not now.

Back.

Yes.

Jane coughed to clear her throat from the countless cigarettes of last night, and loathed herself all over again at the sound. She tried to speak out loud, to see if she could, and it sounded horrible. She had to have a cup of tea before she called Percival and lied to him.

She stumbled over to the kettle. As it boiled with well-watched slowness, she stared blankly at the front page of *The Paper*, which was lying on the worktop. She took in the headlines and the date, glassily, determined to let this day, and these events, burn into her mind for ever: the next time she wanted to go to a pub or have a cigarette (though how could she *ever* want that again?) she would close her eyes, recall this moment, and be saved.

Then something made her look down, at the bottom of the front page, where *The Paper* always had a stupid witty bit.

She froze.

There stood her picture, from off the staff noticeboard at Pontypool University. The witty bit at the bottom of the paper said:

PONTYPOOL MADONNAS IN GOOD
COMPANY
Many Oxbridge dons dream of unearthing the
Great Unknown Work, but a pretty young

female lecturer from the not-exactly-metropol-
itan University of Pontypool has not only
found the gold mine – she owns the rights as
well! Blonde, Welsh-speaking Dr Jane Feverfew, an expert on some of the more obscure
Spanish poets, has joined forces with one of
London's top young producers to put the
notorious, long-banned classic *Las Madonnas
del Cenicero* on the Big Screen, in a production which has already tempted Britpack
idol Marcus Dale back across the water to
don boots and knee breeches once again.
Dale, whose grandmother brought him up
with tales of her native Wales, said of the
screenplay . . .

—Oh my God, croaked Jane.
Famous.
Famous.
Famous.

Famous

—Dad, why is Mam in the newspaper? asked Bryn, tears welling up in his eyes. —Has she been killed in London?

—Duw no, Brynnie bach, love you, laughed Auntie Blodwen, who had been giving Bryn his breakfast.

—What? asked Dafydd, raising his head from his corn flakes. He looked at *The Paper*. He goggled. The phone rang. Auntie Blodwen answered it.

—It's Mam, she said. She had always rather liked Jane. Shame she was English, really.

—Mam!

—What the hell's going on, Janey? asked Dafydd, snatching the phone, as if Jane should have discussed things amicably with him before daring to become famous.

—Nothing much. Is Bryn there?

—Yes. And he's very upset.

—I'm *not* upset, Daddy!

—Dafydd, can I talk to him?

—Well, yes.

—Hello, sweetheart.

—Mam, why are you in the paper? I thought perhaps you was killed in London.

—No, no, sweetheart. I'm fine. Just, someone wants to make a film out of a story I wrote.

—A story for children?

—Well, not really.

—Can I see it when I'm big?

—Of course you can.

—Can Auntie Blodwen see it?

—If she wants.

—We had pancakes for breakfast. Auntie Blodwen can throw pancakes in the air. Dad tried, but his one broke and it fell on the flames. It made loads of smoke. Dad was really cross. Am I sleeping at your house tonight?

—No, at Dad's.

—Oh. All right.

—But tomorrow at mine. For a lot of nights.

—How many nights?

—A lot.

—Four?

—At least.

—Dad wants to talk to you.

—Bye-bye, sweetheart.

—Bye-bye, Mam.

Alan Barony looked at the figures one more time as he munched on his prawn and fennel sandwich. He calculated. He looked again at *The Paper*. After a last pause for thought, he picked up his telephone and dialled.

—Paul.

—Alan, how's The Man?

—I see your Writer has got a one-girl PR machine.

—Fucking great, isn't it? Think how much it would cost to buy those column inches in *The Paper*. Don't you think we should raise her fee?

—My God, you *do* like her.

—Hey, Alan, we all got to settle down sometime. She's a clever girl. Posh. Take her anywhere. Maybe a cottage in Wales would be nice. Log fires, kids, goats and Agas. She's a Writer, she can work from home, and she only has to go to the university a few hours a week.

An au pair or a nanny and bish bosh, sorted. I get to stay in town four of seven and oil the wheels, I come home Friday, maybe even Thursday: she's overjoyed to see me. The kids run out to meet me: immortality. Come Sunday afternoon, when the roast beef's gone down and it's getting boring, I'm already outside in the yard, on the phone, planning my meetings, weddings and bar mitzvahs for Monday in the Groucho. Could be good. Very.

—So cut her in on your fee, Paul.

—Alan, it was only an *idea*.

—OK: if Marcus Dale and Marega Angelina both sign to start next month and you show me the Soft Money and you cut your own fee by £5,000 and the Director's fee by £10,000 you can go out and start hiring people.

—Can we have a Heads of Agreement letter to show people?

—Of course not. You can have a note confirming my interest in principle in the project subject to casting and full budget.

—I have to build the whole show on just that, Alan?

—That's your *job*, Paul, isn't it?

—True. You won't regret this, Alan. OK, so if we come in at £2.9 million, and I promise we will, remind me how much we have to take at the box office before your accounts say the movie has gone into profit?

—About £12 million.

—Yeah, thought so. May as well start dishing out the percentage points then.

—If it makes people happy, Paul.

—It does. Thanks, Alan. Sea's looking tasty.

— . . . So, right, Jane, we got this sexy location and –

— . . . Oh, just a sec, hold on, friend of mine heaving into sight, *must* talk to her, she works for Hal

Scharnhorst, you know, Marega Angelina says he's *terribly loyal* . . .

— . . . Hello, Jane, darling, how *are* you? Well *done*, darling.

—Miranda, darling, how are *you*?

—Bit *fragile*, sort of. But I don't think I *feel* as bad as Marcus *looks*.

—Oh, where's Marcus?

—In Kettners.

—Did he look *that* bad?

—Actually, he looked asleep.

—Asleep?

—Mmm. In his steak.

—What fun.

—Talking of which, I don't suppose you *saved* any from last night, did you, Jane, darling?

—'Fraid not.

—No, nor me. Bugger.

—Excuse me, Miranda, darling, I simply *must* finish this call.

—Important?

—Press.

—Oh well then. See you inside. Shall I get you a Sea Breeze?

—Mmm, please. Put it on Paul's tab.

—Oh, good.

Jane waved Miranda away, and returned to her mobile as she stood in the doorway of the Groucho Club in Soho. Her exhaustion and general feeling of illness had, by now, been very easily outweighed by the fact that she was famous, was standing once again (but now with perfect ease) in the doorway of the Groucho and was talking on her mobile in order to arrange a photo shoot for *Sorted Bloke* magazine, so that they could put her at the last minute into the line-up of their Vote For Your Top Totty Issue (there were twenty categories, and Jane was to be placed in the Brainy Breasty Brit Babes section). The idea had come from Marega Angelina, who had been one of the *very first* to call with congratulations that morning. Jane was to model Marega's new range of retro-designer uplift bras in the photo shoot. Jane had her doubts; but the features editor of *Sorted Bloke* understood them.

—Yeah, yeah, yeah, Jane, of *course* you don't want to look fat. No one does. And our readers certainly don't want to look *at* fat, so we'll make bloody *sure* you don't. It's all in the camera angles, trust me.

—I get approval of the negatives, said Jane crisply.

—OK, OK.

—E-mail that in writing, see your guy at three.

—Done deal.

—Cool, said Jane, and went back into the Groucho, where she now had no trouble getting as many drinks on Paul Salmon's tab as she wanted until her own membership came through: he had besieged her from his bath with voicemail and text messages, and was arriving soon.

Jane tried to suppress the memory of Salmon's hand inside her knickers. Curious. For some reason it did not seem to *matter* as much as it should. She did not *like* remembering it, but she found, to her surprise, that she did not care about it nearly as much as she should. The memory of lying on his bed while he stroked through her jeans should have, normally would have, made her cry out loud with horror and shame. But today, though she could recall it exactly, it felt more like having a small filling in a tooth done under a strong local anaesthetic in an expensive dentist's suite: by no means pleasant, but scarcely a thing to worry overmuch about.

Actually, she would not mind him doing it again. What?

What on earth was going on with her? Was it just the air in W1? Or was it her Fame? She would have asked Miranda, but she did not feel that she had very much to say to Miranda this morning, which was curious, since they had chattered happily away about all sorts of things for several hours last night; also, she could not quite decipher a curious feeling, a sort of numbing around the front teeth and a churning in the guts that she had just got at the mere sight of Miranda, and it slightly unnerved her: surely she could not fancy Miranda?

—Congrats, sweetheart, said Fatty, appearing at her table and air-kissing her. Jane jumped a little bit and also recoiled a little bit because he smelled a little bit. He asked for a cigarette.

—Can't stop, said he. —Just wanted to congratulate you. Very good news. Oh yes, and let me know when you're going back to Cardiff, will you? I can arrange things for you down there, same metropolitan quality, none of your provincial crap, know what I mean?

Jane had not been intending to take cocaine ever again, but for some reason the mere presence of Fatty made her nose start to itch. She could be New Jane again, fully, in five seconds. After all, she was only up in town for a couple of days. And she was bloody famous, for God's sake, she was celebrating, she had to be able to celebrate, didn't she? And she was tired, she was meeting Percival for the first time so she had better be on good form for him, in a way it was just a sort of use-of-time thing. If she took coke again, she would feel better straight away. Of course, she knew she was drawing down an overdraft of sleep, she would feel even tireder tomorrow, obviously, but this was strictly a one-off, it was pretty bloody special day, after all, and when you thought about it, it would really only be a sort of *loan* of energy to herself, from herself, wouldn't it? She could pay it back to herself in extra sleep when she got back to Wales. On one of her many lovely, long, relaxed, famous nights in her little house with Bryn. Or perhaps, her *big* house with Bryn, quite soon. Yes indeed. Her life was perfect, really. It was just that today she needed to make, well, an *investment* of time. That was what it was, yes, an *investment* of energy, because after all, in a very real sense . . .

— . . . Actually, yeah, she found herself saying, while not quite looking Fatty in the eye, —I was just wondering if Uncle Charles was about today? I mean, not now, obviously, far too early, ha ha, but maybe later.

—Uncle C is not only about, but today, for you, he is at home and sitting on the roof.

—Sitting on the roof?

—On the house, sweetheart, smiled Fatty. —Welcome to the club, and, handing back Jane's packet of cigarettes, he left with a wink. —Call me any time. You got my number, yeah?

—I don't think so.

—Oh, I think you have.

—What?

—Call me. Yeah, and have you seen Marcus? He called and said he needed a livener, but he didn't say where he was, the stupid sod. What, does he think I've got a satellite locator for all my friends? Hmmm. Not a bad idea, actually.

—Marcus is in Kettners, I think, said Jane, vaguely, and yet at the same time rather loudly and proudly, feeling like a paid-up member of the Crowd at last, with worthwhile gossip to swap. —And it sounds as if he certainly *does* need you.

Before she knew what she was doing, she found that she had kissed Fatty on his greasy, unshaven cheek without the slightest feeling of disgust. She felt his hand rest for a tiny moment on her lower ribs. Then he rolled off, and Jane checked her mobile-phone book under 'F'; there was no number under 'Fatty'. Then she remembered that 'Fatty' was not actually his name; his real name was Pete and there, sure enough, was his number.

—Anyway, she said, firmly, —just because I've got his number doesn't mean I'm going to bloody call him. It must be this bloody Groucho place. So she decided to go and get some fresh air before meeting Percival. Then, finding that she suddenly did not want to be alone, she called Dicky Emrys (he had phoned several times that morning, in a state of hyperventilating excitement) and they arranged to meet in Soho Square in order to prepare Jane for her date.

—Back soon, darling, said Jane to Miranda. —Just got to go and meet someone.

—Oh. What did Fatty say, darling, I thought, perhaps, did he . . . ?

—He said I could get some free, later.

—Later? Oh. Free? Oh well, I'll see you later then, darling, shall I?

—Of course, darling. I'm meeting a man for lunch here. And Paul, of course.

—A man? Well *done*, darling. Wish *I* could find one. Well, don't *forget* me, will you, darling?

—Of course not, darling.

The Cold Earth

It was now that strangely quiet time, between about eleven and a quarter to twelve, when even the M25 has space to drive in and when there is room to sit and think in the clean, spring air, even in London. Everyone who has got to be anywhere in the morning has already got there, and no one who has got to be anywhere by lunch has left yet: the time of day when starving, hung-over poets emerge blinking into the sun and thank whatever god they write for that they are not working in offices, after all (by six o'clock they will all be suicidal again and wishing frantically for wives and children and steady jobs to give them a good reason to wake up for so that they have not *got* to go out and get whacked again, but right now it feels good).

Jane wandered cautiously up into Soho Square in search of a slice of this curious peace. Everything seemed a little too 3D this morning. She felt dog-tired but totally awake. So this was what being Famous felt like, was it? It was not quite how she had imagined it. She had always thought that if she ever did anything really good, made a splash of any kind, she would be quiet and contented for ever. But instead, she felt nervy and sort of *stretched*.

Jane sat on a bench in the dappling sunlight (amazingly, she had it all to herself) and tried to gloat quietly about her Fame. It was harder than it should have been. She felt as if she had put on a big wig and high heels and everyone was saying tra-la, but actually, underneath, she was still Jane, and her wig was itchy and her heels made it hard to walk. So she thought about money instead. That was easier. That was much better. She could pay off her mortgage, perhaps. A nice house with a big garden for Bryn. Yes, that was better. Even more exciting was the thought that if she made some extra money, she could do what hardly any other academic can afford to do: *take a job in London!* And if she was back in London, in Muswell End, say, maybe she would be able to find a man, after all. An interesting man. A man who liked children. A man who *had* children, maybe . . .

Percival.

She would meet him today, famously.

Tonight, she would be back with Bryn.

By the time Jane had come full circle to this point, however, she also found that she was unconsciously surveying the representatives of Maledom who passed her, trying to work out what Percival might look like, what she hoped he might look like, and why it was that the whole business of meeting him was starting to make her feel sick with anxiety and very unfamous indeed.

Jane thought. She forced herself to analyse herself by using her full, doctoral-level powers of cultural investigation. These powers had been trained by long years of explaining Romantic poetry by reference to Cultural History, so Jane knew what she was talking, or at least thinking, about all right.

—Clearly, thought she, lecturing herself firmly from a virtual podium, —it is because everything feels like it is the wrong way round. Since the dawn of humanity, indeed, since before, since the first primate met another primate and ended up having little primates, we have selected our sexual partners (which has meant, until

253

very recently, the potential parents of our offspring) in a particular manner (*Are you doing your nails, Miz Feverfew? This is a lecture theatre, not a tart's parlour*). This manner holds true whether we envisage (a) one headhunter meeting another in a jungle ten thousand years ago or (b) two people meeting at a Club Nite today. The pattern is the same:

i) Visual. We see them. We note the signs that tell us to which tribe they belong. We choose whether to approach, or let ourselves be approached, or not. If we decide yes, then we move to stage (ii).

ii) Aural. We hear their voices as they *say their name*, the magical sound which will represent them to us for ever. If we like the sheer noise of their voices, we proceed to stage (iii).

iii) Tactile. We feel them by making some excuse to touch their hand or kiss their cheek or flick dust from their shoulder or whatever. At this stage we are now close enough, whether we know it or not, to engage in stage (iv).

iv) Smell. We obtain gigabytes of secret information about them. Then and *only then*, only *after* we have already decided in principle whether this person might be in the frame for possible shagging, do we become fully human and get on to stage (v).

v) Talk. Establish desires. Reveal and Discover.

—But compare and contrast the modern bloody Internet world! said Jane, not quite to herself. —Observe the way everything between me and Percival is arsewise! No wonder we all feel sick when we meet people we only know from e-mails. We went straight to *talking*, for God's sake, we short-circuited all the hard-wired seeing and hearing and touching and smelling, and because we are designed by 400,000,000 years of bloody evolution to assume that we would not even be *bothering* to talk to this person about stuff we care about unless we had already quite fancied them, we assume in our secret hearts, or our secret bloody jeans, that we are going to fancy them as soon as we meet them, because we are already acting *as if* we did. Which means we probably *will*.

—Oh, arse, snapped Jane, not at all to herself. She closed her eyes and breathed deeply. The roar of the traffic in Oxford Street seemed to fade and merge into a natural hum, like bees in a summer forest. If only she could be in a forest now. Alone. Somewhere no one was watching, looking, judging. She felt herself drifting away. The lecture continued in her head, formal, droning, soporific:

—So, really (*pay attention there, Jane, this is serious stuff, you might get a finals question on it*), it's no wonder we are all so confused and scared by everything. We are the first generation in history to be brought up without God and lullabies. No wonder we are all haunted by visions of simplicity and purity and tradition. Every Englishman longs for the timeless summer shadows on the cricket pitch he has never seen, the public school he never went to and the Georgian house he would not know what the hell to do with. Every ordinary Jew feels a secret pang of reproach when he walks out of *Schindler's List* and sees the five-kid Orthodox family walking by, hand in hand, pushchair to the fore and history in every step. Every Frenchman dreams of some lost village in the Vosges where the church bells toll and the cows come home and the priest smiles from the running-board of his Citroën. Dafydd is gnawed by secret doubt as to who he really *is* when he cannot understand Gareth Edwards's Welsh rugby commentary on S4C. And those life-hating hell-hounds who flew the planes into

New York wished they could have been their beloved grandfathers, praying on their mountain tops, with twenty grandchildren and three wives and an ancient Koran to guide every step they took on earth (*OK, read the next chapter for your tutorial groups, see you next week*).

—*We are free and therefore lost*, nodded Jane to herself, quoting Kafka with approval, feeling the pale warmth of the spring sun on her closed eyelids. She felt herself nodding off. God, she could sleep for ever. She wished she was home, cuddled up to Bryn, so she could just sleep, sleep, sleep . . .

—Right, lady: all lost souls.

Jane jumped and found that a youngish man with several troy ounces of silver in his nose, eyebrows, lips and cheeks had come and sat beside her. She vaguely recognised him. Perhaps he was famous? Had she met him in the Groucho last night? She did not feel like talking to some mad actor or whatever right now, so she rose to leave. He did not restrain her, but merely hissed:

—The Saviours are coming, lady.

—Oh, you've heard about it, smiled Jane, famously (*OK, I was right: he's an actor*).

—I'm part of it, princess.

—Me too, actually. Jane. Jane Feverfew, she added modestly (in case he had read *The Paper*), holding out her hand as she had seen Marega Angelina hold out her hand. Skanky merely stared down at her fingers, baffled by this unknown gesture. Then he looked up at her again with his anthracite eyes.

—I'm Skanky, muttered he. —You're *with* him? Mr Salmon?

—Well, we're working together right now on another project.

—Another project? But, Mr Salmon, I mean, I thought this was his big thing, I thought . . .

—Oh, don't worry, Paul was talking about *The Saviours* last night, and yeah, I'm pretty sure it's his, like, next big thing. In fact, I may well be involved.

—You?

—All under wraps just yet, of course.

—Fuck, yeah. Keep the secret, man.

—So, um, are you, er, hoping to take a lead part? Or something?

—I'll do whatever Mr Salmon says, nodded Skanky. —Anything.

—Yes, I can see you as the man with the big machine gun.

—Norwegian Whaling Bastards.

—That's really very good. Very real. Yes, I can see you doing that.

—I'd do anything, lady. Wouldn't you?

—I'm writing it, actually. Well, I'm *slated* to write it, you know, she added modestly. —After all, we're not Green-Lit *yet*. How do *you* know about it?

—*Write* it?

—The film. Paul Salmon's film.

—Film?

—Um, *The Saviours*. Hello?

—Film?

—Well, sorry, must be going. Excuse me. Um, if you grab me, I'll scream.

—The Saviours is just a fucking *film*?

—Well, what do you want? An album tie-in, ha ha? Sorry, um, look . . .

— . . . But I thought . . . Only a film, only a fucking bastard cunting film . . .

— . . . Help!

—Paws off now, lovelyboy.

—Dicky! Thank God.

—They fucking lied to me, man! I believed, I . . . a fucking *film*?! You whores.

—See this, butt? Well, you should have been watching *that* one.

Pow!

So then Skanky ran away with a broken nose and Jane and Dicky Emrys kissed and squealed and planned parties to celebrate Jane's fame in Cardiff and London and maybe even America (Dicky knew a very good Welsh bar called Dylan's in San Francisco). This excitement kept them going for quite a long time, until they were both sitting comfortably and drinking white wine back in the Groucho.

—It's ridiculous, Jane said, —I know it can't Go Anywhere with this Percival because there's no way I could leave Wales and come to London, because of Bryn. Well, at least, not unless I have a definite, guaranteed New Life for him, you know. I mean, with a New Man and a New Home and maybe Other Kids and – . . .

—You straight folk never cease to amaze me. Go Anywhere. *Go?* What on earth do you mean? You can't have a bloody cup of coffee with each other without asking *where it's going*. Nothing *goes* anywhere, lovelygirl, because there's nowhere else to go, is there? We are here, we have already arrived at the only place we are ever going, and the next stop is nowhere.

—You know what I mean, said Jane.

—No, I *don't*. That's the whole point. What *do* you mean? I don't think you even know yourselves. Do you mean you want to shag him up an alleyway? Or do you mean you want to have ten kids and big Sunday lunches? Make your bloody mind up, say I. If you just want to shag him on a beach with your knickers still on, all that matters is if you fancy him or not. But if it's the ten kids you really want, ask him if he wants them as well: if he says yes, result; if he runs a mile, wave goodbye and put an advert in *The Paper* for an arranged marriage.

—It's not as simple as that.

—Yes it is. Except that all you lot still really *believe* in the Happy Ending. You do, don't you? Admit it.

—Don't *you* want to? said Jane, hastily snapping shut the ridiculous telescopes of her spiralling fantasies.

—Want to? Course I bloody *want* to. Why do you think we queers all love Catholic knick-knacks? *Want* the Happy End? Of course I bastard do. Funny: you got a PhD and all, but you still don't know the difference between *wanting* and *getting*. Bloody daft, you all are; you'd be much happier putting shagging in *this* box and the house and kids in *this* box, like posh South Americans or French presidents. But you want it all. It's like me wanting the *same* man to be a snarling little rent boy from Dalston and a distinguished connoisseur of Bellini. Not on, lovelygirl. But still you seek it. Quite touching, really: like children. Time you grew up. Give us a smoke then, I'm gasping.

—Ugh. There you are. I'm giving up.

—Course you are. Oho, what's *this*, you naughty girl.

—What's what?

—Butter wouldn't melt. Look at her. Must be a whole *gram* in there.

Dicky turned the packet of cigarettes around and tilted it so that Jane could see a small, glossy envelope nestling attractively amid the Silk Cuts.

—I didn't know it was there, said Jane.

—Well, I must say, if this is having famous friends, I could start enjoying it. Fancy a quick trip to the

259

disabled toilets in that pub over there? Much more roomy. Well, after all, you want to be on your best form for this man. I mean, what if he really *is* Mr Right?

—I'm not meeting him for the first time when I've taken cocaine!

—True, dangerous. Mind you, you're still buzzing nicely from last night, by the looks.

—I am *not*.

—Whatever you say. Then I shall go to the loo alone for once. And then I must leave you.

—Where are you going?

—Well, I'm not going to sit here and watch two repressed straights acting out *Brief Encounter*, that's for sure. Actually, I've arranged to meet this snarling little rent boy from Dalston. Or was he a distinguished Italian connoisseur of Bellini? Do you know, I just *can't* remember for the life of me. But I'm sure I'll find him in the Admiral Duncan, whoever he was. Or is. Or will be . . .

Professor Evan Evans stumped up the stairs with his face set hard. Beneath his armpit nestled *The Paper* and in his heart burned mighty vengeance. He swept into the Departmental Office and instructed the secretary, Mrs Menna Williams, to commence forthwith writing a note to Dr Jane Feverfew, drawing her attention to the fact that sick leave taken under false pretences constitutes a clear breach of trust and contract.

—And put that last bit in italics, Menna.

—Yes, Evan.

—My bastard grandfathers went on strike so people who had lost their legs in the mines could get sick pay to feed their kids. Not so that posh little spoiled bitches can take a fortnight off to go and ponce about London playing at being media tarts . . .

260

A Man in His Late Thirties

—I'm, um, supposed to be meeting Dr Jane Feverfew, came a deep, English voice from the lobby, and Jane spun round in her chair. A tall man in an old tweed jacket and old cords, with old but polished brogues, was standing before the incredibly beautiful receptionist of the Groucho, looking very out of place indeed.

It had to be Percival.

Jane was sitting nervously at her table. Over the last twenty minutes she had unaccountably begun to feel distinctly grey and desiccated: she was having to try hard to fight off the feeling that she must look like a piece of dried codfish. She rather wished she had taken some cocaine after all. Too late now. She tried to look at Percival objectively.

He had fine brown hair, receding slightly. He also, she noted, had a face. She could not think of anything else to think about his face. It was a face. It did not seem twisted or pursed up or lopsided or anything like that. It did not seem like anything very much. He did not seem to be noticeably fat or unusually thin. He was tall, however. How old? About forty. Jane could not work out what looked so strange about his clothes and his face when you put them together. Then she realised that he was the first man she had seen in W1 in the last two days who looked like a man in his late thirties or early forties and who dressed like a man in his late thirties or early forties.

He turned and looked at her. She knew immediately that he had recognised her too.

—Hello, said he.

—Hello, said Jane.

—May I sit down?

—God, yes.

They looked at each other for longer than normal people would have done. Then:

—I've often wondered what this place is like.

—Yes. It's quite fun, actually.

—I suppose so. All these idiots pretending to be young, eh?

—Yes, said Jane. She had to deliberately suppress the fleeting, treacherous hope that no one would be listening to them. To her horror, she found that she had already begun to master the essential W1 skill of appearing to be dedicating one's entire attention to one's conversational partner while maintaining a state of complete aural and visual Yellow Alert in case someone possibly more useful (and hence potentially more dangerous) walked in. She forced herself to stop it, and to be here with Percival.

They sat there for some moments, the pale beech table between them glowing pink with reflected embarrassment and nervous hope. Eventually, they talked. Their conversation might have been following some Book of Etiquette from an earlier age, when direct questions were forbidden in social chit-chat; they carefully followed leads, as if picking their way towards each other, barefoot and blindfold, across a carpet strewn with shards of glass.

They talked first about their ex-partners, just as a way of confirming, without the other one having to ask, that they were both genuinely free. Then they talked enthusiastically about their children. They were not really talking about their children; but they both instinctively knew that when a parent who is Out There again talks about their child, their hopes for their child, their fears for their child, they are really talking about their own hopes and fears. Which is what they each really wanted to know about.

—It's funny, said Percival. —I mean, all my life, I've only ever bought one kind of sock, so as to avoid ending up with only odd ones, you know. So when I broke up I decided to do the same for my son. Which was fine. I always bought dark blue socks for me, so I always buy him lots of little dark blue socks, too. But now he's six, and last week, I had to buy him a load of bigger dark blue socks, and the next ones up go from size 12 to size 3. This morning, I took all our washing out of the tumble dryer, and everything was all scrunched and dried up, of course, and, well, for a while I really couldn't work out which were his socks and which were mine. I had to lay them out on the kitchen table so I could see them all clearly. And then I sort of *saw myself* doing it, me, if you see what I mean, standing in front of the table, just looking at all these blue socks, and getting late for work. It made me feel, well, funny, I suppose, in a way. I mean, it only seems a few months ago I was carrying him about in a backpack.

—Yes, said Jane. She was thinking about the solar system mobile above Bryn's bed.

—Next thing, he'll be reading books on his own in his room. I suppose your boy can read already?

—No, actually.

—Oh. Oh, good. I mean, you know: I don't really like all this forcing-house stuff. Do you know any eight-year-olds that *can't* read? Let them do it when they're ready.

—Definitely. Actually, my boy's being brought up bilingually, so –

263

—Oh, so's mine.

—Really?

—Yes. Yours is learning Spanish, I suppose? I mean, it is Spanish you lecture in, isn't it?

—Yes.

—That must be great. Such an important language, I mean.

—Yes. I mean, no. He's not being brought up bilingual in *Spanish*, actually.

—Oh. So . . . um, *French*, I suppose?

Jane could not bear it any longer. The very thought of Bryn being brought up to speak Welsh seemed so utterly laughable here in Soho, W1. More than laughable. Insane. Abusive, even. But even worse was the way that the very word, *Welsh*, opened up the dreadful gate she had been trying to keep closed in her mind: the iron gate of geographical impossibility.

She found that she liked Percival.

She found that she liked him very much.

She found that she liked him more than she wanted to.

She had been trying in vain for the last few minutes to stop herself thinking insane thoughts like *Hmmm, his kid must be nice. His kids would be nice.* And there was no point. None at all. Because she lived in Wales and would never be able to move.

—Well, she said, covering her sense of hopelessness, —let's have a drink shall we? she said: —Sea Breeze?

—Why not? Never had one.

—It *is* quite fun here, isn't it?

—Yes.

After they had sipped their drinks they talked about how rarely they drank during the day and cagily began to admit to sometimes (just sometimes, of course) feeling sort of, not exactly lonely, of course, but, well, you know, just occasionally, in the evenings . . .

—It's worse in summer, said Jane, bravely.

—Yes, it is, isn't it? said Percival, admiringly.

—In winter you can snuggle up and put on big jumpers and say to yourself: *at least I'm not out in the rain*. It rains a lot, where I live.

—Me too. Log-fire weather.

—I'd love a log fire.

—I used to have one. I lived out in the country. It was nice. But she didn't like it.

—Right.

—Oh, but of course I'm much happier now, log fire or not.

—God, yes. Me too, I mean. After all, most religions and that sort of thing say that spending time *on your own* is really important.

—Do you think so?

—Don't you?

—I suppose. But it does seem a bit . . . a bit of a waste, sometimes, doesn't it?

—Yes, it does, said Jane, avoiding his eyes studiously. They had both finished their drinks by now, and without Sea Breezes to hide behind, the gentle flutter of cards being thrown on to the table was all too clearly audible.

—Look, Jane . . .

—. . . Yes?

—Um, I just mean, God, listen, it's just, no, the thing is, oh Christ, all right then: do you just want to call this a day?

—What?

—I mean, I've never done this before, have you?

—No.

—So, well, I suppose, if we had just met in a bar or

265

something, we'd know by now if we wanted to talk or anything, talk, I mean, or want another drink, so, really, I, well, *I* do.

—You want another drink?

—Eh? No, no, I mean, yes, actually. But no. I mean, not that. *I* do. Know. What I think, I mean, about, oh God, *us*. Oh Christ, I sound like a bloody lunatic, don't I? I'm not. It's just, this is all strange. What I mean is –

—If you mean that you already know that you don't want to run off and it would be nice to have another drink and get to know each other, said Jane, with desperate courage, —then I know what you mean and so would I.

—Right. Yes. Oh, good, said Percival.

So then they laughed hastily and concentrated swiftly on not being boring or sad or intense for a bit.

It was pretty clear from some things Percival said that he lived in north-west London, but Jane tried hard to ignore this ghastly truth (after all, she had always known he would live there) and, without exactly *lying*, she made it sound as if she came to Soho pretty often and quite possibly lived in Muswell End. Then she realised that even if she wasn't exactly lying, she was being insane.

She was liking him more and more the more they talked, but all that could happen was that it would be even worse the moment she told him that she actually lived *in Wales*. She knew that she would see his face, his kind, open face, try in vain to hide the pointlessness of it all as soon as she told him. *Wales*. He would be nice, he would pretend not to be hurrying his drink, and as he left he would say that they should definitely keep in touch, certainly, and he would even believe it himself as he said it. And then they would never meet again because there would just be no bloody point, would there?

So Jane absolutely made her mind up that the very next time he mentioned some place in Portobello Road or whatever, she would say, bravely and suicidally: Oh yes, I sort of know that area, I sometimes go by there. When I'm going to Paddington, *to get my train to Wales.*

Where I live, unbelievably.

Where I can never move from, indubitably.

Where I may as well go back to alone, immediately.

The more she thought about this, the louder it sounded in her brain. Percival's voice, his light, pleasant, English baritone, became merely a river of agreeable noise that was heading inevitably towards a sea of uselessness. She tried to listen to the words, but, having made her decision, she was merely on watch for her cue to destroy their warm illusion of possibility.

—Oh yes, he was saying (*shit, this is so unfair, he has really nice eyes*) —I try to feed him organic as often as possible, too. I mean, to give him some kind of chance against BSE and microwaves and stuff, eh? After all, we'll probably just about miss out on gene therapy and all that amazing new stuff, but at least our kids will live to see it. By the time they're old it'll probably be possible to download entire brains and things like that, maybe they'll look at old photographs of us poor buggers and think: My God, what was it like to *know you're going to die*? It all seems pretty bloody unfair, doesn't it? But I suppose it always was, I mean, all those people who dropped dead of TB, when they only had to make it through another couple of years and they'd have been cured with an injection. Anyway, yes, there's a really nice organic shop in Westbourne Grove, I sometimes go there when I'm –

—John?

—Yes?

—Look. I need to say something right now. The truth is that I, well, I live –

At this point, Jane was suddenly air-kissed by the designer she had met the night before.

—Darling, *congratulations!* Hel-lo. *Love* the tweed, mate: so witty.

—Oh, hello, Max. This is John Percival.

—Great name.

—Thank you.

—Look, Jane, what do you think of this? You see, John Percival, Jane *gave* me this idea last night. *Such* a nice present. You've no idea how *tight* people are with their ideas here, John Percival. Such a good name, that. But Jane just sort of *flings them off*, don't you, darling? Here, look.

Max opened his large leather document case and drew from it a poster, which he unrolled with a curious mixture of religious care and practised ease, as if he were a renowned professor of Egyptology unwrapping a rather, but not extraordinarily, valuable papyrus in front of TV cameras. The poster, now fully revealed, showed a teenage girl with many piercings, filed teeth, ultraviolet hair and a very flat stomach: she was caught in the act of screaming abuse at the camera, and seemed about to physically assault the photographer. In retro-punk lettering, the slogan said: *'This Is Not A Look It's the Way I Am!!!!'*

—What is it an advert *for*? asked Percival, politely, amid the general awe.

—For? Well, it doesn't really matter, does it? I thought cars, perhaps. Or tampons, of course. There's the BBC's new under-eights kiddies' channel, it would be just right for that, wouldn't it? Or that new campaign that's supposed to persuade young single mothers that the best thing the government can do for young single mothers is stop giving them any money. I'm really not sure. Obviously, we wouldn't go putting any *information* on it anyway, would we? Spoil the impact. Oh, and about our in-car rear-facing LCD screen thing, Jane, darling, we've got a meeting with someone from BMW tomorrow.

—Actually, said Jane, wishing that an individual-sized, portion-controlled earthquake would immediately devour her, chair and all, —that was John's idea.

—Oh. I see. Oh well, *you'll* sort his back-end deal out, then, won't you? Out of your cut, obviously. Must fly, Dorian's opening, you know. Congrats on *The Paper* again, darling, *very* astute.

Jane sat and tried not to feel cross with Percival because she now had to feel embarrassed and ashamed.

—I'm sorry, I would have told you about the LCD screens, I just forgot about it completely, we only talked about it last night and everyone was, well, you know, *drunk*, and then we –

—Oh, never mind that. It was only a joke. Like your stupid screenplay thing, eh? If some idiot takes that sort of stuff seriously, let them.

—Right.

—So, what were you about to say before that idiot came over? Something about *living*?

—Oh yes. Yes, yes, just, excuse me a minute. I'll be right back.

Jane, fearing that she might get tearful, grabbed her bag and fled to the toilets. In the mirror, she checked for bags under her eyes and so naturally found bags under her eyes. She searched for redness in her eyes and of course found it. She looked at her skin to see if it had any life, and it inevitably had none. She told

269

herself that she was famous now, but her eyes seemed unimpressed. It was no good.

She would have to tell him there was no future.

The future's grey; the future's Wales.

Arse and death.

But perhaps Dicky was right. Who needs a future? Here he was. Here she was. Who said they had to have a future? There was always the present, that easily forgotten thing. Where we who have no future are forced to dwell. OK, then.

Fuck the future.

Alleyways, then.

But she could not sit opposite him looking *like this* and expect him to fancy her *like that*. OK, so she was doomed to single motherhood in bloody Wales. Well, not all the bloody time. She was on holiday now. And she was famous. No more kiddy talk, then. Time to stop looking like a windblown cod. Time to bloom again.

—Go get him, girl, said New Jane to Jane.

Jane made sure again that the door was locked behind her, and took the little envelope out of her cigarette packet. After all, the whole of life was artificial these days, nothing was natural and organic any more. She and Percival would never have met at all if they had waited to meet naturally. It was all just a question of modern solutions for modern problems. Simple. You were lonely so you went on the Net and got your social circle electronically enlarged. Or you were tired so you took some coke and got your pupils chemically enhanced. Just this once, just once more, to get you through . . .

. . . By the time Jane had finished this fine, detached and objective analysis of her actions, the cocaine was biting into her nose again and within seconds she felt three inches taller. Already, her worries were falling from her, like cherry blossom. She rinsed her face with cold water; she looked into her now-large eyes and smiled her new-large smile.

—Right, said she, and:

—Hi, said she, as she sat down again with Percival.

—Let's have another Sea Breeze, shall we? *Much* better . . .

(*Hmmm, wonder how Marega does that thing with her eyes. God, that was a good line. I could take him upstairs, they have rooms here. Or Hazlitt's, it's just up the road and Marega says the rooms are fab . . .*)

—Sorry? he said.

—Oh, I was just thinking, you see that lovely little blonde over there? The one who looks like she's stepped out of an advert for countryside and freshness? Well, I heard last night that she sucked, I mean, she *gave oral sex* to some producer to get that part, you know, in that film, whatever it was . . .

— . . . Oh yes. Her. Well, I'm not surprised.

—Oh. Aren't you? (Jane felt that slight annoyance that always comes when some tasty piece of gossip fails utterly to shock.) —I was.

—Actually, he smiled, —I've always felt a bit sort of, you know, *Cromwellian* about actors. People whose job is pretending they have just lost their lovers, or they are dying of cancer, or something. I mean, why would they *want* to do that? What kind of a life is that? What kind of person would do that? I suppose someone who has no idea who they really are.

—Well, yes. Except I think that quite a lot of people sort of feel like that, these days.

—Do you? Do you really?

—Well, I suppose so. From what one reads, I mean.

—Yes, of course.

There was now a curious silence. Percival eventually broke it suddenly.

271

—I read *Las Madonnas*.

—You've *read* it? Wow.

Jane smiled devastatingly. (*OK, so me and Wales would never get a man like this for keeps. But me and my Uncle Charles can get him right now for sex.*)

—I found a translation on the Internet.

—And you *liked* it? How funny.

—Very interesting. I liked that big chapter when they're all having dinner and discussing religion and nationalism and things. Way ahead of its time, isn't it? Or isn't it?

—Yes, yes it is. Actually, that bit's gone.

—Gone?

—From the film version.

—What film version?

—I'm making a film of it.

—A film? Of *Las Madonnas del Cenicero*?

—Yes. That's why I'm here. In town.

—Oh, I see. You're making a film *about* it?

—No, *of* it. Of the book.

—Um, well, that's wonderful.

—Yes, it's quite fun. That's what the thing in *The Paper* was about today, you see.

—Oh, I didn't read *The Paper* today.

—Oh. Well, why should you?

—What, you mean you were *in* it?

—Yes.

—God. So, you're actually going to write a *proper* screenplay now? That's great.

—No, actually. We're making it pretty well as it stands.

—What? That thing on the website? But you can't make it like *that*, Jane.

—John, darling, you see, I'm sorry, but it's all *process*, and well, at the end of the day it's the male sixteen

272

to twenty-four age group who decide what plays and what doesn't.

—Yes, but, Jane –

—And anyway, we have to get people to *see* it, or we may as well be making *home movies*, right? You call that clever? And if that means we have to give the lads some tits and ass to consider, obviously, hey, I mean, if we're looking at a three-figure throughput deal and a 17 per cent sale-and-leaseback on a back end of seven point five million let's just run it up the flagpole and see if the cat decides to chew it and –

—Jane.

—Eh? What? Sorry?

—What *is* a sale-and-leaseback?

—A what? Oh. Yes. Well, um, I'm not sure exactly, but it's, anyway, it's something good.

—Jane, are you OK?

—OK? Me *OK*? Hey, I'm on, like, fifty points of net.

—It's just, well, you, you sort of, you've *changed*. Is this what you want to do?

—It's a fantastic break.

—But into what?

—What?

—I just mean, nothing leads to anything else.

—Lost me, sorry.

—I'm good at lawyering, so I get more lawyering to do. A good doctor gets more doctoring to do. Nothing *leads to* anything else. This break just means that you'll get more of *this* to do, so you see? So: do you actually *like* it? I mean writing stuff like *that* and sitting about in places like *this* and talking to people like *them* and –

—You listening? Fifty points of net. You know another Writer getting *fifty points of net*? If you have, you been further than anyone NASA sent up yet.

—Jane, you look awful.

—Hey, thanks a bunch.

—No, no, I don't mean that way. Oh shit. Look, I think, I think, actually I think you're very beautiful, actually, um, there, said it.

—Oh.

—Oh God. Look, Jane . . .

— . . . Yes, John?

—Jane, can we go somewhere else?

—Somewhere *else*? What, Soho House, you mean? The Colony? Oh my God, I'm sorry. What am I talking about? Oh God, John, I don't know what's happening. I want to go home. This is all pointless, isn't it? Um, yes, perhaps, perhaps we could get some fresh air, there's a nice alleyway up the road, I mean, a nice café, and –

—Let's. Here, I'll take your coat. Are you OK? You seem . . .

— . . . Thanks. God, I feel all cold, I . . .

— . . . It's OK. Here, let me help you.

Her eyes met his kind eyes. She felt her huge pupils sucking her towards him, or him towards her. She stretched out her hand and laid it on his big, clean hand. She opened her mouth to say something, she was not sure what. Percival's arm came down gently around her shoulder. She felt the weight of his bones, but it did not feel like weight. It felt like an uplifting wind. She wanted to stop him and tell him she lived in Wales, and cry.

—John, I'm sorry, I –

But once again, they were interrupted.

—Janey, lady, stuff the Sea Breezes: Guy, my man, house champagne, lots of it.

—Yes, Mr Salmon.

—Paul, oh, Marega, darling, hello, um, I was just leaving actually, I don't feel very –

— . . . Jane, darling, I'm so *thrilled* for us all.

—This is my friend, John Percival.

—Hiya, John. Paul Salmon.

—He-*llo*, Mr John Percival. I'm Marega. *So* good to meet you.

—Oh, hello, um, so, Jane, shall we . . . ?

—What's happened? Paul? Marega?

—We're Green-Lit is what's happened, Jane.

—We are?

—Alan Barony just pressed button 'A'. We are going. Jane, you just became a made lady.

—Well *done*, Jane.

—Oh my God.

—Um, Jane and I were just going to get some air, actually. Jane?

—Well, I mean, I can't go now, John, can I?

—Darling, you aren't posh, are you?

—Yes actually, Marega, darling.

—Jane?

—Hey, my friend, give the girl a break. She just hit oil.

—Would you like to escort me to the disabled loos, Mr John Percival? I like a man in tweeds. So . . . solid.

—Jane . . .

— . . . Look, John, you could stay here *with* me.

—Darling, you *must* stay with Jane. And me.

Marega Angelina did the thing with her eyes. Percival hesitated. Then he looked at Jane, and frowned, but not as if he was cross.

—Look, I'd better be off. Let me know how it went, Jane?

—John, I . . .

But he was already going. Jane took one step after him, but Marega was already leading her towards the toilets with feline arms, through a vague mass of backslapping, smiling people. Jane was forced to say fast hellos and to return swift kisses. She turned around, searching for him: already, his dark green tweed was almost lost in the sea of black clothes and white teeth. Again she moved to follow, but he was out of the door now, in the street. Marega smiled as the toilet doors swung closed behind them.

—*Now* then, let's *celebrate*, darling. You did say you had some, didn't you?

—Sorry? Oh yes, yes, of course.

—You aren't *upset* about anything, are you, darling?

—No. No, it's just . . . Oh, it could never have worked anyway. Shit. Come on then.

—After you, darling.

Patagonia

Richard Watkin Jenkins approached Paddington in the second class of the 11.00 from Swansea. He had been on the phone most of the journey, in Welsh and English. At present, English was his language of choice.

—Look, Marc, I'm sorry, I know you wanted the play for the summer season, but I got to do this bastard film, haven't I? Why? Well, *because*, mun. We got to break out, take Wales to the world, put ourselves on the map of reality and come up to the daylight from the mines and quarries of our old language and our old hearts and our full ashtrays and our slack, frightened cocks and . . . Marc? You still there Marc? Marc?

Beside Jenkins sat his long-time producer, Cerys Llyn, a short and strong woman of such dark beauty that she was often addressed familiarly, if unsuccessfully, by Cardiff shopkeepers who, when she spoke to them in English with some effort and a ferocious accent, assumed that she hailed, like them, from the wide plains and fragrant hills of Asia rather than, like her countless forebears, from the bleak fastnesses of Gwynedd. Tough, she was dressed in one of those soft cotton zip-tops, hooded and bestrewn with imitation soccer-team patches, which one sees often on teenage boys. Usually the big white letters which straddle the zip on such jackets say BRA ZIL or ITA LIA. Hers, however, was custom-built and said PATA GONIA.

Cerys Llyn conversed with Rich Jenkins in the measured Welsh which both had received from generations of chapelgoing antecedents. All languages have their limits of expression, however, and there were naturally times when they had to slip from this elegant and formal tongue into the occasionally more useful, if less poetical, words of the hated Pink Ones, the Thin Language itself:

—Well, fuck him then *and may the Lord of hosts desert him in his hour of greatest need, that little lamb's penis and cat's abortion*, said Jenkins, snapping shut his phone.

—*By the Eternal Lord, Richard Watkin Jenkins, what did you* fucking *expect? Lord, Lord, it is incumbent on you to deport yourself more like a* bloody *man and less like a* dull wanker. *Our nation was always distinguished by a certain necessary tendency to abhor earthly success, and he who travels on affairs of the world to Llundain, the high city of the despised* bloody *Saxons, must expect to hear hatred whispered from the doorways of his homeland. Well,* thank fuck for that, *we are arrived at* bastard Reading *at last.*

Real

Meanwhile, Jane had somehow got into a taxi with Marcus Dale, because they could not find Fatty and everyone had taken all Jane's free cocaine by now and Marcus Dale needed company to go and buy some more for them all in a pub near the National Theatre, on the South Bank, where the young actors go to score.

Jane had been feeling unaccountably nervous ever since watching John Percival leave the Groucho, and had welcomed the excuse to get out into the afternoon light. Once again she had the curious feeling that she had put her life down somewhere and forgotten about it. But she put this down to lack of fresh air. Marcus Dale agreed with her.

—Sometimes, he said, —the Actor needs to feel the breath of reality.

—Mmmm, said Jane, blocking off all thoughts of Percival and allowing the G forces of the cornering taxi to press her closer to Marcus Dale's famous bum as they spun round Waterloo. She could sense the warmth coming through his trousers. Two years. How had she not had sex for two years? And what good was a man in tweeds anyway? Especially one who lived in London. She just needed a little livener and she would forget about him. Perhaps she would go with Marcus into the loos. Perhaps, in the loos, Marcus would . . .

—Sorry, Jane? Did you say something?

—Oh no, I was just thinking about, um, my next script.

—It sounded wonderful.

—Marcus, how do you *do* it? Act, I mean?

—How do any of us do it, Jane? Are we gods or madmen? Or a little bit of both?

He kissed her gently, looking into her eyes all the time.

—Silly, said he, and smiled.

—Glurrrrk, said Jane.

—Thirty quid please, guv.

—Hello, Marcus, ya cunt, ha ha ha.

—Marcus, ya cunt, ha ha ha. Hello, Doll.

—Fred, Batesy, boys boys boys, how are you?

—Your usual waiting behind the bar, Marcus. Ya cunt. Ha ha ha. Where you been, Marcus: up Soho House?

—Soho Arse, you mean, mate, ha ha ha!

—Been Up the Arse, eh, Marcus, ha ha ha!

—Is Jack Garlic about, Fred?

—Sure, Marcus, sit down, I'll call him. Gissa hug then, Princess. See these?

—Aha, said Jane, detaching herself from the man's rough, beery, sweaty embrace with some difficulty, though for some reason feeling no moral revulsion. She looked dutifully at the three roundish, livid scars on the large beer belly that was revealed as one of Fred's pals hoicked up his Union Jack T-shirt.

—What *fun*, said she.

—But what happened to the *other* guy, Jane? asked Marcus. —Eh, Fred?

—Fucking right, Marcus, ya cunt, ha ha ha! Fucking Yardie, see, Princess. Dead Yardie now, ha ha ha. Only good sort, ha ha ha. Well? You got a name, gal? What you drinking? Marcus's usual here is a pint of Strongbow and a couple of g's, ha ha ha, eh, Marcus, ya cunt? Writer, are you? Well, if you want to hear some stories, you come to the right place!

—So *real*, said Marcus Dale, softly, into Jane's ear. —The simple, human pleasure of being called a *cunt*. Such a relief after all that *falseness*.

—Mmmmm, said Jane. —Do you think we'll have to wait very long?

The Dark Mother

On the gum-spattered, ash-sprinkled grass in Soho Square, Skanky was letting fate decide whether he, too, would take drugs that night. In his case, it was a question of how to spend today's tenner: a large meal of fish and chips and a couple of beers, or a single, small, pink E?

Skanky was not good at deciding things in general, and this was no easy choice to make: he had debated it endlessly for the last half-hour. He was very, very hungry, having got consummately trashed on an empty stomach last night, and was now doomed to a night spent in either hunger or sobriety. Tough call. It seemed only right to let Fate decide.

Skanky had developed his own particular technique for divining the commands of Fate. It involved the passers-by in Soho Square and the ends of cigarettes. Skanky had saved the end of his previous roly, and, sucking on the last of his present smoke, he sat down cross-legged against the wall of the half-timbered toilet block and flicked each butt a roughly equal distance from himself, out on to the path. He now began to count the number of times a passer-by trod on, or kicked, each one.

Today, the left-hand fag end represented Drugs, the right-hand one, Food. Whichever one reached twenty first, would win. As he waited expectantly for Fate to give its answer, Skanky reminisced fondly about certain epic decision-making battles of the recent past: Porn versus Drink; Fags versus Porn; Cornwall versus

Amsterdam; Drugs versus Fags. Fate had always spoken, and Skanky had always obeyed.

Almost immediately, the fag end representing Drugs was kicked from one passing foot to another in impossible succession, and after some thirty seconds had taken the lead by the ludicrous, the inexplicable margin of eight to nil. Skanky stared, and discussed with himself the implications of the possibility that the very laws of Nature themselves had been suspended for the benefit of Drugs. Perhaps Gaia herself wanted him to take the pill? Ten–nil now. There was no way back for Food. Skanky began to lick his lips at the thought of his pill. Drugs was in the Golden Zone, all right. Fate was speaking. Soon, Skanky would be happy.

—Hey, fuck, man! he screamed, as the whole game suddenly changed completely. Drugs took a thin edge from a passing brogue, skidded some three feet, and was then squashed flat by the twin of the brogue, which unbelievably stopped and stood still right upon it. Eleven – nil now, but Drugs was right out of the fairway and covered by a shoe. A shoe which was now quite still. This had never happened before. No one ever just *stood* there like that, in Soho Square. —Fuck you, man! Skanky yelled at the owner of the brogues, a tall, sad-looking man in an old tweed jacket. He, however, did not seem to notice, though several other passers-by jumped and hastened to swerve away from Skanky. The tweedy man just stood there, looking up at the vortex of starlings which, for some reason, had begun to swirl wildly above the little patch of trees and grass.

And now, as if by invisible command, Food took a swipe from a motorbike boot which skidded it right into the narrow flight path across the square where most footsteps seem to funnel themselves. Food was squashed and kicked repeatedly, and though Skanky managed to call for the video referee successfully on several occasions, each time coming up with a 'No Score', he could not ignore the voice of Fate for ever. Meanwhile, the tweedy bastard just stood there, his foot parked firmly atop Drugs.

—Fifteen–eleven, moaned Skanky. Why had he ever trusted Fate? He must be crazy. He had forgotten the obvious logic: as soon as he took a pill he would not be hungry anyway. This was ridiculous. It was not fair. It was wrong. How could the game be played if some sad old git insisted on just standing there and looking at the fucking sky? Seventeen–eleven. Skanky could bear it no longer. He leaped to his feet, bounded over and shoved the old git out of the way.

—Fucking move, will you, you mad fucking bastard? he yelled.

The next thing he knew was that a large firework had gone off between his eyes, his knees had stopped working, and the ground had shot up to meet his back.

—Fuck! he shouted weakly. Around Soho Square, a modest ripple of applause followed the tweedy man off as he went blushingly on his way towards Oxford Street. No one cared to ask if Skanky was all right.

Cunts.

But clearly, the game was over. No way was *that* fair. In fact, it was obvious that the Dark Mother had tried to intervene. Yeah, that guy had been an Agent of the Darkness all right. They had tried to stop Skanky taking his pill. Yeah, because when you took a pill you found Love. And Love was what the Dark Mother hated most.

—Found you out, FuckerMother, yelled Skanky, at the sky, and he raced away, through the hastily parting crowds, towards the little alley off Great Windmill Street where, he knew, his only Love was to be found.

*   *   *

The tweedy man leaned on a wall in another, similar alley, and said:

—Oh, Jane. He said it softly and with the miserable certainty that it was for the last time. There was just no point, was there? After quite a long while standing there, he looked at his watch, and set off towards Holborn, to buy a new wig, because his old one had been irreparably damaged during a recent case when he had taken it off and thrown it at the judge in fury.

—Oh, fuck it all, he said.

—Right, Sheina, we all set for lunch?

—All set, Paul.

—Make my day and tell me that *for once* I don't have to eat bloody fennel?

—The chef absolutely *promised*. I think it hurt, but he promised.

—Great. And remember, you and Miranda be extra bloody nice to this arty Welsh git. He brings the Soft Money with him, so we need him for now.

—Leave him to us, darling. His feet won't touch the ground. Is Jane safe with Marcus, do you think? I shouldn't think she'll stand much chance, poor little country girl.

—I suppose not.

—Paul, this is all such fun. Green-Lit at last!

—So, how about you and me celebrate later, Sheina? Just the two of us and Uncle Charles?

—That would be . . . Oh, Paul, that would be lovely.

Jane and Marcus Dale did not have to wait long. Once their cocaine was delivered, Marcus Dale stood up and said: —Quick one here? and headed for the toilets.

Jane stood up and followed. As she crossed the unheeding pub, she could feel nothing but the slow, inexorable push of Fate in the small of her back.

—Whatever will be will be, she nodded profoundly to herself.

Welsh Not

Rich Jenkins strode boldly into the Groucho, his long leather coat slapping firmly against his boot-cut jeans, his sideboards resplendent and his cigarette at a fine, if somewhat dated, Parisian angle to his lip. His complete un-Englishness, which was already beyond any reasonable doubt, was confirmed by the Welsh in which Cerys Llyn, bustling at his side, holding her documents like a farmgirl with a basket of carrots, gave him final warnings on the innate duplicity of the Hereditary Enemy. Jenkins nodded wisely, and then switched tongues without seam or effort.

—All right, babe? he challenged the Kensington girl at reception. —Lunch for *Las Madonnas del Cenicero*? Richard Jenkins and Cerys Llyn, babe.

Somewhat bowled over by the first unreconstructed seventies man to have entered the Groucho since Howard Marks last week, the Receptionist led the way delicately upstairs, towards where Paul Salmon had laid on a light but distinguished lunch and plenty of vodka.

On the South Bank, Jane smiled fixedly as she watched Marcus Dale cut lines of cocaine in the Gents' lavatory.

In a little alley off Brewer Street, Skanky sat on a cold stone step, watched the hookers inviting richer-looking passers-by to enter their garish heaven, and waited to feel his pill, his salvation, begin its well-known work.

He could hardly wait to feel his brain start to tingle, as if a warm, primeval rain were pattering down upon his skull; he longed to feel the all-embracing arms of the Goddess about him. He waited.

And waited.

And could fool himself no longer: he had been sold a dud; he had spent his last money on nothing. Without that chemical theatre playing out inside his brain, he was himself alone.

Alone, for the whole night.

Alone alone alone.

It felt like for ever.

It had come, then, at last, to this.

The heavens screamed about him.

Salmon was on the phone again, he paced the room as Sheina and Miranda supervised the setting-out of lunch with practised ease. He had his earpiece in his ear and his mobile held away from his head so as to avoid baking his brain with microwaves: he had read a newly alarming report about radiation that morning, while trying to shit on the loo, and had dug the hands-free kit out yet again from beneath archaeological piles of socks and pants. He *must* train himself to use it all the time, not just when he was a bit, you know, *stressed* . . .

—Well, Paul, mate, I can talk to Gary about taking over as Director, but the project has to be free first.

—Steve, how can I make it free until Gary says yes?

—How can I offer it to Gary until you kill this Welsh arsehole off?

—How can I kill him off until I know Gary's on board?

—Hmmm.

—Hmmm.

—Tell you what, Paul . . .

— . . . Hit me, Steve.

At this point, Salmon looked by accident into a mirror as he walked, and saw that he was yet again holding the handset two inches from his balls.

—Christ!

—Sorry, Paul?

—Oh, no, Steve, nothing (Salmon now patrolled around the room with the phone held at arm's length before him). —Look, can't talk here now. See you in the House later, yeah?

—Will do, Paul. Oh and, any sign of the *Bonny Prince* today?

—Na, bloody Fatty's away again.

—Fuck him, that's no way to run a business.

—Too right. But Marcus Dale is shopping in bulk down the South Bank, so we should be OK for a while tonight.

—Great. Get your board waxed, Paul.

—Goggles on, Steve.

—Paul, darling, Richard Jenkins is *on his way up*.

—Right. Hey, lunch looks great, girls.

—Guaranteed fennel-free, darling.

—What are those things?

—Which?

—Those things in the little bowls.

—Artichokes, of course, darling.

—Oh yes, of course. Good idea. OK, Miranda, get the door. Remember, no one mention windbags, sheep or the All Blacks. Rich, my man! Sheina, Miranda, meet Rich Jenkins. Our Director.

—All right, babes?

—Richard, *delighted* . . .

— . . . So *excited* . . .

—And this is . . . ?

—Cerys Llyn, Producer, said she.

Sheina bent low to air-kiss her.

—Hel-lo (sniff). —Oh I'm so sorry, just a touch of *media flu*, you know, darling, sounds like you've got it too, eh? Ha ha!

—Me?

—Oh, well, you sound a bit *bunged up*, too, and I just thought –

—No. I haven't got a cold and I don't take drugs. I'm just a Gog.

—Me too. *Absolutely* agog to hear Richard's take. Aren't we, Miranda, darling?

—We certainly *are*. So, how's Cardiff, Richard? I hear great things about it.

—Well, we're still a few legends short of a city, babes, nothing to write *Ulysses* about just yet, but there again, it wasn't *Ulysses* that put Dublin on the map but the other way around, right? So, until we believe in our own bastard freedom, how can we expect to live in a real city, eh, babes?

—Mmmm. Interesting. Isn't it, Sheina?

—It certainly *is*. Fascinating. Yes, my friend Pete's just starting a business in Cardiff, actually, *media-related stuff*, you know, and *he* says it really *doesn't* feel, you know, *provincial* at all these days.

—That's because it's not, said Cerys Llyn, her un-plucked eyebrows bristling. Through her impenetrable accent, the menace failed utterly to make itself plain.

—Exactly. And I think that's perfectly wonderful, darling. I mean, it's only the size of, well, *Coventry* or somewhere, isn't it? So I think it's *terribly* exciting that you've got so much *going on* there. I *must* come up one day.

—No, you see –

—Cerys, mun, drop it for now.

—I will not. It can't be provincial, can it, love?

—Sorry, darling?

—She means, said Jenkins, pacifically, —that it can't be provincial because we're not a *province*, see?

—Well, I suppose yes, a *regional capital* . . .

— . . . Reg-io-nal?

—Now now, Cerys.

—Well, I mean, obviously, *regional* in the sense of a modern, *European* region, you know, *Europe of the Regions* and all that, I mean, and, um . . .

— . . . Miranda, check the vodka, will you, darling?

—Yes, of course. (*Shit, sorry, darling. God, who is that ridiculous little bitch?*)

—Sorry about that, Richard, Cerys. Now . . .

— . . . That's OK, babe. Forgiven and forgotten. But we're not a *region* of anywhere.

—Oh God, no, of course not. We know *that*, ha ha. You're a, what do you call it, a *principality*, aren't you? Much better altogether. All that, sort of, well, *prince*-ishness, eh? Such fun. No? Oh. Um, Paul? Could you . . . ? Anyway, as I was saying, Paul is *so* excited to meet you and –

—Mr Salmon (Cerys Llyn pronounced every conceivable syllable of the name), —I have a few minor concerns regarding the extent of Mr Barony's formal and binding commitment to the project, Mr Salmon. Oh, and the word you're looking for is *country*, love. *Nation* would do, as well.

—Miz Clean, no need to worry, Alan's word is his bond, he is the rock on which we build our tower, and let me tell you that Alan Barony has never, as in never *never*, been known to welsh on a deal. Shit, sorry, fuck, I mean . . . Sheina, are we, er . . . ?

—I think, Richard Jenkins, the time draws near for me to leave.

—Cerys, mun, listen –

—Ah! Yes. Right. Let's, um, sit down, shall we? Marcus and Jane should be back any minute with, well, *pudding*, you know, ha ha, I bet we could all do with a nice bit of *pudding*, eh? I certainly could, but anyway, do let's start lunch without them. Miranda?

—Well, yes, now, in honour of the script we thought we'd start with something a little bit different . . . Um, is that OK? Sorry, did someone say something? Richard? Oh God, don't you *like* artichokes? But I thought . . . Paul? Um, would you rather have fennel . . . ?

Rich Jenkins surveyed the artichokes with disbelief. At his side he could feel Cerys Llyn, already boiling rapidly with a patriotic rage he himself could not deny. He felt the call of his homeland.

—Come on, Cerys, babe. This is bollocks.

—Hey, Rich, my man, what you mean?

—Thank you *so* much for your proposal, Mr Salmon. We regrettably decline. We'll pay for our own train tickets, don't worry: in Wales, we buy our *own* knickers. Good day to you: *hwyl fawr*.

—Whoa, whoa, hold on there, lady, where you think you're going?

—Hey, pinkyboy, you touch this babe's arm again and I'll rip your fucking spine out, all right?

—Oh dear. Miranda, darling . . .

—I suppose we should be getting back, said Marcus Dale.

—I suppose so, said (Dr) Jane Feverfew, porn star, rubbing his famous cock through his black jeans. She was thinking about him walking into her office during a tutorial; of sending the gaping students packing (*cool, huh*?); and of laying herself across her kneel-down typing chair . . .

*　　*　　*

The world roared in Skanky's ears as he passed Mc-donald's in Shaftesbury Avenue. There they queued. The meat-munching scum. Chewing on carcasses.

Driven by some unknown force, Skanky went swiftly in and headed downstairs towards the toilets before anyone could be bothered to question him.

What? said Owain Hughes-Evans.

—What? said Alan Barony.

—What? said Marcus Dale's agent.

—What? said Marega Angelina's agent.

—The West is untrustworthy, said the Serbian Media Delegate.

—Sorry, mate, said Baz Andrews, and

—It's all right it's all right it's all right, said Paul Salmon to everyone. But he could hear his house of cards falling about him like dead, dry moths in a dusty attic.

—Shit, said Fatty.

Shit-deep, sewer-level in the unmapped tunnels that lead from cellar to cellar beneath Soho, those lower depths known only to those who have fallen straight through the map of the world, Skanky squatted and nodded. All his life he had been putting this off, he now realised: every so-called friend he had ever had, every Movement he had joined, every Tribe he had hitched on to, they had all just been moments of brief evasion. The Dark Goddess had him, she had always had him, and here he was, in her womb itself.

Skanky picked idly, vaguely interested only, with his clasp knife, at the gas pipe beside his head. After a while it gave out a powerful hiss. Skanky smiled. Still like a sleepwalker, he ambled into the next dark room, where he had found the countless drums of cooking oil required each day by the McDonald's restaurant somewhere above him. He looked at one of the drums for some time, then, suddenly and experimentally, he stabbed it hard with his knife. The metal yielded with a dull, ringless noise, quite unlike metal at all, and a stream of oil poured forth like glistening blood. That was good. Skanky went from drum to drum, thrusting, lungeing, bayoneting the enemy all around him.

At last, he was fighting back.

Jane and Marcus Dale came out of the Gents' toilet in the pub at Waterloo. Jane sniffed, and tasted the sour backflow of cocaine as it mixed with the aftertaste of Marcus Dale's spunk. She could still feel where his fingers had been inside her. She felt nothing very much; if she felt anything, she felt wicked, dark, outrageous: free. What the hell did the *normal* people know? Marcus Dale was already calling a cab. Of course. Public transport? Don't *think* so. Time to get back to the real world of Soho. Rich Jenkins would not have his girlfriend with him tonight. Hmmm. Maybe. Why not? Christ, what had she been doing all these years. She was filled with a dull, aching pain: she wanted to suck the cock of the world and shove it up hard inside her.

As Marcus called for his cab, two of the big Union Jack T-shirted men appeared, smiling. Jane smiled back, a vixen.

Then the two men firmly took Marcus Dale's arms and carried him away out of the pub. Jane stopped smiling. The man who had showed her his scars earlier came up and put his hand on her bum in an avuncular manner.

—Princess, you paid for those last two grams?

—No, I, um, Marcus said they were going on his tab.

—Mmmm. Good old Marcus. Thing is, Marcus don't got no tab no more, see? Marcus has just got overdrawn with making proper arrangements, know what I mean? He appears to have misled my West End associates about his financial position.

—No, no, no, they obviously haven't heard, he's the Lead in my, well, *our*, film. We're Green-Lit.

—Na, na, na, you obviously haven't heard: you ain't got a film no more, Princess. Some stroppy Welsh git blew it up for you.

—What?

—So mind if I take payment right now?

—What happened?

—Don't ask me. That's one hundred pounds, love.

—But I, oh Christ, I left my bag in the Groucho Club, I haven't got it, I –

—Pockets. Come on. Hey, don't get funny with me. Pockets, girl.

—OK, sorry, um, I . . . look, I've got about, yes, seventy pounds here, but obviously I need to get a cab, I've got to find out what's going on, and –

—Need? No, *want*. But who said we get what we want, eh? Hard old world. Thanks. For you, this once, seventy quid will do. Marcus can look after the rest.

Jane let the twenties and tens flutter down, dead leaves, into his big, ringed hands. As they fell, she saw them as a slow, silent waterfall of organic fruit, small toys, summer days out in museums and parks.

—Tell you what, since you didn't make no fuss, I'll leave you the bus fare. Nice ride up West, this time of day. Lovely view from the bridge. No offence, princess, come along any time, always find me here, always the same quality, always the best price. But best bring a geezer with better credit next time, eh? Well? You should be off. Not the kind of place for a posh bird half off her tits to go drinking on her tod. Especially not when she's wearing spunk for lipstick. Off you toddle, Princess. Don't worry about Marcus. No one's talking bin bags just yet. We just want a word. Make him aware of the situation, know what I mean? He won't be long. And he'll all be there, no worries! Go on, off you toddle.

Jane toddled.

—Everything all right, Mr Barony? asked Alice the receptionist.

—Mmm. Is Kate downstairs?

—Yes. And your limousine is waiting. Very nice young lady.

—She is, isn't she? Good night then.

—Good night, Mr Barony. Have a nice time in New York.

—Oh, and Alice?

—Yes, Mr Barony?

—If Paul Salmon rings *before* my flight leaves, and promises me a new project by Cannes, put him through to my car, will you? If he doesn't, never put him through to me again. And when Sheina calls, tell her I'll want to see her when I get back, will you?

—Yes Mr Barony. (*Nice young lady. I should say so. At his age anyone that's young is nice, lady or not. And a lady she ain't. Still, got to hand it to her.*)

Paul Salmon was ringing and ringing. He was pacing the little roof garden at Soho House, calling every writer he knew, boldly careless now of the micro-waves basting his eardrums. He kept on looking at his watch. Barony's flight was at six. The clock was ticking.

Inside the loo some twenty feet away, Sheina was chopping lines of cocaine with grim, professional determination. Time to invite people, quickly. Time to smile and dish it out and save the day.

At Paddington Station, Cerys Llyn took Rich Jenkins's arm as they prepared to board the train back to Wales. She made him turn and look at her. Solemnly, she looked up at an acute angle (for she stood precisely as high as his navel) and spoke in Welsh.

—Your choice of ways is not yet definitive, Richard Watkin Jenkins. Decide otherwise if you wish; the position is not yet irreparable; if you alter your course now, all may be saved. But by the setting of this day's sun, your path will be defined.

—Fuck them, babe, said Rich Jenkins in English.

—There we are then. But be aware that in this moment you choose the small land of your fathers for ever. You will never again be taken by the hand of wealth and power in this city of Llundain, nor will you cross the Western Ocean in triumph.

Jenkins looked into her dark eyes and saw that all she said was true. For a moment, he hesitated. From the ancient early-eighties diesel locomotive, twin jets of foul, black, particulate smoke roared clatteringly into the air and drifted slowly down around them. Jenkins's hand was still frozen upon the door handle. Then a small and stocky scrap dealer from Merthyr Tydfil came barging up.

—You getting on or not, boys? Come on, let the dog see the rabbit, I got to . . . Hey, Rich, mun, Cer, all right? Remember me? Glyn Rhys. You used my scrapyard for some bastard film three years ago. Remember that night we set fire to that caravan?

—Fuck, aye, Glyn, mun.

—Hello, Glyn Rhys.

—Well, how the fuck are you, boys, what you doing in bastard London? Me? Bit of this, bit of that, you know, selling some knackered bus engines to China, actually, whatever, hey, drinks on the train, is it?

—Are we climbing aboard, Richard Jenkins?

—Oi, boys, come on, fair play, don't you start speaking bastard Welsh now, or I'm off.

—Here we go again, said Rich Jenkins, and took her arm. —Come on, boys: home.

Jane sat on the front seat of the top of the bus, frozen. The bus seemed to have taken approximately six years to get to the bridge. She was going to die. She could not think. This could not be happening. It was just some misunderstanding by those horrible low-life blokes, obviously. If only she could call someone, to make sure everything was OK really.

She could not call anyone, however, because her phone was in her handbag, in the Groucho.

She was alone, knowing nothing, penniless, lost.

Her son was in Wales. She wanted to howl like a beaten dog. She wanted her mother.

She wanted more cocaine.

Well, at least she had that. Yes, that would clear her brain, at least: yes, if she took some more cocaine, then she would be able to think about something else except how she wanted more cocaine; and then she would be able to work out what to do. Yes indeed. Anyway, this was London and the bus was empty and everyone did cocaine in London and she was a Writer on her way to the Groucho Club so that was OK.

Jane lined up her cocaine with her fingernail on the little window ledge in front of her. Night was falling over London; the river ran dark; the lights were coming on. Jane, admiring the view with the cool, philosophical appreciation of someone who is about to take the line of cocaine they are dying for, looked in her pocket for a note and then remembered she had none. She rolled up her bus ticket instead. A hand tapped her on the shoulder.

—Excuse me, madam.

—Oh, for God's sake just a minute, snapped Jane, and snorted.

It was a policewoman. Behind this policewoman stood a policeman. Behind the policeman stood a rather smug-looking bus conductor.

—Oh, all right, said Jane, —sorry, sorry, sorry, *not on the bus*, I understand, I wasn't thinking, so-rry, point taken. She put the envelope back into her pocket and rose to leave the bus, arms and hands held up in mock, posh surrender.

—Where do you think you're going, madam?

—Well, the Groucho actually. But I'll walk it from here. Clear the head. Oh. Oh dear. Oh God. Oh my God. Oh Christ. Please, I just want to go home, I didn't mean, I was only . . .

— . . . Come along, madam.

—Hello, Paul, hello Sheina, said Fatty, as he strode out on to the little roof garden of Soho House.

—Pete, my man, said Salmon, covering his mobile briefly. By means of complex hand signs and eyebrow waggles, Salmon gave Pete to understand that he was listening to someone of unusual importance. But Pete simply walked up and killed Salmon's phone.

—We need to talk outside, said Fatty.

—Hey, fuck, Pete, my man . . .

—Peter, darling, I'm sure you understand . . .

Behind Fatty, two large and not very English-looking men had appeared.

—I understand, Sheina. But I'm having trouble convincing my Ukrainian partners. Outside. Hey, Paul, we can always wait outside for you, until the club closes. But the longer we wait the more it costs. You choose.

Skanky had read a lot of books, if only because he had spent countless days alone. Who else has time to read so much? So Skanky knew the theory, and discussed it now with himself as he splashed about knee-deep in cooking oil, with the gas hissing merrily about him.

—When I need a drink, I want a drink. Why? So that I *don't* need a drink any more. Right. When I need drugs, what do I want? To not *want* drugs any more. Say I want a shag. *Why* do I want a shag? So that I *will have* shagged. So that I do not *want* a shag any more. Fucking right. When I want to live, what do I want to live for? So that I don't *need* to live. Peace, that's what we all want. Buddhism, see? All we seek is peace. Freedom from desire. All I want is to want nothing. To *need* nothing. *Thirst* wants to *not be thirsty* any more. Life wants to *not live*. To be free of life. Free of need.

Skanky looked at the matches which had somehow appeared in his hand. A brief unpleasantness, that was all. He considered this brief, sharp unplesantness when weighed against the grey endless horror of the life ahead of him. It was no contest. His face relaxed at last into something that was surprisingly like a nice, normal, slow, human smile.

—Free, said he, and lit the match. —Om.

The following unpleasantness was no doubt very unpleasant, but since it was so very short that Skanky's nervous system did not even have the time to register

300

the unpleasantness before it ceased being a system at all, there is probably a strong argument for saying that it cannot really be called unpleasant in any meaningful sense.

At any rate, that was the end of Skanky

But it was just the start of the fireball which now, seeking the air and the upper world, raced out in every direction along the unknown depths of Soho. And in every direction, found new powers.

You sure you don't want a solicitor, madam?

—No.

Jane shook her head slowly. It felt as though her skull was swaying on a long stalk, quite apart from the rest of her body. She sat with her plastic cup of tea, in the blue-tinged iceberg of her own head, and pondered the destruction of her existence.

She was still detached from all reality, but the shadow was already growing. She swallowed with abstract dread at the knowledge that as soon as her cocaine wore off, she would want to hang herself. It would be hard to find a reason why not, this time. There was Bryn. But wouldn't it be better, even for him? What would he miss? A vague haze of Motherliness? But we all miss that, in the end, anyway. He would not see her shamed, destroyed and wrecked. She could save him that. If she did it now, she would even get a small notice in the papers: *tragic end of cokehead bluestocking.*

—*Woe unto those whom fame's enticing shade tempts from the quiet circle of their own*, said Jane, softly.

—*The best time to die is the one time you can get an obituary*, discuss.

Inside her anaesthetised skull, the stalactites glistened and rang.

Hmmm. If she did it carefully, the very generous

university pension scheme would pay up her benefits as if she had worked right up to age sixty-five. Bryn would be cared for. It would have to look like an accident, then. Simple. Fall off a cliff. Not *easy*, but simple. Who could ever say it had not been an accident? Once, she remembered, she had been to the edge of a very tall sea cliff in Donegal, the tallest in Europe they said, and, legs turning to jelly on the sea-blasted grass, deaf from the winter wind and blinded by the low, cold, yellow, Atlantic sun, she had stared down at the wheeling seagulls a thousand feet below her.

Not easy, but simple.

As she whirled and fell she would think of little Bryn, her Welsh son, being sorted out for his unknown life. She would leave a secret note for him.

—*The best time to die is the best time to die for your children*, discuss.

Bryn would be all right in any case. Dafydd's family would look after him. He would never have to move. He would be saved. She had done her bit; she had broken the vicious circle of wandering; she had brought a boy into the world, and given him a homeland; now she could quietly disappear. Let go, slip hands and let herself slide gently into the dark, warm river of forgetfulness . . .

. . . She would have liked more children. More children to die for . . .

. . . Hmmm. But of course, she could not do it until the drugs were totally out of her system. Her pension funds and insurance policies might well exclude drug-related mishaps, so she would have to wait until they would be unable to prove anything. How long until there is no trace? Two days? A year? What did it matter? She could wait.

—I must get clean enough so that I can die, said Jane

302

to herself, stoutly. And then, to her own surprise, she added, rather Welshly; —There we are then.

They were still waiting for the Inspector to come. Jane was feeling very cold. She was feeling very like crying. She wanted to howl at the world. Bugger suicide. She would find something to do, some great Action. She would go out in a blaze of glory, or peppered by bullets. She had destroyed her own life, but she would Do Something that would make sure that Bryn and Bryn's children and their grandchildren would be bought drinks and given jobs by people not even born yet.

—*The best time to fly a 767 into a skyscraper is the best time for your great-grandchildren*, discuss.

Then Jane decided to stop thinking mad thoughts. Instead, she tried to turn off her brain and let it reset itself quietly. She sat and imagined her head as a hard disk being defragmented; except soon she found herself hypnotised by her own internal vision, stuck staring at the colourful little chunks and bytes as they cascaded unstoppably, crazily downwards towards some unplumbed depths. She got hastily to her feet and approached the duty officers.

—Um, excuse me, but, I don't know, you see, you asked if I wanted to see a solicitor and I said no.

—Changed your mind, have you?

—No. I still don't want a solicitor. But I'd like to call a barrister, if that's OK?

—A silk? Most unusual. What do you think, George?

—Very unusual.

—But may I?

—May she, George?

—I dunno. I think they just changed the rules. Never happened before though.

—No, I mean, it's just a friend of mine, really, but he is barrister too.

—Don't see why not then, George.

—Suppose not. If he's friend. What number, then, *Doctor*?

—Actually, I don't know.

—Not much of a friend then.

—Well, no, I mean, yes, but quite a new one.

—Look, Doctor, I'd go for a solicitor. More usual altogether. If you want one, that is.

—Wait. I'll remember.

Jane shut her eyes. She had a good memory (well, that is all you need to get a first and a PhD). She imagined she was back in her finals, trying to remember a long quotation from Spanish literature. She saw the start of Percival's mobile number, not as a series of figures, but as a visionary whole. Gradually, it extended to form a full series. She called it out loud three times. It was safe. She would know it for ever, it was burned into her for as long as she lived, like the postcode of the house in Scotland that she had left when she was seven: EH10 5BL. It was locked away as one of the bright, secret numbers of her life.

She watched the policeman dialling the number. He listened sceptically.

—Good evening, sir. Are you a barrister, sir? No, this is not the Law Society Appeal Fund, sir, it's Holborn Police Station. Oh, you *are* a barrister then. Thank you, sir. Here you go, madam, *Doctor*, rather: one barrister for you.

—Hello? John? said Jane to the phone, trying not to burst into tears.

—Jane?

—Oh, John, said Jane. And for quite a long moment,

she could not be quite sure whether she was calling the only person who could help her, from Holborn Police Station, or calling the only person she wanted to call, from a doomed aircraft.

Prenuptial

Fire burns upwards.

The Great Fire of Soho, kindled low beneath the greasy streets, now blasted its way through jerry-built, single-brick, eighteenth-century cellar walls, and leaped from restaurant basement to pub cellar to porn-video stock room. It discovered the Malt Whisky Merchant with particular joy and delighted in the off-flow from the Angus Steak House kitchen; it bounded like a lamb from oily kitchens up via woodchip-papered staircases into garrets and airy passageways; peepshow cabins became instant, private furnaces; secluded, dubious bars were overwhelmed in seconds; spacious restaurants fell with single, great crashes into the flames.

Hell came home to roost.

—Christ almighty, said Dicky Emrys, as he struggled through the smoke and dived into the first car which crawled past him down Old Compton Street. —Sorry, lovelyboy, but I'm taking a lift.

—Absolutely, said a soft Italian voice from the front of the car.

—Carlo Bennutti! squealed Dicky. —Oh my God, I *adored* your *Clemenza*, I saw it at the Welsh National Opera last year. Oh!

—Ah, always the Welsh people I love, shrugged the distinguished Mozartian conductor, and smiled, showing impossibly white teeth. —I think I get us out of here, no? Is the end of Soho. You come with me, Hampstead, have bath, relax.

—Yes *please*.

As they moved off, however, the other door to the back of the car was flung open and a second figure, small, lithe and speedy, dived gasping and snarling in from the acrid chaos outside.

—Fack me, what the fack's going on, black as Newgate's knocker out there, put your facking foot down, mate, the whole facking place is going up. I just lost my facking trade in the smoke. Fack it. Oh. Nice wheels. Leather. Ve-ry tasty. Hel-lo, gents. Well, so, we looking for anything particular tonight, are we? Fancy a party, gents?

—Yes, I think we three make good party. You think?

—Let's, boys. Well, there's lovely. Who'd have thought it? Both sides of life, and both at once. Fair play to it.

Jane was shaken gently awake from an antarctic almost-sleep, and found herself in front of John Percival. As she stood up, she found herself instinctively straightening out her skirt, like a schoolgirl about to be told off.

—Jane, he said.

—Hello, said Jane.

—I, I came as fast as I could, I –

—It's fine, I'm fine, thank you so much, I –

—No, God, I was so happy when you called, I mean, not happy because of *this*, obviously, but –

— . . . God, no.

— . . . Just, you know . . .

— . . . Yes.

—So, how are you feeling?

—Horrible. I don't really want to go to prison very much. I want to look after my little boy. Can you help me?

—Jane, that's so sweet. We can go right now.

—What?

—They aren't going to press any charges.

—What, just like that?

—Of course. They haven't even told me what it's about. What is it about?

—I'd rather not say, actually, John.

—Righto.

—It won't happen again.

—No, of course. Whatever it was. I don't care what it was, by the way.

—John, look, are they letting me go because *you* came?

—Well, I suppose it does sort of, you know, make them *think twice*. But, I mean, look, I assume you haven't got any sort of record or anything, have you?

—God, no.

—And I don't suppose that whatever it was you did, was, well, *that* unusual, these days. In W1, anyway.

—Well, no, I suppose not.

—Well, that's why, really. And, well, you haven't got, you know, *tattoos* and things, have you?

—What, you mean they'll just let me go because they think I'm, you know, sort of . . .

— . . . Certainly.

—Because I'm *posh*?

—Well, yes, if you put it like that. This is England, after all, Jane.

—Oh. Yes, I suppose it is.

—Um, so well, I was thinking, perhaps, I could take you home. To *your* house, I mean, of course. If you'd like?

—I'd like that very much. But my house is rather a long way and –

—But nothing. You look like you need looking after tonight.

—Do I?

—Yes, said Percival firmly, —you do. Oh, I mean, I didn't mean you look *bad* or anything. Not at all. In fact you look . . . yes, well. But you still need looking after tonight.

—Oh.

—Anyway, it's all pretty chaotic out there tonight, some sort of huge fire in Soho, so I'm not leaving you to go home on your own. So there.

—Right.

—Right then, that's settled. I'll just . . . I'll let you get yourself . . . Um, I'll see you outside in a minute, then, Jane. Don't worry. It's all fine now. Everything, I mean.

And, blushing to the roots of his fine, sandy hair, he strode manfully out of Jane's cell, pausing only to collide briefly with the door. Jane watched him go, champed her teeth a bit, and thought about being looked after and about everything being fine after all. But as soon as she thought about that, she burst into hopeless sobs, so she swiftly covered her head again in her rough, grey, penitential blanket.

Alan Barony's long American limousine had left Soho Square some minutes before the firestorm began, and was one of the few cars to battle its way through to Oxford Circus without suffering very much real damage at all from the exploding glass and concrete all around.

In its roomy back seats, Kate from Walthamstow crossed her white-cotton-stockinged legs and leaned on Barony's shoulder.

—What an evening.

—Kate?

—Yes, Alan?

—I want to ask you something serious.

—Yes, Alan?

—Do you still want my money?

—Oh yes, Alan.

—But is it just for now?

—No, Alan. For always.

—Always?

—I will always want your money, Alan.

—Promise?

—As long as it lasts.

—It will last a lifetime.

—Then I shall always be here, Alan. I shall never leave you.

—Kate?

—Yes, Alan?

—Will you, would you . . .

— . . . Yes, Alan?

—Would you sign a prenuptial agreement?

—Oh, Alan, I was waiting, hoping . . . of course I will!

—Everyone out? demanded the Senior Fireman as the last stragglers left the Soho House club.

—I think so, said his junior colleague, removing breathing apparatus. —I'm not bloody going in there again, whatever.

—What is it, another fucking knocking shop?

—Yeah, by the looks. Upmarket. Kitchen's a bloody death trap, fucking extra virgin olive oil everywhere you look, barrels of the bloody stuff.

A large, fat man dressed in leather trousers bowled head over heels down the stairs and out of the door, then ran screaming away, his long, greasy hair ablaze, wads of smouldering cash spilling from his hands and pockets, smelling curiously of caramelised fennel. As if obeying some learned instinct, he raced off blindly

310

towards the Groucho, which was by now itself a mere crematorium of journalistic and theatrical talent, before throwing his arms skywards and collapsing in the gutter with a cry that seemed more of deep irritation than of mortal pain.

—Call it a day here then, said the Senior Fireman, as the paramedics gathered, palpably useless, about the smoking form. —Come on, they say there's a dozen old upper-class tarts trapped upstairs in that bloody French pub. Better *try* to get them out, I suppose.

Jane was summoned to the reception desk, where the Inspector kept her standing for almost ten minutes while he talked about other matters with his colleagues, in order to let her feel the weight of his stately power. Jane stood in a vague imitation of a military At Ease posture, and looked squarely at the clock, trying to look the way she imagined a female soldier taking a well-earned rebuke might look. In the corner of her unmoving eye, she could see Percival calmly looking through his papers.

—Well, Dr Feverfew, said the Inspector at last, —you've been a naughty girl, haven't you?

—Yes, said Jane, watching the clock steadily.

—Are you going to be naughty again if we let you off tonight?

—No.

—Do you think we should let you off?

—No.

—Well, I'm going to.

—Thank you, sir. I mean, Inspector.

—Good night then.

—Good night, said Percival, and got quietly to his feet behind her. Jane thought: *I shall always remember how quietly he rose to his feet just then*, but then she stopped thinking anything very much, except for relief and joy, because now Percival was leading her softly by the arm out into the grey London morning, and freedom.

As she clambered numbly into his leathery car, she was only vaguely aware of the red glow over Soho, and the wails of the fire engines. Instead, she saw, much closer, the soft, warm glow of the instruments on his dashboard. It reminded her of her father's car; of being carried, wrapped in a plaid blanket, in Scotland, into her father's Rover car.

It reminded her of home.

As soon as her smooth seat belt clonked into place, she turned her head, looked once at Percival, smiled, and slid quietly into a dark lake of sleep.

In Salmon's flat in Kentish Town, Paul Salmon and Sheina had binned their scorched clothes, dressed their burns and were now fumbling vaguely with one another's pants, their attention being focused mainly on the four fat, creamy lines of cocaine that Salmon was preparing with almost his usual flourishing skill upon the little wooden bog-roll cupboard. His grip on the slightly molten Greenpeace card as he lined up the powder was scarcely affected by the crude splint and bandage around his right hand. Sheina had made it for him as they fled the inferno: the two Ukrainians who had been busy breaking his fingers had both been killed before their eyes by an avalanche of Georgian brickwork in Greek Street.

—I'll call Alan now, catch him before he boards the plane, pitch the ecowarriors thing at him, Marcus's scared shitless, he'll do it for five grand a week, he's got to get a pay day before they come looking for his balls. Ha ha! Thank fuck we didn't stay in the House, eh? Most of the Producers and Talent and PR in Soho just got barbecued, sweetheart. Think about it. Are the wheels going to stop turning? Are they fuck. No way. You got any idea how much UK studio space the US big boys have got booked and pre-paid this year? You reckon they are going to just write it off? No way. You know who we are, Sheina? We are the two peasants that just survived the Black Death. Tough on the rest of the suckers but hey: *we* can charge what we like to cut their hay, this year.

—My God, Paul, you're right: we're going to be the only game in town.

—We'll be able to cut a sale-and-leaseback deal at a forty/sixty split of 33.3 points of the back end under a throughput umbrella refinancing package territory-by-territory with cable TV and format rights reserved to ourselves on a Most Favoured Nation basis and Marega will be *extra* nice to Hal Scharnhorst if she made it out of the fire and –

—God, you're good, said Sheina, squeezing his cock absently, as she watched him hoover up his two lines, and —Mmmm, she said, as he handed her the rolled-up note. Salmon leaned back against the wall, idly slipping his hand between Sheina's bum-cheeks as she bent to snort, and blinking with the hit of the coke. Then he blinked in a new way, looked very surprised, clutched at his left arm and said: —No, Christ, no. Not yet. Not *the bottom line*, please.

—Mmmm? said Sheina, dabbing her nose and about to start on line number two. —Not the bottom one? But these are both *mine*, darling, you just *had* your two, you . . . Are you all right, darling?

—Yeah. Yeah. Whew. Fuck, that was weird. OK, look, I know this writer, really talented, broke as fuck, two little kids, all we need to do is raise a few grand for him to write *The Saviours* on a buyout, we'll see the bank tomorrow, take out a mortgage on your flat and –

—*My* flat? Why? What about *yours*?

—Well, *I* can't. I'm leveraged at 110 per cent as it is.

—What? But, Paul, I thought you were loaded.

—Me? As if. OK, so ask your daddy for a few bob.

—My *father*? What few bob?

—But I thought you were, you know, posh.

—Me? I wish. Mum and Dad worked night shifts to send me to the right school. What you see is what you get, darling.

—Oh.

—Oh dear.

—Um, listen, Sheina, hey: don't *tell* anyone I'm broke. It'd ruin me.

—Well, Christ, Paul, don't tell everyone I'm *common*, who'd ever give me a job?

—OK, OK. Shit.

They looked at the half-empty wrap of coke.

—Oh, Paul.

—Do you ever want to stop this shit, Sheina?

—Yes. Do you?

—Yes. Do you like goats?

—Goats?

—And Agas.

—God, yes. I mean, if I could ever *afford* one of the bloody things.

—You and me, Sheina.

Salmon took her in his arms. He moved his hand slowly through her golden hair. She nestled closer to him, laying her head on his chest.

—It's going to be OK, Sheina. I may not be posh, but I can work.

—I know you can, Paul. And I'm pretty good at looking the goods.

—You're great. Sheina, I . . .

— . . . Yes, Paul?

—Look, we are going to have those goats and Agas, I promise you. This project I was talking about, this one will *make* us, you know that? But we just need to raise a few grand *fast*.

—What shall we do?

—Well, I was wondering if you, you know –

—I am not *being nice* to people, Paul! You bastard!

—OK, OK, I was only *thinking* –

—Bastard!

—Ow! Christ, watch the coke, you silly fucking tart, you've knocked it everywhere –

—Quick, get the hoover. And a clean dust bag. Don't tread in it, you fat idiot!

Jane awoke as Percival's car jolted to a stop at a set of lights. She came to and looked vaguely around. At last she recognised Chiswick flyover.

—Sorry, sorry, said Percival, —I didn't mean to wake you up. Go back to sleep.

—Are we going to the M4? asked Jane, somewhat thickly.

—Look here, said Percival, —I'm sorry, you were asleep, and, well, I don't know where you live, so I was going to take you back to my place. But now you can tell me where you live, of course. Sorry if I've taken you out of the way.

—Actually, this is the way home for me too.

—Oh. Oh, well then.

There was a telescopic silence. Jane allowed her tired brain to suggest that some people *did* commute from Wales to Reading. It might be possible. Or perhaps he even lived in Swindon? Or even, maybe, Bristol? Bristol was not really that far from Wales, it would only be like driving across London, really, if he lived in Bristol. Or Swindon even. Anywhere along the M4 corridor would be within the bounds of possibility . . .

The lights stayed red.

Jane decided.

She wanted to wake up in his house, wherever it was. M4 corridor or not. She wanted to be looked after. By him.

—Well, yes, it's, um, quite a long way to my place, said Jane. —So, look, if you've got a sofa or something, perhaps I could stay.

—I've got a bed. A *spare* bed, I mean. But it's quite a way to my place too. I think I should take you home. And drop you off, obviously. I wasn't, you mustn't think I'm, I just meant, well, I could just, you know, *tuck you up* and get you something warm, some cocoa maybe –

—Some *what*? said Jane, horrified.

—Some cocoa.

—Oh. Oh yes, of course. Cocoa.

—Unless you don't like cocoa? I mean, I could make you –

—No, no, said Jane, —cocoa would be lovely.

So that's that, thought Jane, looking into his eyes: *this is the man I want. But he thinks I am posh, like him. I don't want to live a lie. But I want him. This is so unfair. I don't want to have to tip my soup plate away from me and eat bloody artichokes. I don't want to mind my Ps & Qs, whatever they are (note to self: find out what Ps & Qs are). I do not want him to want me because he thinks I am like him. But if I tell him I've been lying, what will he think of me? That I am just a bloody* actress *or something? How can I explain? Can I tell him that nothing is Authentic*

316

and Real any more, that we choose the person we would like to be, and make them up like a 3D puzzle. Roots? We haven't got roots. Vegetables have roots. We were born to walk deserts and cross mountains, always in search of a new home. Will he understand that? How could he? Of course he can't. Who could? No one. What's the point of explaining things cleverly? You can explain and explain and be right and be right and it all means nothing. Christ, why wasn't I born pretty and stupid?

—Are you all right, Jane?

—Yes, yes. Look, thanks for saving me, John.

—That's OK.

—But there's stuff you should know about me. So you know what a mess I am.

—I don't care.

—Well, you should.

—Everyone's a mess, said he, stoutly.

—Don't be nice, please. You'll make me start snivelling. And if I start to get all snotty, I'll end up sounding like . . . like a Gog with the flu.

—A *Gog*?

—Oh, sorry, it's just something they say where I live. Sorry, don't look so worried, I'm not rambling, honestly, it was just a joke. John? Are you OK?

—But, Jane, I *am* one.

—A joke? Don't be silly.

—No, a Gog.

—A Gog? You?

—Yes. But, but how do *you* know about Gogs? Do you, I mean, do you, live in, in . . .

—I live in Wales.

—Wales? he breathed.

Jane looked at him, amazed. In his eye she saw something that looked like hope, or fear, or perhaps it was the fear of hope. Inside her head, she could feel a strange, deep, echoing sound, as if the great flywheels and secret pendulums that ran her life were meshing and locking into place at last.

—Yes. I live in Cardiff, she croaked.

—Oh my Gog, I mean God. Jane, I, well, so do I. Live in Cardiff.

—But you're a barrister.

—We have barristers in Cardiff, you know.

—Do we? Do we, in Cardiff? said Jane, faintly, as though Percival had just murmured the name of some lost, fabled city of magic and romance.

—I'm from Anglesey, you see.

—Anglesey, I see.

—I know, I know, I've got this fucking stupid posh English accent. There we are, blown it, haven't I? Sorry. Sorry, Jane. I'm not posh at all, sorry.

—You're not?

—No. I was going to tell you. But I couldn't.

—You couldn't?

—No.

—Why?

—Because, because, well, because I like you, sod it. Already. There. Oh bollocks.

—Oh.

—Well, there we are, now you know. And the truth is, I don't *even* want to be bastard English or bastard posh and I don't like you just *because* you're English and posh, right? So don't think *that* of me whatever you think of me.

—Right, said Jane, very faintly indeed. —I won't.

—We moved away from Anglesey when I was eight, I couldn't speak a word of English then and now I can't speak anything else. I lost my own language and I had to stop talking English like an idiot to stop getting beaten up and I suppose I overcompensated

318

and . . . Oh God, now I've fucking stalled, oh shit shit shit, sorry, OK, fuck off hooting, will you, you stupid fucking little wankers?

Jane looked around at the outraged Golf GTi full of Young People behind them who were screaming and shouting insane abuse because they might now be two minutes later getting to their Club Nite in Slough.

—John, she said.

—Sorry, it's just, the little shits –

—Stop it, John. I know what you mean.

—You reckon? Start, you pile of Swedish junk! If those little sods hoot again I swear to fuck I will –

—John, listen: I'm not posh.

—What?

His hand fell, as if paralysed, from the ignition switch. The hooting had stooped now that the lights had turned to red again, and in the silent car, only a distant *whumpa-whumpa-whumpa* of music could be heard. Slowly, Percival turned to look at Jane. He seemed to be holding his breath with his mouth open. He blinked several times. Inside Jane's head, the cogwheels strained and clattered, then hung poised: the great bells swayed gently, ready; the silent, dusty cloisters of her life held their breath.

—I'm not. Posh. Not at all. And I was brought up in Scotland.

—Scotland?

—Yes. I'm really and truly not posh.

—And, well, you, you're not even English?

—Well, half. Three-quarters, actually.

—Yes yes yes, but I mean not *English* English. Are you?

—Oh no. Not. Certainly not. Not like *that*. No.

—Oh my God. Thank Christ.

There was another longish pause.

—But *John Percival*, well, it doesn't sound very Welsh, I mean –

—It's not my real name.

—What?

—I'm really called Ioan Persiwl. I changed my name. You try being a boy called *Joan* in a playground in south London when you're eight. I just wanted to seem, I don't know, just . . .

—. . . You wanted to seem normal, said Jane, firmly.

—Yes, that's it. That's it. Just *normal*. How did you know?

—How do you think I know? When I was seven everyone called me *Wee Janey*. Then we moved to Leeds. You try being called *wee* anything in the playground, in Leeds, when you're seven. So I became Jane pretty sharp. Plain Jane.

—Not plain, Jane.

—Oh, Ioan.

—Jane, you say it almost perfectly.

They kissed once, slightly, swiftly, hesitantly, fearfully. Then they kissed again, not. Jane felt the past and the future hang fire for a second. She pulled away from him and looked him in the eyes. The great bells hung for a second in the air as they swung and turned.

—I'm not quite properly divorced yet, Jane said. —Are you?

—Yes. Will you be, soon?

—Very soon.

Jane looked at his nice, solemn eyes. Then she sort of nodded to herself mentally and said: —There we are then, and kissed him again.

The towers rang with light and life.

As the driver of the Golf GTi, cursing with disbelieving impatience, tried to edge his way lunatically out into the endless stream of cars at Chiswick roundabout, the driver of the white, curiously scarred-looking limousine behind him (it was hurrying on its way to Heathrow) began to sound his horn as well; and soon all the assorted cars queueing up beyond had joined in the chorus, because above the absurd, middle-aged couple who were snogging like teenagers in the Volvo ahead, the lights had long since turned again to green.

Fair Play

—Here, I had that Paul Salmon on the phone again today, Dai.

—Never. Still after our Soft Money, is he?

—Aye. Something for Marega Angelina, he wants. *Co-Producership*, he's giving her this time.

—Good on the girl. Welsh angle, has it got?

—Bloody will have.

—There we are then. Oh, come on, give the boy a clap then, girls.

Dai Jones-Hughes and Aled Morris-Evans half turned from their wines and their actresses in order politely to applaud the latest Award-Winning Set Designer (as his agent would henceforth forever call him) to have been created by virtue of winning his class at the thirteenth annual Cymru-Wales Oscwr ceremony at the Millennium Stadium in Cardiff. Since they themselves had decided upon the recipient of the award over lunch some six months before, it came as little surprise to them, but the boy deserved his applause: fair play to him.

The newly minted Best Non-Fiction Set Designer (English Language TV Production) descended from the podium to the stirring waves of the national anthem, and the fifty images of himself on the vast TV array behind were seen to return to his congratulating table (no more mortgage worries for him!). The happy audience, still basking, as was the whole nation, in the three tries by Rhys Williams (the new J.P.R., they were calling him) which had buried England and won the first Grand Slam since 1978 on this very turf a mere three months ago, turned their contented attention back to the Weathergirl and Sports Commentator who were hosting the event and who now introduced the next award: the Cymru-Wales Oscwr for Best Adaptation of a Non-English Foreign Short Story (English Language TV Category).

There were few entries in this particular field. There was, in point of brute fact, only one. But the Host and Hostess made no secret of this: the Jury, they smilingly explained, had decided that, in the absence of any Competition (that dubious Anglo-Saxon concept?), the Cymru-Wales Oscwr Committee had felt perfectly at ease, indeed in a certain sense more completely happy, with judging on the more classical (and perhaps more truly European?) grounds of Objective Excellence alone. The audience heard this reasoning (they heard it first in Welsh, then in English) with approval or benevolent neutrality; certainly, they heard it without any shock, for the same logic had been applied to seven of the thirty-one Oscwrs to have been given out so far this evening.

And so it was that (visibly pregnant) Dr Jane Feverfew, of the Department of Communications, Journalism and European languages at the University of Wales College of Pontypool and Writer/Translator of the film (it was an adaptation of the only Spanish-language short story to have been published in Patagonia the previous year), ascended, air-kissed the Weathergirl and Sports Commentator, and took her Cymru-Wales Oscwr in one emotional hand while steadying the microphone with her other.

Jane stared from the podium, out into the vasty hall.

She found herself at the centre of a bright, white

sea of light, within whose brilliance she could clearly see the table where her Tribe was seated. Professor Evan Evans was engaged in what appeared to be a red-wine drinking contest with the Head of Public Relations at BBC (English Language Section), while Dicky Emrys and a young actor had returned to take their places, just in time, from what had evidently been a most enlivening trip to the disabled toilets. The producer Cerys Llyn entwined her strong, workworthy arm anew about the waist of Rich Jenkins: he had directed Jane's film and had already carried off the Cymru-Wales Oscwr for Best Director in that category, as well as another for his creation of the Best Culinary Documentary (Welsh Language), a studied meditation on the history of the artichoke in Welsh society. Jane's ex-husband, Dafydd (their decree absolute had come through very amicably last year) sat hand in hand with his new wife (she had been his schoolboy sweetheart), looking up at Jane with a rather satisfying expression of admiration, disbelief and secret regret.

Jane smiled at them all, as if at one single person, and then let her gaze slide along and lock fast on to the deep eyes of her beloved husband, the crusading barrister Ioan Persi, who was currently electrifying the Welsh Assembly with his campaign to force every business west of the A470 to have a Welsh speaker on the payroll. Upon his proud lap sat two seven-year-old boys, her Bryn and his Cai, both half-theirs now. Later, long before the partying was over, when others were grouping off and heading out towards hotel bars, grubby clubs and late-night dives, she and Ioan would drive back out beyond the sodium-orange sprawl of Greater Cardiff, leaving the slip roads and roundabouts far behind them, into the silent, unlit darkness of Mid-Wales, to their large, very old and fully Internet-ready stone house in the small, notoriously traditional and utterly Welsh-speaking village of Tal-y-ban.

The boys would soon be in bed, storyed and sung to sleep; the log fire would soon be bright.

That night, she would feel Ioan's sideboards scratching her cheek as they curled up to sleep: it would remind her again of when she was a girl, of resting her head against the horsehair that used to peek roughly through the arms of her Scottish grandmother's old sofa. She would feel the hard swell of her belly in his arms, and the cold of his hairy thighs on her warm bum. His gentle, rolling snore would drown out the world, like the roaring of the endless ocean on a measureless, pebbly beach . . .

. . . Beyond this happy table, half-known faces gazed benevolently up at Jane. Further still, the light faded in the arena. Jane stared out past the limelight and into the comforting darkness.

A horizon at last.

An end to the unbearable hauntings of infinite possibility.

A home.

So much for freedom.

Jane cleared her throat as the applause died down. As soon as she started to speak, she had to stop again, somewhat overcome with feelings. Neither the audience nor the Host and Hostess showed any sign of impatience, for the Wales-Cymru Oscwrs have no truck with the stage-managed timings of the Hollywood version. People understood. Give the girl a fair crack, for God's sake. Fair play to her. It was not an easy moment, they all knew. Why should it be easy? How could it be easy? To stand up here and explain not only to your own loved ones, down there below you, but also to *several thousand human beings* whom you have never met (the event was being broadcast live, on S4C and BBC2 Wales) that tonight you are as happy as it is possible to be.

Not easy.

Especially when you also have to make sure that amid all this emotion, you also say thanks to all the right people, in just the right order, so that no one is missed out or miffed and so on and so forth.

Especially when you are saying it all first in Welsh.